MAXWELL

A BROTHERS INK STORY

By

Nicole James

To Rosa —
Love isn't always easy —
but its always worth it!
— Nicole James ♥

MAXWELL

BROTHERS INK
BOOK 2

By

Nicole James

Published by Nicole James

Copyright 2017 Nicole James

All Rights Reserved

Cover Art by Viola Estrella

Photography by Reggie Deanching / R+M Photography

Model: Alfie Gordillo

Edited by CookieLynn Publishing Services

ISBN#: 9781548831592

CHAPTER ONE

Maxwell bent over the arm of a client, twisting and leaning to get to a difficult area of shoulder. The bell over the front door tinkled, drawing his eyes up for one brief glance. He saw the back of someone in a hooded rain jacket as they turned to close the door. A cool mist blew in as the sound of the pouring rain traveled through the shop.

His eyes flicked to the clock; it was lunchtime, and they'd called their order in to Thai Garden two blocks away. He hoped this was the delivery boy with their food.

His eyes again darted to the entrance and did a double take as the hood of the raincoat was pushed back.

Holy hotness.

She was a petite, Asian beauty with long silky hair and big dark eyes—not too much eye makeup, just thick dark lashes and a bit of liner. Her skin was flawless. She stepped toward the far wall; her eyes up on the framed art, and her body came into view from around the reception counter. The rain slicker hung open in front revealing a slender, boyish frame. Low-slung jeans hugged her hips and exposed a teasing inch of skin between them and her tight top. Nice rack.

Clicking off his machine, his eyes returned to the client in his chair. "Give me just a minute, Ryan."

"Sure, no problem. I could use a break anyway."

Max smiled and got up to greet their new customer. He moved to the lobby and around the front of the reception counter, leaning an elbow on it. His eyes swept over the young woman, again falling to that gap between her jeans and top. Her belly was flat and toned, and her skin looked like silk. He hoped she wanted some ink. He'd love to work on her.

His gaze followed hers as she leaned closer, examining the art and photographs of tattoos the shop had done, her eyes moving all over the colors on the wall.

"See anything you like?" he asked. When she didn't respond, he spoke a little louder. "Miss, anything I can help you with?"

Then his eyes dropped to the bag that hung by her side, and the aroma of the best Thai food in town found him. His eyes moved back up to her face. She wasn't the skinny Asian kid who usually delivered their food. Kiet was his name; they knew him well, as they ordered so often. But in all that time, this girl had never delivered their food.

"How much do we owe you?" he asked. She still didn't answer, so he stepped closer and repeated it a little louder. "Miss, how much for the food?"

Just then she turned, bumping right into his

muscled chest. Her eyes got big as she stared up at him, taking a step back, obviously startled by his proximity. He reached a hand out to steady her, but she flinched back as if she were afraid of him. He was a big man with muscled arms covered in tribal ink, and he knew that could be intimidating, especially to a petite girl like her.

He smiled, hoping to put her at ease and put his hands up. "Sorry. I'm Max. You're not the usual kid who delivers our food. Kiet. Do you know him?"

She stared at him, but didn't answer, and Max wondered if she didn't speak English. She held out the food and pointed to the receipt stapled to the bag. He took it, hoping his smile would reassure her. His eyes moved over her face. Her beauty took his breath away. *How had a girl this beautiful been reduced to running food deliveries?*

He twisted to set the bag on the counter, checking the receipt for the amount, and then he dug his wallet out. As he thumbed through for the money, he called over his shoulder, "Liam, you got a ten? I'm short."

When he turned back, he noticed the girl's attention had returned to the art on the walls.

"Do you like our art?" he asked.

Liam walked over, handing him a ten, and they both studied the woman as she stared at the wall.

"Maybe she doesn't speak English," Liam murmured.

"Damn, right about now, I wish I spoke Thai," Max

whispered back and Liam grinned at him. Max reached for the bag, and his elbow knocked a glass candy bowl to the floor. It shattered with a loud crash.

"Shit," Max jumped back. As he looked down at the broken glass, he felt an elbow in his ribs and glanced up to find Liam nodding toward the girl. Max's eyes swung to her and noticed she hadn't even flinched.

"I think she can't hear, bro," Liam whispered.

Max took the ten from Liam, added it to his own, and tapped the girl on the shoulder.

She whirled, startled.

He held the bills out to her, nodding toward them.

Just then, Liam made some gestures with his hands. Max frowned, watching him. "When the hell did you learn sign language?"

"A kid in my high school class was deaf. A lot of us picked it up over the four years."

The girl looked relieved and gestured back, a big smile breaking across her face. They continued signing back and forth.

"What is she saying?" Max asked.

"Says her name is Malee. Kiet is her brother. He's sick and couldn't make the delivery, so her father sent her."

Liam signed some more, gesturing to the wall. She signed back, a shy smile on her face. "She likes the colors."

He signed some more. She signed back.

"She likes to draw. The art fascinates her."

Max watched her closely.

"Can you read lips?" Liam asked her, and she waggled her hand before signing. "Says she tries, but she still has trouble with it."

Max gestured up to the art on the wall and spoke clearly to her so she could read his lips. "You want a tattoo?"

Her eyes got big, and she pointed to herself.

He nodded.

Max ignored the broken glass, too consumed with speaking to this beautiful girl. "Ask her if I make her nervous?"

Liam signed to her, laughing and making symbols that had Max thinking his brother was calling him a big gorilla. The girl giggled and blushed, and then she shrugged and held up two fingers about an inch apart.

He smiled, understanding that sign, and asked, "Why?"

She made a motion with her hands, like she was trying to wrap them around a large bowl, and then pointed to his bicep. "Big," she tried to say the word that seemed foreign to her mouth.

He took her hand gently in his and brought it to his muscle revealed by his short-sleeved shirt. He smiled at her as her eyes got huge as she touched his skin, and suddenly she pulled back, embarrassed, and he was left wondering if she hadn't touched a man before.

Then suddenly, she backed up a step. She dipped

her head down, her eyes looking up from under her brow. Then she turned and dashed out of the shop.

Max followed to the window, watching her hurry down the street. "She was beautiful, wasn't she?"

Rory walked up, taking in the glass on the floor and Max staring out the window, then turned to Liam. "What's he looking at?"

Liam grinned huge. "Big brother is in love."

"Say what?"

"I just saw it happen, right before my eyes. He fell hard."

Max swiveled his head back. "She's pretty is all I said. Don't make a thing out of it."

"Yeah, right. Why do I suddenly feel like there's a lot of Thai food in our future?"

Max shoved his shoulder as he walked past him toward the back. "Speaking of… Clean up the glass and maybe I'll let you have some of it."

"Me? I didn't break the damn bowl, you did!"

Max laughed and kept walking.

***

Malee turned and glanced back at the tattoo shop, studying the name. *Brothers Ink*. She'd never been there before. She'd lied to the man when she'd said her brother was sick, and her father had sent her. Her father rarely let her out of the restaurant, preferring to keep her back in the kitchen, like her deafness somehow made her flawed and she should be hidden away. Her mother said he was just being protective of her, but sometimes she wondered if he wasn't ashamed of her disability. She wasn't perfect like her brother, who could do no wrong in their father's eyes.

She glanced back at the shop. She wasn't supposed to make that lunch delivery. She'd grabbed it and ran out the door while her brother was busy, glad to escape the confines of the restaurant, even if it was only for a few minutes. Her father may beat her for her disobedience when she returned, but it had been worth it. She'd never seen art like that before. All the colors and designs had taken her breath away. She'd been fascinated. Tonight, in her room, she'd pull out her hidden sketchpad and colored pencils and try to duplicate the beautiful designs.

Her mind turned from the art she'd seen in the shop to the big man who'd spoken to her. Max, he'd said his name was. Tonight, when she was alone in her room, in addition to her drawing, she'd also practice saying his name out loud until she got it just right, so if she ever got the chance to run into him again, she could say hello to him, and he wouldn't think she sounded funny.

She knew her lack of hearing distorted her voice and didn't sound exactly like other people. But it was hard to form the words correctly, when you couldn't hear how they came out.

Her mother wanted her to get an implant that the doctor said would help her to hear, but her father forbid it, saying it was too risky and too expensive.

Her eyes again strayed back to the tattoo shop as she stood on the corner in the rain, waiting for the light to change. She'd seen that man before — Max. She'd seen him in the gym on Fourth Street where her brother took martial arts classes. MMA, they called it; Mixed Martial Arts. She'd seen Max in there working out on the bag. He had powerful arms, and she'd been mesmerized watching him. She wasn't supposed to go there either, but sometimes she'd sneak down there when her brother went and watch through the big storefront windows. No one ever noticed her. She made sure to stand off to the side, trying to be as inconspicuous as possible.

And now she knew where the big man with the powerful arms worked. Brothers Ink. She smiled a secret smile as she jogged back toward her parents' restaurant, happy for the first time in a long time.

CHAPTER TWO

Max and Liam sat in the break room. Liam was flipping through this month's copy of *Inked Up* magazine, and Max was drinking an energy drink when Rory walked in to grab a drink out of the refrigerator.

"Hey, Rory," Liam said, not looking up from his magazine.

"Yeah?"

"Keller's is having a sale on guitars."

"Yeah?"

"You buy one, they'll throw in free lessons."

Max laughed, and Rory flipped Liam off as he walked back out.

"Why do you constantly antagonize him?" Max asked.

Liam grinned. "Why, you jealous?"

Jameson walked in and collapsed into a chair.

"They've got handbooks for everything these days. I know because I just spent the last two hours in the bookstore with Ava. Handbooks for names, handbooks for pregnancy, handbooks for motherhood, handbooks for fatherhood, handbooks for smart babies, handbooks for city babies…"

Liam glanced up from his magazine. "Livin' the dream, huh?"

"Shoot me now."

"Where is she?" Max asked.

"Up front, talking to Rory."

A minute later, Ava walked in with a bookstore bag in one hand and a twin-pack of muffins in the other.

"How are you doing, sweetheart?" Max asked as she sat down.

"I'm doing well. Just starving."

Jameson looked over as she unwrapped the package. "You gonna share?"

She took a big bite of one. "Nope."

"There are two huge ones. Are you sure you need to eat *all* that?"

She glared at him with a look that promised to go nuclear. "Are you calling me fat?"

Even Liam looked up from his magazine at that comment. "Oh, dude, you just hit the button that launched all the missiles."

She stood up and stomped out of the room.

Jameson called after her. "Baby, I'm sorry. You know I get cranky when I'm hungry."

"He's never gonna dig himself out of that hole," Liam murmured.

"Yeah, there's no handbook for that," Max put in with a grin.

"What, you don't think she's gonna forgive me?" Jameson asked.

Liam continued flipping pages. "Maybe in a parallel universe. Where you aren't a dick."

Max tried to stifle his laughter. "I'll go talk to her. Smooth things over for you."

"Thanks, man. I'm exhausted, and you always did have a way with calming her shit down."

Max winked. "You're not the only one with special skills, superstar."

He found Ava sitting on the big couch in the lobby, eating her muffins and quietly fuming. He sat down next to her and patted her knee. "You know he didn't mean it. You're the most beautiful girl he's ever seen. He's just tired and irritable."

"He's always tired and irritable. *I'm* the one carrying this baby."

"I know, but he's been working long hours on the house, trying to get it finished in time, plus his work here."

She dropped the hand holding the muffin to her lap. "I know. You're right. I'm just so emotional right now."

Max grinned at her. "Well, don't let him off the hook. Make sure he makes it up to you tonight. That rates at least a foot massage or a back rub."

She slouched back against the cushions, closing her eyes. "Oh God, Max. What I wouldn't give for a foot massage right now."

"Your wish, my lady." He pulled her foot up on his leg, turning her sideways on the couch as he slipped her shoe off. "Babe, you think you should still be wearing these high heels?"

"I've given up everything for this baby, Max. I'm not giving up my heels, too."

Max grinned. "Okay, Ava." He rubbed her foot, pressing his thumbs into the arch until she moaned.

"My God, that feels great. Why aren't you married, Max? If the ladies knew you had this skill, they'd be lining up out the door."

He chuckled. "If you say so."

After a few minutes, she rolled her head on the cushion and looked at him. "Are you happy here, Max?"

He turned his head to look at her. "Sure, I guess."

"That's not an answer."

He shrugged. "I'll never be as good as Jameson, but I get by."

"Is there something else you'd like to do? Did Jameson twist your arm into a career you didn't want?"

"Not at all. I enjoy working here, but…"

"But what?"

"For Jameson this is his passion, but for me… it's just a job."

"And what's your passion, Max?"

"I thought about MMA fighting at one point but that ship has sailed. For the longest time I didn't think I was good enough, and I let that hold me back. I'm too old now. You gotta be a kid for that. Now? I don't know."

"Max." She leaned forward, touching his arm. "Don't ever let feelings of inadequacy keep you from going for your dream. Don't ever let anyone tell you that you aren't good enough to have what you want. And don't let negative thoughts stand in the way of getting it."

"Guess that worked out for you, huh?"

"It did. I have everything I've ever wanted."

"I'm happy for you, girl, for you and Jameson, both. So, don't be too hard on him tonight, okay?"

"Well, since you just gave me a fabulous foot massage, how can I tell you no?"

"You can't. That's part of my charm."

She laughed, but then touched his arm again. "Max, seriously, if there's something more out of life that you find you want, don't wait for 'someday' to make it happen. If you do, 'someday' will never come."

CHAPTER THREE

Malee carried a tub of dishes she'd bussed from a table in the restaurant dining room to the kitchen. Once again, a customer had grabbed her arm, trying to ask her for something. It happened at least once a week. It was frustrating because she couldn't understand them, and they couldn't understand why she didn't respond. This one had gotten mad and shoved past her, almost knocking her down. It was scary—the way he'd grabbed her.

Her father always told her never let the customers know she was deaf. He told her it was for her own safety; he didn't want any of them to follow her in town, targeting her due to her disability and using it as a weakness against her. She was a pretty girl, her father told her, and she must guard against men with bad intentions who may prey upon her.

She thought he worried too much, but every once in a while, like today, a man would scare her into believing he might be right, that it was something she should be on guard against.

Malee set the tub down in the kitchen and turned, plowing right into her brother, Kiet, who was carrying two plates of food that crashed to the floor. They both quickly bent to pick up the pieces, and she whispered, "I'm sorry."

Kiet signed to her. *It's okay. It's my fault. I wasn't looking.*

He glanced at their father, and she followed his gaze. Her father was shaking his head, grabbing another plate and dishing up another entrée. Malee knew he was probably muttering under his breath about how much money he'd just lost.

Her eyes met Kiet's and glazed over with tears. He squeezed her arm and signed, *It's okay. Don't worry. I'll clean this up.*

Malee dashed up the backstairs to throw herself on her bed, crying into her pillow. Sometimes she hated her life.

CHAPTER FOUR

Max walked through the back door of the old building on Fourth Street. The painted sign on the brick said Fourth Street Gym, but everybody called it Pops' Gym. Pops was the cantankerous old man who owned the joint and held a very special place in Max's heart. If it hadn't been for the old man, Max would have probably headed down the wrong road as a teenager. It had been Pops who had taken the time with him, and given him a direction and goal, way before Jameson had opened up the tattoo shop — long before Brothers Ink became the glue that held them all together. No, back then, it was Pops who was the guiding hand that steered Max in the right direction.

Pops had come into his life at a time when Max had just lost both his parents in a tragic car accident. Suddenly, it was the four brothers all alone in this world. They had no one but each other. Jameson, who was just eighteen at the time and was supposed to head off to college that fall, had immediately given up all of that and stepped up, fighting tooth and nail against the legal system to keep his brothers from being split into different foster homes. He made sure the family stayed together. He'd worked his ass off, shoveling feed at

Ryerson's Feed Store all day, then apprenticing at night with a local tattoo artist until he was able to learn the craft, hoping it would be a marketable skill with which he could support his brothers.

Max, being the second oldest at fifteen, did his part as well, making sure the two younger boys—Liam who was ten and Rory who was seven—were taken care of while Jameson worked. Max helped them with their homework, cooked them dinner, and put them to bed.

But in his free time, he had plenty of opportunity to get into trouble. At fifteen, it was easy to rebel against all that responsibility, especially with the anger that brewed inside him over losing his parents. Life wasn't supposed to be like this. It wasn't supposed to be this hard. He'd been tempted by the wrong crowd, tempted to take up petty theft—five-finger-discounts, they called them. He and some other rowdy boys from town got into their fair share of scraps, too, fighting openly in the back alleys of downtown. Until one day, Pops saw them and broke the fight up. He told the boys if they wanted to beat each other to a pulp, they'd might as well come inside and do it in his Gym.

They took him up on his offer, and everything changed for Max that day.

Slowly, but surely, Pops' brand of tough love seeped into the edges of Max's hardened heart. Through the art of boxing, the old man taught him respect, discipline, how to rise above failure, and that working hard toward a goal made it that much sweeter when you finally achieved it.

He gave Max simpler things, too, like a place to go after school, and a place to hang out other than the street. He gave him attention, something Max craved, and he gave him a strong adult role model... Not that Jameson didn't strive to be one, but he was barely older than Max was himself.

The old metal door banged closed behind him as he entered the dark cool Gym, and the familiar smell of stale sweat hit his nostrils, shaking him from his memories. Max glanced over to the teenage boys taking a mixed martial arts class. That wasn't part of the offerings at Pops' back in Max's day. Back then they'd learned boxing. But last year, Max had talked Pops into giving it a chance and hiring a guy to teach a few classes. It had turned into a success. Then Max had talked Pops into giving the boys off the street free classes over the summer, a time Max knew when idle hands could get a boy into trouble. There'd been quite a response, and now some of those same boys were so hooked on the sport, they worked afterschool jobs in order to pay their way for advanced classes.

Max moved to the metal staircase in the back and headed up to the small office Pops kept on the second floor. He pushed open the door without knocking. The old man was kicked back in his chair, dozing.

Max grinned. "Go home, Pops. I'll lock up."

Pops startled awake. "Huh. Oh, Max." He ran a hand over his face. "I was just resting my eyes."

Max chuckled. "Right. Go on home to Eleanor."

He looked at the time. "Gotta close the place up. They should be done soon."

"I can take care of it. Go home and get some rest."

Pops nodded and stood, pulling his jacket on, his motions slow.

The old man looked tired, his age showing more and more recently. And Max knew the reason. "How is she?"

Pops looked off at the small window as raindrops began pelting against the glass. "She's doing as well as can be expected. She's starting to need more and more help, though. We've got a nurse comin' by twice a week now."

"I'm sorry, Pops."

He nodded. "Been thinkin' about takin' her down to Florida. Our Katy is there. She'd be a big help."

"What about the gym?"

Pops huffed out a breath. "Close down, I guess. I don't know who'd want an old busted down place like this anymore. What do you call 'em? Millennials? They go to the fancy places now, the ones with saunas and spin classes and all that crap. They don't want to go to an old school place like mine."

Max grinned. "Old school is cool, Pops. Haven't you heard?"

Pops chuckled. "Yeah. Right."

***

Malee secretly watched from the shadows of the

corner of the gym as her brother's MMA class finished up. She'd followed him down the two blocks from the restaurant, like she often did, and snuck in the door. But it wasn't really the MMA class that held her interest or had her coming down here every week. It was the big man from the tattoo shop. The one named Max. He had enthralled her from the first minute she'd laid eyes on him. But he'd been missing the last few times she'd snuck down here. And as she looked toward the punching bag hanging in the corner, it appeared he was a no-show again.

The class wrapped up, and the students headed to the locker room in the back. The big cavernous space with the boxing ring in one corner, the MMA area with its large matted floor, and the exercise equipment in the other corner seemed dark and still.

Malee eyed the punching bag as the frustration in her simmered. Her eyes darted around, seeing no one. She moved quietly toward it as thoughts of all that had transpired that day rolled through her—the encounter with the customer, the accident with Kiet, her father's disappointed look. Then on top of everything, she missed getting to see Max. It was a stupid crush, she knew, but still, it had become one small highlight she looked forward to every week. Disappointment melded with frustration, and she pulled her arm back and punched the bag. It felt good, and soon she was pummeling it, her arms swinging hard and fast, her face tight with anger. She let it all out, releasing the flood of feelings until the torrent of emotions rolling inside her boiled over, and she found herself clinging to the bag as she burst into tears, her shoulders shaking silently as the bag swung slowly.

It was then that a large hand appeared just above her head, steadying the bag. Her eyes moved from the hand up the strong muscled arm, and her head twisted to see the face that haunted her dreams.

Max.

Startled, she took a step away.

He smiled down at her. And then the smile faded as his eyes swept over her cheeks, wet with tears. But then he did the most unexpected thing. His hand lifted, and he began to sign to her. Just letters. Slowly made, as someone who was just learning the skill would do, spelling out the words.

You okay?

She was so shocked that she could only stare at him through her tears.

And then that same hand lifted to her face, and his thumb gently brushed the wetness from her cheek. His eyes searched hers as he signed again.

Tears. Why?

She covered her cheeks and turned her back to him, embarrassment flooding through her. She was mortified he'd seen her crying.

She felt his hands close softly over her shoulders, turning her back around. He cupped her face, tilting her unwilling eyes up to his. When she finally looked up, she saw the questioning expression on his face as she read the word on his lips, *why?*

For some reason, the fact that he was showing her any sympathy had her breaking down again, her shoulders shaking with sobs.

He looked a little out of his depth, like he wasn't sure what to do with the silly girl who was falling to pieces right in front of him. But then he surprised her. Almost as if it was an instinctive reaction, he reached out and pulled her up against him, his arms wrapping tightly around her in the shadowy corner. They stood there a long time, until her sobs faded away.

She had time to realize all sorts of things. Like how comforting his arms were, how good he smelled, like the wind and rain, and some manly soap combined with his own scent. She was cuddled up against this man she barely knew, as if she belonged there. He was warm beneath the soft fabric of his shirt, and she could feel the vibration of his heart thudding under her ear.

His hands were soothing as they smoothed up her back. She'd never had a man touch her like this. His touch was calming and tender. She didn't want to lose the feeling as she stood there with her face buried against him and her hands pushed under the warmth of his arms. She felt safe, protected, sheltered, in a way she hadn't felt in a long time, maybe ever.

But then she remembered she barely knew this man, so she pushed back away from his body, and he let her go, but his hands still held her arms lightly. She looked up at him, studying his face. It was dimly lit in the cavernous room, but she saw the genuine care in his eyes and the question there, too. He still had no idea why she was upset.

Just a bad day, she signed. She tried to laugh it off and then, daring to admit her attraction, she signed to him. *You haven't been here in a while.*

He shook his head in confusion, not catching all her signs, so she tried a simpler version. She pointed to him. Then signed three letters *N O T*. Then pointed to the floor.

That had a smile pulling at the corner of his beautiful mouth. Her gaze dropped to his gorgeous lips for a moment before returning to his eyes as he tilted his head and signed slowly.

You noticed.

She nodded shyly.

He signed some more, his fingers fumbling slowly over the motions.

I had work.

It seemed he had a lot he wanted to say to her, but signing every letter was slowing him down. She knew the frustration he felt. She felt it every day, trying to communicate with the hearing world. But he was making the effort. She couldn't believe he'd actually learned the alphabet. Had he done it for her? Because when she'd delivered lunch that afternoon several weeks ago, he hadn't known any sign language. The thought that he had done it just for her had a thrill of pleasure shooting through her. It had been a long time since anyone had done anything like that for her, put actual effort into something like that, just to be able to say hello to her if he ever chanced to see her again.

He held up a finger, indicating to wait a minute.

She frowned as he reached into his pocket and pulled out his cell phone, his thumb moving over the screen. She assumed he had a call or text come in, but when he didn't put it to his ear, she knew there'd been no ring that she couldn't hear. After a moment, he turned the phone toward her to see.

She looked at the lit up screen. He'd pulled up his notes app and had typed out a message to her. She grinned at his ingenuity and read the words.

Are you okay? Why were you crying?

They began passing the phone back and forth.

It's nothing. Just a bad day. You learned sign.

Just the alphabet.

Why?

So the next time I saw you, I could say hello to you.

That had her face lighting up as she pointed to her own chest and mouthed, *for me?*

Yes, ma'am.

Thank you.

You're welcome. Are you waiting for your brother?

She shook her head, her eyes darting to the locker room as she stepped back.

Max frowned and typed out a message.

What's wrong?

He doesn't know I snuck down here.

Snuck?

I'm not supposed to be here.

Why?

My father is very strict.

Oh.

I should go before Kiet sees me.

Max looked over his shoulder as the locker room door opened, and he heard voices. He pointed at a door behind Malee and opened it. He motioned for her to enter and held his finger to his lips, signaling her to remain quiet.

She nodded and stepped into the storage closet. He closed the door, but left it ajar an inch so she could peek through. He moved away, waving to several of the students as they exited the gym. She saw Kiet leave the building with the last of them. Then the class instructor came out. He shook hands with Max, and she could see their mouths moving as they spoke to each other, then both smiled and laughed.

The teacher went outside. With the door opening, Malee could feel the chilly night air sweep into the building and with it the clean scent of the rain she knew was now falling outside.

When the students were all gone, Max moved to check the locker room, then came back and motioned her out.

He typed another message to her.

They're all gone. Do you want me to show you how to

punch the bag correctly?

She read the message, and her wide eyes flicked up to his. Her first instinct was to shake her head no and run home, but she didn't want her time with Max to be over. So she gathered her courage and looked over at the bag.

He held the phone up for her to read, the dare in his eyes plain. *Or are you afraid of me?*

That had her chin coming up. She'd never been one to shy away from a challenge, so she did the only thing she could do. She shook her head, gestured to the bag, and spoke, forming the words carefully, "Show me."

His eyes sparkled at her response before he stepped away to fetch a pair of gloves. He helped her slip them on, patiently lacing them up for her. She watched, mesmerized by his callused fingers and strong hands as he worked.

His eyes flashed up to hers, and he smiled. Warmth spread through her chest, and she couldn't help the answering grin that broke across her face.

With big gentle hands on her shoulders, he positioned her in front of the bag. His hands closed over her forearms and brought her gloves up to jaw height, tucking her elbows in. He demonstrated with his own hands, making fists tight to his face, indicating that she should keep her hands up, close to her face.

She mimicked him, and even as she did so, she couldn't help letting her eyes drift over his bulging biceps. They were covered with the most beautiful ink she'd ever seen, that scrolled up under the short sleeve of his T-shirt.

He bounced on his feet, dancing toward the bag and away, pivoting right and left and jabbing at the bag to show her. Then with a lift of his chin, he indicated for her to try it.

She bounced around on her feet and swung at the bag.

He grinned and shook his head at her pathetic attempt.

She didn't take offense, and they both laughed.

He moved behind her, and she felt his hands close over her hips as he repositioned her stance, his heat upon her back and his breath on her ear as he reached around her to take her wrists in his grasp. He guided her movements, making the punching motions with her in slow motion. With every jab at the bag, he made sure she touched her jaw with the opposite free hand, indicating she needed to remember to keep both hands up at face level. Then he stepped back and nodded for her to try it.

She did, and he nodded, mouthing, *yes, good.*

She knew it was a small thing, but his praise lifted her spirits, and she felt something blossoming inside her. A radiant smile burst across her face. It had been a long time since anyone had paid her such attention. A long time since someone really seemed to enjoy her company, rather than just tolerate it.

He worked with her on technique for a while,

showing her how to jab and how to follow through with several shots. He was a good teacher, extremely patient and encouraging.

A flash of lightning lit up the rain-streaked windowpanes pulling her attention. She glanced up at the clock, high up on the wall. It was getting late, and she needed to get home before someone missed her. She gestured toward the window.

Max frowned, not understanding.

With her hands in the gloves, she couldn't sign or type on the cell phone. She was forced to use her voice. It still embarrassed her, the way her voice must sound, but she made herself do it, speaking slowly. "I have to go home."

Max nodded. *Okay.* He reached for her hands, and she turned them wrist up so he could undo the fat gloves.

She waited patiently until he tugged them off, but when she turned to go, he caught her arm, stopping her. He held up a finger and began typing a message.

It's raining. Let me drive you home.

She shook her head, then took the phone and responded.

I can't. If my father saw us together…

I could drop you off at the corner or in the alley behind the restaurant.

She glanced toward the window. The rain was coming down pretty hard. Reluctantly, she turned back and nodded to him.

He typed a message, holding the phone out.

Why don't you use your voice? I can understand you.

She licked her lips, debating, and then formed the words, "I sound funny."

You sound fine.

She read his words, and her eyes flicked to his. She found only sincerity there, but still she bit her bottom lip. She'd been teased so often as a child that she had just stopped trying. Now he had her rethinking that.

He typed again.

You don't have to if it makes you uncomfortable. Only if you want to.

They stared at each other. She wanted to trust him, but she knew if he, of all people, ever teased her about it, she'd be devastated.

He typed again.

My truck is in back.

Then he jerked his head toward the back door, and she followed him, waiting while he turned out the lights. She stood beneath a small overhang as he locked up, and then hit a button on his key fob, and the headlights to his big black pickup flashed on as he unlocked it. They darted out into the rain, and he opened the passenger door for her, helping her inside.

She liked the courtesy he showed her. No one had ever held a car door for her before. It felt nice. It felt special. She grinned. He definitely earned some points with that move.

The interior of the pickup was like a warm cocoon

against the stormy weather outside, and she had a few seconds to glance around. A person's vehicle told a lot about a person. Max's truck still had that new-car smell. It was obviously a late model with all the bells and whistles. She also noticed it was immaculate on the inside, no clutter or fast food wrappers or empty soda cups. That showed he respected his belongings and took care of them, just as holding the door for her had shown he respected her.

The driver door opened, and the truck rocked as he hoisted himself inside. Raindrops sparkled on his shoulders as he started the engine and cranked up the heat.

She had on just a light jacket and rubbed her hands over her arms. He noticed and reached in the back, grabbing a black fleece jacket. He tucked it around her like a blanket and mouthed the question, *warm?*

She nodded, smiling, and realized it wasn't just the jacket that made her warm; it was the way he cared for her. Once she was cuddled in the soft fabric, he reached across her and buckled her seatbelt.

She breathed in the scent of him that clung to the fabric as he threw the pickup in reverse and headed out. It smelled of some delicious scent, like a woodsy soap that blended with his own manly aroma, one that she was instantly addicted to. She knew that smell would be imprinted on her brain for a long time, maybe forever.

He rolled down the street and made a right. A

thought suddenly had her straightening in the seat.

She unburied one arm and reached over to tap his shoulder. He turned his head.

"Do you know where I live?" she asked, forming the words slowly.

He signed back, *above the restaurant?*

She smiled and nodded. "Not too close."

He made the okay symbol with his hand and then patted her knee with a grin.

They didn't have far to go. Her family's restaurant was on Main Street, just a couple of blocks from the gym, but Max drove a block out of the way and came up on the Main Street intersection two blocks down from the restaurant, stopping at the red light. Malee glanced down toward her family business in the distance. Main Street was pretty much deserted at this hour of the night. The lights were out at Thai Garden, but she knew her parents were probably still back in the kitchen cleaning up and preparing for tomorrow.

The light changed, and they rolled through the intersection. Max turned right into an alley that ran behind the businesses. He pulled to the end where it came out at the cross street. If he continued across and drove farther down the next section of alley, her parents' restaurant would be the third one down on the right. She could see the green dumpster that sat beside the back door. Her brother's red Kawasaki Ninja bike was parked next to it.

Max put the truck in park and cut the lights. They

were tucked back from the street, nestled on the narrow alley between two brick buildings. In the dark of night, no one would notice them. The only faint light was the glow from the dashboard. She shot a glance over to his hands on the steering wheel. One reached to turn a knob on the stereo, probably turning down a song she couldn't hear. She noticed the size of his hands. They looked powerful, but they had been gentle when he'd touched her. She hadn't expected that gentleness from someone as big as he was.

She tore her eyes from his hands and looked out the window, trying to think of something other than his hands and how they might feel if they touched her bare skin.

Breathe, she told herself.

Rain pelted the windshield, and with the wipers turned off, it soon became a mottled glaze of streaks that turned everything into an abstract watercolor. Down to the right she could see the stoplight on Main, changing for an empty intersection. There was something forlorn about a stoplight that changed for no traffic. She could see it from her bedroom window and often watched its blinking colors late at night. She could also barely make out the Fourth Street Gym from her second floor window that sat at the corner of their building. The gym was down two blocks, but she could make it out. What she couldn't see from her bedroom window was the tattoo shop where Max worked. She'd tried, but it was too far east, and there were trees in the way. Sometimes she heard the motorcycles roar past, though—the ones that often stopped at Brothers Ink. She'd memorized everything about the colorful shop since meeting Max. It fascinated her, but not half as much as the man himself.

And now there she sat, alone with him in the dark of his truck. It made her stomach knot up. She didn't have much experience with men, and she wasn't sure what to do.

He tapped her knee, drawing her attention from her passenger window to the phone he held up to her.

I'm glad I met you the day you delivered our food.

She smiled and replied to him. *Me, too.*

They traded the phone back and forth.

I'm glad you came to Pops' tonight.

She nodded. *I was hoping I'd see you again.*

You can always come to Brothers Ink.

I don't leave the restaurant very much.

If I order food, would you deliver it?

She shook her head. *My brother does the deliveries. My father doesn't like me to leave the restaurant.*

Why?

She shrugged and looked away, not wanting to talk about it. He must have sensed it. After a moment he tapped her knee and, she looked back.

Can I get your phone number? You have a phone, right?

She shook her head.

No, I can't have it?

No, I don't have one.

He frowned. *Why?*

She pointed to her ear. *My father thinks it would be a waste of money.*

But you could text.

She shrugged. *It's expensive.*

Max nodded, not pressing her on the issue. *I like talking with you. Can I see you again? Will you come to Pops' next week?*

She bit her lip. *Maybe.*

Will you try?

She smiled and gave him a saucy look. *If I can.*

He chuckled, then his grin faded as he studied her. *Why aren't you allowed to go anywhere?*

Malee sobered and looked away for a moment before typing her answer. *My father is strict. It's for my own safety. He thinks it's better if I stay close.*

Is it because you can't hear?

She nodded, and could feel Max studying her as if he wanted to say more, but in the end, he stayed silent. She glanced at the clock on the dashboard. It was getting late and she needed to get inside before her parents came upstairs from the restaurant to the apartment above and found her missing. Her older sister would probably cover for her, but she didn't want to risk it. *I should go now.*

Max looked to the back door of the restaurant and gestured toward it. *Will you get in trouble?*

Not if I can sneak in. She waggled her eyebrows at him, and he grinned.

She undid her seatbelt and reached for the door handle, but he laid a hand on her arm, stopping her. He searched her eyes, and then slowly signed with his hand. *Can I kiss you goodnight?*

She couldn't stop her eyes as they dropped to his lips in the shadowy truck. She thought about the way it felt when he'd pulled her up against him, and she'd fit like she'd belonged there. Her hand dropped from the handle, and she nodded once.

His warm palm reached up and cupped her cheek as he tilted his head and touched their mouths together. It started out as just a soft, gentle press of his lips to hers, before he pulled back an inch, their eyes connecting. Then he went in for another kiss, this time his lips parting, his tongue seeking entry. She opened her mouth, and his tongue slid in to stroke along hers. Her hand crept up, sliding up and around his neck. He took that as encouragement and the hand that cupped her face, slipped around to cradle her head and pull her body closer.

Malee had never been kissed like this before. There had been a few boys in high school, but none kissed like this, and none had ever gone farther than a kiss. They had been boys; Max was a man, and she was finding there was a big difference. She was completely out of her depth here. And it felt wonderful. She didn't want it to end.

As soon as that thought crossed her mind, he pulled back, his breathing heavy. He typed on his phone, his thumb moving with maddening speed. Then held it up to her. *I don't want to stop, but you're a sweet girl, and I like you. I want to treat you right. So we better stop.*

Okay, she signed.

I want to see you again. Say you'll come next week.

She read his message, then nodded and spoke the words, "I'll come."

He glanced out the windshield. *It's still raining. Can I roll the truck up closer?*

She shook her head. He didn't look too happy with her answer.

You'll get wet.

I'll be okay.

His hand closed over the black fleece, and he pressed it toward her. *Take my jacket. Cover your head to keep the rain off.*

She looked down at the fabric and then back at him. "You're sure?"

He nodded with a look that told her she was taking the jacket, no arguments.

She took his phone and typed, *I'll bring it to you next week.*

He grinned. *Deal. Goodbye, Malee.*

"Goodbye, Max." She said his name, like she'd practiced in her room late at night. By the sparkle in his eye, she could tell he liked it.

He leaned toward her for one last kiss. Then she climbed reluctantly out of the truck and dashed through the rain toward the restaurant, holding his jacket over her head. She paused at the back door and looked back. He was still there, watching to make sure she got in safely. He'd turned the wipers back on, but not the lights yet. She could faintly see him through the windshield. She waved and saw his hand lift from the steering wheel at her, returning her gesture. A feeling of euphoria rushed through her as she quietly crept inside and up the back staircase.

***

Max watched her go. He already felt bereft without her, the empty truck feeling suddenly colder. *Jesus Christ, you barely know her.*

Didn't make a difference. Didn't matter one bit. He was sunk. One kiss, one sweet touch of her lips, and he was done for.

He'd known he was in trouble when he'd positioned her in front of the punching bag earlier tonight and touched her hips to get her stance correct. Hell, his big hands had almost circled her tiny waist. Standing so close behind her, he'd breathed in the scent of her long dark hair that hung in a glossy sheet to her waist. It smelled like fresh blooming honeysuckle. When he'd kissed her a few moments ago, and she'd slid her hand to his neck, he was sure she could feel his pulse beating a mile a minute beneath her gentle touch. It spurred him on to thread his fingers into that silky hair, finally touching it, like he'd longed to do since the moment he'd laid eyes on her. If she were any other woman, he'd probably have fisted it in his hand, urging her for more, and taken much more than a kiss. But she wasn't any other woman. She was like no one he'd ever met before—sweet, a little shy, but with a spine of steel. He'd seen that at the gym as he'd thrown down that challenge, and her delicate chin had come up, her determination and maybe a touch of stubbornness shining through. He had a feeling she'd been beaten down in life a time or two, but he bet she always got back on her feet, always willing to give her best shot. He liked that. He liked all of that.

But he had to face the fact that she came from a different culture. Her family obviously was very close-knit and protective of her. He could tell that much just from the few tidbits she'd shared with him tonight. Duty, responsibility… he knew about those. But he had a feeling it went deeper with her. He had a feeling she didn't ever want to disrespect, disobey, or shame her family. He'd have to be very careful if this relationship proceeded as he hoped it would. He'd have to treat her with the utmost respect. And another thing he'd have to do was take it slow. He could sense an innocence about her. It was in her eyes, in her body language, and especially in her kiss. That innocence drew him like honey. And he realized he wanted to be the one to change that someday.

He couldn't wait to see her again next week. Suddenly his Mondays were looking a whole lot brighter. He grinned as he flipped his lights on and put the truck in gear, pulling out onto the street and heading home to the farm he shared with his brothers. It was good to have something to look forward to. It had been a long time since he'd felt this kind of joy and excitement.

CHAPTER FIVE

Malee slipped off her shoes and crept up the back staircase to the second floor apartment. Her father owned the building, and the place was quite spacious. There was a small kitchen at the back, a dining room, and a large living room that looked out over Main Street. There were three bedrooms, one for her parents on one side of the living area, one for her brother in the back next to the kitchen, and one she shared with her older sister.

She crept through the quiet apartment. Her sister was in the living room. The TV was on, but Lawan wasn't watching it. She looked up from a magazine when Malee came into the room. She signed, *Where were you? Did you follow Kiet to that smelly gym again?*

Yes.

He came home a while ago. Where have you been?

Does he know I wasn't here?

No, he went to his room. I told him you were sleeping.

Mother and Father?

They haven't come up yet. You're lucky, Malee. You know I can't keep covering for you. Why do you want to sneak down there anyway? Do you want to take the class Kiet is taking?

She shook her head. *I just like to watch. I get bored sitting at home all the time. Why are Father and Mother afraid for me to go anywhere? It's not fair.*

Her sister patted the couch next to her.

Malee sat down, and Lawan pulled her into her arms, tucking her feet under her. She rubbed Malee's arm and signed with the other hand. *I know, baby. They are just trying to protect you.*

I don't need to be protected. I'm twenty years old.

Lawan's hand stroked her upper arm and hugged her. *What do you want to do? You're not happy working at the restaurant, that's obvious.*

Father will leave the restaurant to Kiet someday. Not me and not you. You know that. He won't even take any of the suggestions I make. I can't wait tables in the dining room, like you. I don't like to cook. What is there for me? I bus tables and wash dishes the rest of my life?

I think father wants you to marry.

So I can be someone else's responsibility.

You know that's not it. He wants you to be happy. But, Malee, he's a traditional man. He wants us both married. He thinks if we were wives and mothers it would make us happy.

Would that make you happy?

Her sister seemed uncomfortable with the question. She signed. *I overheard them talking. Father is bringing some boys from Thailand, supposedly to help with the restaurant. But I don't think that's why.*

What do you mean?

I think he's trying to arrange a marriage for me.

Malee sat up straight. *What? No.*

Lawan nodded. *I think he is.*

But you've been dating that paramedic. What about him?

Lawan shrugged. *He's not Thai.*

So?

Jake and I have been having problems. I think he cheated on me. I don't think he's the one. And besides, you know Father wants us to marry a nice Thai boy.

And you're going to go along with that? Marry some boy he picks for you?

I haven't even met him yet. Maybe I'll like him. Mother showed me a picture. He's very attractive. Mother says Father might leave him the restaurant, if I marry him and if Kiet doesn't want it.

Kiet doesn't want it? This was news to her. She'd always assumed…

I think he wants to go to college. He's brilliant, Malee. He wants to be an engineer. Maybe even work for NASA.

Our brother, the rocket scientist? Malee grinned.

Don't laugh, Malee. He's serious. He doesn't want the restaurant.

There's no money for college. Father says so.

Kiet thinks he can get a scholarship.

If he did, Malee would be happy for him. She didn't begrudge her brother that. She herself had wanted to go to art school, but there was no money for it. *So, you marry this Thai boy…*

His name's Kai.

So you marry Kai, and the two of you run the restaurant?

Maybe. Someday. She shrugged. *I don't know.*

Tears formed in Malee's eyes. It wasn't supposed to be like this. There had to be more to life than letting someone else plan out her life for her. And suddenly Malee longed to be free of it all—the restaurant, her father's expectations, a future that held no joy for her...

It's not just Kai, Malee.

What do you mean?

Father has plans for you, too.

Me?

There's a boy. Mother says his name is San'ya...

Malee looked at her sister. She knew Lawan felt the same pressure to please their parents as she did, to not disappoint them, to not shame them, but that wasn't the life she wanted. She had always confided in Lawan, so she told her about Max.

I met someone.

Lawan's face lit up in a surprised but bright smile. *You did? A boy?*

Malee couldn't hold back the giggle that bubbled up as she nodded.

Tell me. Lawan was almost ecstatic.

I met him when I delivered food to the place he works.

You took a delivery? I didn't know that. When?

A couple of weeks ago. I just grabbed the bag and ran out. I couldn't take being in that kitchen one more minute.

Tell me about him.

He's very tall with big muscles, but he's very kind, very considerate. And guess what?

What?

He didn't know how to sign when I delivered his food. But when I saw him again today, he had learned the alphabet. Just for me.

Lawan smiled. *That's so sweet.* Then she frowned. *Wait, you saw him today? How? Did you deliver food again?*

Malee shook her head. *No. He was at the gym where Kiet takes his class.*

Lawan's chin came up, and she gave her a knowing smile. *Aha. That's why you want to go there.*

Malee blushed and admitted, *Maybe.*

Is that where you made the food delivery? Is that where he works, the gym?

Malee looked down, plucking at a thread. *No. Where does he work?*

She stared into her sister's eyes. *He's very nice.*

You said that already. Why won't you tell me?

Father won't approve.

Lawan frowned. *Why not?*

Malee straightened her shoulders and lifted her chin. *You know the place a block down and on the other side of the street? He works there. Brothers Ink.*

Lawan signed in a jerky motion, a stunned expression on her face. *The tattoo place?*

Yes.

The place where all those bikers go? Malee, what are you thinking?

I like him.

Is that why you've been gone so long tonight? You were with him?

He was at the gym. I talked to him a little, that's all. Then he drove me home.

You went in his car? Malee, that could be dangerous. You hardly know him.

He'd never hurt me.

How do you know?

I just know, Malee signed angrily, her motions abrupt.

He dropped you off here?

Malee shook her head. *At the end of the alley so no one would see.*

Malee, you need to be careful. Sometimes men want to take advantage.

She rolled her eyes. *I know! But he's not like that! He held the door for me and gave me his jacket and everything.* She held up the folded black garment that was clutched in her arms.

Lawan frowned. *He gave you his jacket?*

Malee stroked the fabric lovingly. *So I would be warm. So I wouldn't get wet in the rain. See how sweet he is?*

Malee, are you going to see him again?

Maybe. Okay, yes. I promised him I'd come to the gym next week.

Baby sister, please be careful.

I will. I'm not a child anymore, you know.

I know. Lawan touched her cheek. *Father will never approve, Malee.*

We're just talking.

Is that all?

Well, he kissed me goodnight.

Lawan held her tongue, but Malee could tell she was worried. This time she made no foreboding statements, instead she asked, *How was it?*

Malee couldn't help but smile. *It was amazing.*

At that admission, her sister grinned. *My little sister is growing up.*

I'm already grown up!

I know. But you'll always be my baby sister. And I'll always worry about you.

I know.

I love you.

I love you, too.

Just please promise me you'll be careful.

I will.

They hugged.

I'm going to bed. Malee stood.

Lawan nodded. *Goodnight, Pumpkin.*

Malee walked into her room. It was in the front corner of the apartment with a turret window that overlooked the intersection of Main and Fourth Streets. It was the largest room and had the best view. That was compensation for having to share it with her sister, not that she didn't love Lawan, but it would be nice to have her own space. At least her sister had allowed her to have the bed next to the window.

Malee went into the connecting bathroom and changed into a sleep set with a spaghetti-strap tank and matching short bottoms. Then she washed her face, brushed her teeth, and climbed into bed. She grabbed Max's jacket that she'd laid on her bed and pulled it under the comforter with her, hugging it to her chest and breathing in the scent of him that still lingered on the fabric.

She gazed out the window at the lights of town. A vehicle moved up the street, its tires kicking up a wet spray, its wipers moving back and forth. She looked into the distance and could barely see the old-fashioned gooseneck light that hung over the door to Fourth Street Gym. Usually that light was out this time of night, but Max must have forgotten to turn it off as they ran out the door into the rain.

She thought of how he'd hidden her in the closet, of how he'd taken the time to show her how to punch the bag, and of the ride home he'd given her in his pretty black truck. But especially she thought about that kiss. Pressing her fingertips to her lips, she swore she could still feel the sensation. He had a beard, and she'd been surprised at its softness when he'd leaned in that first time to gently brush her lips with his. And then the second time, when his tongue had sought entry to her mouth, and the way he'd pulled her closer. She hadn't wanted it to stop, but he knew they shouldn't go too far. He'd been respectful. He'd called her a sweet girl and said he wanted to treat her right.

She believed him. Every word.

But Lawan was right. Her father would never approve of him. And it wasn't even the fact that he wasn't Thai. Her father would never approve of him because of what he did for a living, of who he was and who his family was. He would look at Max and see only the ink that covered his body.

Malee knew well that her father hated Brothers Ink. He hated the bikers and other clientele it brought to Main Street. He thought they were nothing but trouble, and not a respectable business. He'd even been one of the downtown businesses that had fought hard to get rid of them. He said those O'Rourke brothers were no good, had never been any good, and had never been anything but trouble to this town.

He'd even gotten some other business owners to agree with him, and they'd tried to see that the shop's business license be revoked. That had all changed when Max's older brother had become famous. Now he was the darling of the town, and her father knew he would never be able to get rid of that shop.

Sometimes Malee would see her father sweeping up on the street in front of the restaurant late at night when some motorcycles would ride past, headed to Brothers Ink, and she would see him shake his fist and mutter angrily.

No, her father would never approve of Max. So, she just wouldn't tell him.

Lawan was right, she needed to be careful, and not just about Max, but about making sure her parents didn't find out. Malee knew this wasn't the proper behavior expected of her, but as much as she tried to squelch it, she had a rebellious streak. Most days, the only thing holding it in check were the responsibilities of being part of a family business, the expectations of her parents, and a ton of guilt that she'd never measure up to those expectations.

She always tried to do what was proper, what was expected of her, but sometimes she just wanted to do what she wanted and to hell with all of the rest.

She didn't, though, because one thing that was ingrained in her from a very young age was that you never acted in a way that would bring shame to your parents. Seeing Max would shame her father.

But she wasn't ready to give Max up... not that she really *had* Max. They had only spoken twice now. And he probably wasn't looking for a real relationship with her, not one that would go anywhere. A man like him may tolerate her disability, but would he really want a wife who couldn't hear him? She didn't think many men would. There were only a couple of boys in high school who would go out with her, and they never went out more than once. Things with Max probably would never go very far, but whatever happened, she would enjoy the time she could.

Malee inhaled deeply, taking in Max's scent once again. No, she wasn't ready to give him up yet.

CHAPTER SIX

Max and Malee's next meeting didn't go as well as the last.

Kiet was late getting to the MMA class, and he'd been in a bad mood all day. Malee had noticed it earlier. Lawan said he hadn't done well on a test in school that day.

She'd asked if she could accompany him down to the gym, making the excuse that she wanted to look into a self-defense class that was offered. Her father, for once, thought that was a good idea and made Kiet take her with him, which made him even more annoyed.

While he was in the class, she sat on the sidelines and pretended to peruse the pamphlets. She'd noticed Max as soon as they'd walked in the door. His presence was magnetic, and she found her eyes immediately drawn to him. He was a big man, tall, muscular, and intimidating with all that ink, and maybe that was part of it, but there was something else, too. It was in the way he carried himself, the way he stood, the way he moved. But especially it was in the way his eyes scanned the crowd, searching her out…and when finally they locked on her, the beautiful grin he tried to hold back but couldn't.

Through the entire class, as he worked with the teacher as an aid in his demonstrations, she couldn't keep her eyes off him. That kiss they'd shared had left her restless. Some part of her awakened, making her feel alive in a way she hadn't before. The pull between them had been that strong. He'd branded her with that single kiss until she'd dreamed of it, over and over. Staring at him now, watching his body move, his muscles flex, the smile on his face… It was all like a dose of a drug she was newly addicted to.

The hour was over much too soon. While Kiet was in the locker room, she moved to the bulletin board on the wall to scan the different classes offered. But it was just a pretense, and they both knew it.

Max joined her. With both their backs turned to the room, he signed, grinning over at her. *Hello, beautiful.*

She peered behind to see the stragglers who were drinking water and chatting before heading to the lockers. In a soft unsure voice, she spoke. "Hello, Max."

That had him smiling even bigger, showing perfectly straight white teeth. He lifted a hand and signed to her. *You came.*

She nodded.

His eyes strayed to the board. *Are you thinking of taking a class?*

"I told my father I wanted to see about a self-defense class. He thought that was a good idea and made Kiet bring me."

I see. And do you really want to take a self-defense class?

Her chin came up, and she murmured, "Maybe."

He turned back to the bulletin board and pointed to the calendar.

She read the listing.

Sundays 2pm
Self Defense for Women.
Instructor: Max O'Rourke

"Then I definitely want to," she said.

He laughed. She could see his chest shake with it. She couldn't hear it, but she imagined it must be the most beautiful sound.

He signed slowly. *I thought about it a lot. About…you, and about* — his eyes dropped to her mouth — *everything.*

The kiss. He'd thought about their kiss! Happiness burst inside her.

He reached over and let their hands brush, his little finger hooking hers. Then he winked, and she felt her heart melt a little.

Max twisted, looking behind him. Malee followed his eyes to see Kiet was tapping him on the shoulder. His eyes moved between the two, and Malee wondered how long he'd been watching, how much he'd seen. He didn't look happy.

He jerked his head toward the entrance, his eyes on her, and signed, *Wait for me by the door.*

Malee was disappointed that her brief time with Max was cut short, but she did as her brother said. Even though she was two years older than Kiet, her father had made him responsible for accompanying her tonight, and he took his duty seriously.

She handed Max the jacket she'd promised to return tonight. "Thank you."

With Kiet standing there, he could do nothing more than nod and accept it.

She walked toward the entrance. Turning back, she saw Kiet speaking in a firm way to Max, who was clenching his jaw like he was holding back a comment. Instead he just nodded respectfully. His lips moved, but whatever he said, it was short.

Then he turned and walked away. Kiet followed him with his eyes, before swinging back to pin Malee with a look. He moved toward her, coming to stand in front of her.

Father would not want you associating with men like him.

We were just talking, Kiet.

Let's go, Malee.

She glanced over her shoulder as Kiet held the door for her. Max was wrapping his hands with tape in jerking motions as he stood before the punching bag. His eyes flicked up in time to catch hers as she moved through the door. There was anger there, but they softened for a moment. She tried to communicate with her eyes that she was sorry.

***

Max watched the metal door with the red peeling paint slam shut behind them. He finished wrapping his hands and then slammed a fist into the bag, taking out his frustration.

Kiet had warned him off Malee, telling him to keep his distance and refrain from speaking to her. Max wanted to argue with him, but he knew it would get him nowhere. If he wanted in the good graces of her family, arguing with Kiet was not the way to go about it. All he could do was assure the boy he meant no disrespect. The kid had moxie, though; he gave him that. He was twice Kiet's size, and the boy didn't even flinch in telling him there'd be trouble if he didn't keep his distance. Something told him that was going to be easier said than done.

CHAPTER SEVEN

Max walked out of the Main Street Diner and stood under the awning, waiting while Liam paid the check for breakfast. His eyes flashed up to the sun. It was after ten, and they needed to get back to open the shop by eleven. His gaze dropped back to scan the street as he lifted his to-go coffee to his lips. He paused, the cup half way to his mouth, his eyes doing a double take across the street.

Malee.

His piercing stare focused in on her like a hawk's.

She was walking down the sidewalk, an empty reusable shopping bag over her shoulder and a girl who must have been her sister at her side. Her hair swung and her hips moved in an enticing sway as she walked. He felt a kick in his stomach.

She didn't see him as they approached, so he eased slowly back against the wall and surveyed her.

He took pleasure in watching the way she moved so carefree and easy down the sidewalk. It occurred to him that she must enjoy the bit of freedom from the restaurant, even if it was just to run to the Asian grocery the two stepped into. He decided he'd wait a while, just to get another chance to see her when they exited.

Liam came out, but Max wasn't ready to leave just yet, so he instructed, "Go on ahead, I'll be along in a few minutes."

Liam gave him a funny look and noticed where Max's eyes went. Once he saw the Asian market, it only took him a second to put two and two together.

"Ah. Is the girl from Thai Garden in there?"

Max gave him a piercing look that told him to shut up.

Liam chuckled, punched him in the shoulder, and headed down the street. He got about five steps before turning back and shouting, "We could use some soy sauce, if you want to stop and pick some up!"

Max ignored him. He would be content to just catch another glimpse of Malee when she came back out. So he leaned against the wall and sipped at his coffee, his eyes repeatedly darting to the market's glass doors.

Two groups came out of the restaurant and brushed past him. And still Max waited, barely mindful of them. When the market door opened, he straightened. The wait had been worth it. It had been a week and a day since he'd seen her last, yet she was every bit as beautiful as she had been when he'd first stared down into her eyes.

Another group of diners exited behind him, and the sun's strong morning rays hit the glass door as it swung open, and a blinding flash reflected across the street onto Malee.

She looked up quickly, eyes drawn to it, and that's when she spotted him. There were maybe a hundred feet between them. It didn't matter. Even across that distance with people passing by and cars driving past, he saw her flush and swallow, and look away only to glance back again.

He could read her expression — she remembered, just like he did, how that kiss had been between them.

She turned back to her sister, walking away, pretending a nonchalance he knew she didn't feel. He knew it, because he still felt what they'd shared. And she felt it, too. She glanced back once more, giving herself away. He'd been right. It was just an act. She was as affected by the sight of him as he was by the sight of her.

He stared after her, letting her see that he watched her still, followed her every move with his eyes as she walked away and disappeared up the crowded sidewalk.

***

The restlessness that flowed through Max the rest of the day wouldn't leave, no matter what he did. Finally, as evening closed in, he walked into the break room.

Liam was bent at the waist, his head in the fridge. He looked up as Max dropped himself in a chair, folded his arms, and leaned back, a scowl on his face.

"What's your problem?" Liam asked.

Max stayed stubbornly mute.

Liam reached and grabbed an energy drink from the top shelf and joined his brother. The only sound in the room was the pop of the can opening with a fizz as Liam cracked it open. "You gonna be like this all week?"

Max flipped him off.

Liam chuckled. "Now that's the only sign language you'll ever be any good at."

Jameson walked in, took one look at Max and asked Liam, "He in another mood?"

"Yup."

Jameson pulled the carafe from the burner, poured himself a mug of coffee, and turned to lean back against the counter. He paused, the rim at his lips. "You want the girl, do something about it. Otherwise, you need to shake this funk you're in."

Max stared at the tabletop until both his brothers' remarks sank in — *really* sank in.

They were right. He needed to put up or shut up. And if he wanted Malee, he was going to have to earn her, , he was going to have to show her he was worthy, and he was going to have to learn sign language. Not just the alphabet — the real stuff like Liam knew, so he could converse with her at a conversational speed, his hands and fingers moving as quickly as he'd seen Liam do when he'd signed to Malee.

So, there it was: the big decision. Did he want a real chance with her?

"So what's the verdict?" Jameson asked. "You goin' after her or not?"

Liam huffed out a laugh and teased, "He'd need to learn how to communicate with her first. Not sure he's a good enough student. Can't teach an old dog new tricks, and all that."

"Who are you callin' an old dog, dickhead?"

"Either she's worth it or she's not," Jameson stated.

Max's pissed off eyes swung from Liam to Jameson. "She's worth it!"

Jameson nodded, then grinned over at Liam. "Guess that makes you his new tutor."

Liam's brows shot up as he pinned Max with a look, the front legs of his chair hitting the linoleum with a bang. "You serious, dude?"

"Yes, I'm fucking serious."

Liam grinned. "Well, hell. I wondered how long it'd take for you to come to your senses."

Jameson looked at the calendar on the wall. "Eight days. Rory wins the pot."

"What pot?" Max asked.

Liam was only too happy to inform him. "We each put in twenty bucks. Rory bet you'd take ten days or less. Jameson said two weeks."

"And you?"

Liam's face split in a wide smile. "Me, I said six months."

"You suck. You all suck."

Jameson let out a laugh as he walked out of the

room.

Max slammed a fist into Liam's shoulder. "Asshole."

"Hey." Liam rubbed the spot. "The student doesn't hit the teacher."

"This one does."

"How much does this gig pay, anyway?"

"I'll give you my tips."

"You realize it takes years to learn."

"Are you shittin' me?"

"Nope."

"Christ, I can't wait that long."

"Well, you pay attention and practice a lot, and maybe I can teach you enough phrases to say a few things to her in a month."

"A month? She can talk to me; I don't need to be able to read what she signs. I just need to be able to sign what I need to tell her."

"Well, I suppose if you write down a list of some sentences, you might be able to learn them in a couple of weeks."

Max nodded. "Okay. I can do that."

Liam stood and tossed his can in the garbage. "Decide what you want to say. We'll start tomorrow."

Max stopped him at the door. "Liam?"

"Yeah?"

"Thanks."

His brother paused to study him. "She better be worth it."

"She is."

Liam winked at him and walked out.

***

Good to his word, Liam used any free time they had teaching Max as much as he could. Every day for two weeks they worked together until Max was a natural at signing the twenty odd phrases he'd asked Liam to teach him. Liam called them Max's two-a-days, just like they'd had to do in high school football. Only this time it was two phrases a day that Max had to learn. And Liam cut him no slack, drilling him endlessly until Max's frustration would boil over and he'd flip Liam off.

Max would then run his hand over his head, take a deep breath, shake it off and start again.

His determination to learn this stuff for a girl had all his brothers watching him with admiration. They ribbed him, but they encouraged him, too.

CHAPTER EIGHT

Two weeks later —

Max stood at the front window of Brothers Ink, sipping a cup of coffee. He stared past the cheesy Halloween decorations—that Ava had insisted they put up on the glass—to the street beyond. The holiday was a week away, but with the snap in the air, it already felt like November.

Max eyed the sky. It was early yet. The shop didn't open for another hour, but Jameson had taken Ava to her obstetrician's appointment, and Max had promised to open up. He'd left the farmhouse right after the two of them. His brother was a nervous wreck the closer she got to her due date, and Max found that hilarious. Jameson was totally out of his depth.

And he wasn't the only one. Ever since Max had met Malee, he couldn't get her out of his mind; it kept straying back to the way she had felt when he'd pulled her up against him in his truck, the way her lips had felt under his. Hell, it had been almost a month, and he still couldn't forget the delicate, sweet taste of that innocent mouth.

"Max!" He turned at the sound of Liam's sharp voice.

"What?" he snapped, pissed to be shaken from his sweet thoughts.

"Jesus, dude. I called your name like three times. Are you spacing out again over that chick?" Liam came to stand beside him.

"Just trying to enjoy my fucking coffee. That okay with you?"

Liam huffed out a laugh. "Yeah, right." He folded his arms and leaned against the window frame. "When's Rory due back in town?"

"Fuck if I know. Call him and ask."

"He's not answering."

"Typical. Whenever he's on the road with his band, he's notoriously hard to reach. Text him. You might get a reply in a day or two."

"I bet if Jameson called him, he'd fucking answer."

"Yup. He's smart enough to know better than to piss off big brother."

At ten in the morning, Main Street already had a lot of foot traffic. Maxwell sipped his coffee and watched absently as people moved past on the sidewalk.

"Look, there's Steffy," Liam pointed out. Maxwell's eyes swung to the coffee shop across the street and two doors down, spotting Ava's sister. She came out juggling a tray of coffees and a bakery bag. But it wasn't her that had him straightening; it was the person on the street she bumped into, sending the coffees spilling and crashing to the pavement.

Malee!

"Whoa, shit! Did you see that?" Liam shouldered away from the door.

Malee was shaking her hand like the hot drinks had burned it.

"Come on!" Max snapped, and both brothers went out the door and dashed across the street.

Steffy was apologizing profusely. "I'm so sorry, Miss. I didn't see you. It was my fault entirely. Are you okay?"

Max's voice was calm as he said, "She can't hear you, Stef."

Steffy frowned. "What?"

"She's deaf," Liam informed her and began signing to Malee. *She apologizes and wants to know if you're okay.*

Malee nodded, but she was holding her hand tucked to her waist and there were tears in her eyes.

Max knelt before her and reached for her hand. "Liam, tell her I want to see her hand."

Liam signed the words, knowing that was not in the list of phrases he'd taught Max.

She shook her head.

Max looked directly into her eyes and mouthed, *please.*

Reluctantly she let him pull her hand free and held it out. It trembled with pain and was bright red.

His eyes lifted to her. *I'll fix it. I promise. Okay?*

She nodded, a tear rolling down her face.

Max rolled back her long sleeves. The burn appeared to be only the back of her hand and wrist.

"We need to get this tended to. Tell her to come to the shop, and I'll take care of her, Liam."

Liam signed and pointed across the street.

"Maybe she should go to the hospital," Steffy suggested nervously. "I'm so sorry."

There were fresh fruits and vegetables scattered around their feet, and Max realized, with a glance at the bag, that Malee had just come from the Asian grocer. He stood and pulled her toward the curb, ordering Liam, "Get her things and bring them, okay?"

"Yeah, sure thing."

Max led Malee across the street and up into Brothers Ink, but she pulled back. He could tell by one look at her face, that besides the pain, she was very nervous about being in the shop.

It's okay, he signed.

She shook her head, but he ignored her, knowing time was of the essence. He pulled her to the back, led her into the room they used for piercings and straight to the sink. He turned on the cool water and put her hand under it.

She tried to pull it out, but he held it firm, trying to sign with the other hand. *It will help.*

Liam stuck his head in the door. "She okay?"

"Tell her she has to keep her hand under the cool water for twenty minutes."

Liam signed to her, and she nodded. He set her bag of groceries down on the padded table. "I'll get her some Ibuprofen.

When they were alone again, Max grabbed a tissue and wiped Malee's tears. He nodded to the water running over her hand and signed, *Better?*

She nodded and slowly said, "I wasn't looking."

Max grinned and shook his head, mouthing, *nope.*

That had a smile pulling at the corner of her mouth.

He lifted his chin to the grocery bag. *Shopping?*

She nodded. "Every Tuesday and Friday morning."

Max nodded, thinking he'd start making it a point to be standing outside twice a week, just to get to watch her walk past.

Her sorrowful eyes met his. "I'm sorry about what my brother said to you."

Liam came back in with a small bottle of water and two caplets in his palm. He held them out to her. She popped the pills on her tongue and then took the bottle, swallowing them down.

Max motioned for her to drink more, so she turned the bottle up again with a roll of her eyes.

"Tell her I saw that," he said to Liam.

Liam chuckled and signed it to her.

That got him a smile and another eye roll.

Max waved his finger in front of her face, teasing her that she'd better not do that again.

Liam signed something to her that had Malee laughing. Max didn't know what it was, but he assumed it was some joke about him. He didn't mind, for once. As long as it distracted her from the pain, she could laugh at him all day.

Liam glanced at his watch. "I think that's been long enough."

Max nodded and turned off the faucet.

She reached for a paper towel from the dispenser, but he grabbed it out of her hand and tossed it aside. Before she could respond, he grabbed her waist and in one quick motion he hefted her up onto the padded table.

Her eyes got big.

"Tell her it's better to air dry," Max said.

Liam signed the explanation to her.

She sat facing him, her legs dangling as he rolled over a stool and sat in front of her, then gently took her hand in his, examining it. Lifting his eyes to hers, he swore he could get lost in those beautiful soulful depths. He winked. "Tell her she'll be okay, but to keep it uncovered and not to put any ointment on it."

Liam signed to her, and then asked Max, "Anything else you want me to tell her, Dr. Max?"

"I've got it from here, smartass." He twisted to give Liam a look that told him to give him the room. Liam took the hint with a grin and closed the door quietly as he left. Max signed to her.

I've missed you.

"Me, too." She took note of the fact he was no longer using the alphabet to sign. "You're learning sign language?"

He nodded. *I've been practicing some phrases.*

She seemed pleased and pointed to herself in

question.

Yes, for you.

Her face brightened.

I want to see you again. Can you meet me?

"I don't know."

Please.

"Maybe."

I wish you had a cell phone so I could text you. Maybe I'll buy you one.

Her eyes got big, and she shook her head. "It wouldn't be right to accept it."

Can you come here to the shop, just to talk sometimes?

She shook her head. "The restaurant is down the street. Someone might see me."

He was tempted to ask her to come in the back door, but even as he thought it, it sounded wrong. She didn't deserve to be relegated to coming in a back door like she wasn't worthy of the front. *After the gym closes, could you meet me there?*

She bit her lower lip and hell if he didn't want to kiss it. "Maybe. If I can sneak out."

What time?

"I don't know." She searched his eyes. "How will I know if you're there?"

I'll leave the outside light on, the one over the red door. If it's on, I'm there.

She nodded. "Okay. I'll try."

If the light's not on, don't come. I don't want you wandering the streets. It's not safe.

"Okay. I can see the door from my room."

How will I know you're coming?

"I'll put a small lamp in the window."

He nodded, happiness flooding through him for the first time in a week.

"I better go. They'll wonder what's taking so long."

He nodded, the smile fading. Then before she could hop down off the table, he stood, planting both his hands on either side of her hips, leaned in, and kissed her. She was only surprised for a second, before her mouth opened under his, and he swept inside, and it was just as sweet as he remembered. He pulled back a fraction to search her eyes.

She grinned, reached up, and tugged the bottom of his beard, pulling him back to her mouth for another kiss.

Max kept his hands locked in place on that padded vinyl. Determined not to scare her by doing what he wanted—which was to wrap his fists in her hair and pull her body flush against his, pushing his hips between her knees to spread them wide. It all flashed through his mind, every move he wanted to make, and his fingers curled into the padding in absolute control of the urge, fighting it back with every ounce of willpower.

He broke away, his breathing heavy, and pressed his forehead to hers. She was breathing hard, too. Her delicate uninjured hand came up to cup his beard-covered cheek.

"I should go, Max."

He straightened and helped her down, but paused to sign. *Tonight.*

She nodded, grabbed her bag, and walked out.

He stood in the room, knowing if he followed her to the door, he wouldn't be able to resist hauling her back into his arms for one more kiss.

He'd see her tonight. He could wait that long.

CHAPTER NINE

Three days later —

Max walked into Thai Garden along with Liam, whom he hadn't had to coerce too much into accompanying him; just the offer of buying him lunch had done the trick.

Max had never been in the place before; they'd always ordered delivery. A hostess station was in front with a middle-aged woman that had to be Malee's mother. She was attractive for her age, her hair pulled up in a bun. She gave them a slight bow.

"Two?"

"Yes, ma'am," Max replied.

She grabbed two menus and led them to a booth against the wall near the kitchen door. The red vinyl creaked as he slid his big body in.

"Your waitress will be right with you." The woman smiled and departed.

Max took a moment to survey the place as he picked up the menu she'd set before him. It was dim, the front windows tinted against the bright sun. A large golden Buddha sat on a pedestal against the back wall, flanked by bamboo plants. There were a few booths along each sidewall and about a half-dozen tables in the middle of the room. The place was not packed, but they did good business.

His eyes found Malee. She was across the room, busing a table, her hair braided down her back. She wore a white double-breasted restaurant shirt with the sleeves rolled to her elbows.

Max knew he should stay away, that it was risky coming here—where her family was, where her father and brother were—but he couldn't help himself. He couldn't wait any longer. For three nights, he'd gone to the gym and left the light on above the door. And for three nights, no lamp had shown in her window.

Max knew he couldn't speak to her here, not where anyone could see, but he had a plan.

Their waitress appeared at the table, setting down two glasses of water. Max studied the girl and knew in a moment she was Malee's sister—the same girl he'd seen walking with her. The resemblance was undeniable.

She took in the tattoos running up their arms, then her gaze lifted to the *Brothers Ink* logo on their black T-shirts, and her eyes got big. She maintained her demeanor, though, pulling her order pad out.

"What would you like today?"

Liam scanned the menu. "I'll have the Pad Thai and an order of spring rolls."

Max's eyes strayed back to Malee while the waitress was waiting on Liam. He saw her turn, her eyes sweeping the restaurant, probably searching for other empty tables that needed busing. They landed on him, and her mouth dropped open, and damned if she didn't almost drop the gray bin full of dishes she was holding.

"And for you, sir?" The waitress addressed him, drawing his attention and forcing him to break eye contact with Malee, but not before the girl noticed and glanced over her shoulder. When she looked back to pin him with her eyes, she knew who he'd been looking at.

"I'll have the same." He handed the menu to her, wanting to get rid of her. He waited until she left, his head twisting to make sure she was through the kitchen door before he turned back to search out Malee. He didn't have far to look; she was heading for the kitchen herself, passing right by him. He only had a moment.

He reached out and touched her arm, halting her in her steps. Her eyes flashed to his, and she darted a look around the room. He slipped a note from his pocket and held it out near her hand.

Her fingers extended, just enough to grab onto it, and then she disappeared through the same swinging door.

"Smooth."

Max turned back to see Liam grinning. "Shut up."

"You see the look the waitress gave us?"

"Yup. I don't think they think too highly of where we work."

"Or maybe she was fascinated by our beautiful ink," Liam suggested with a waggle of his brows.

"Did that look say 'fascinated' to you?"

Liam chuckled. "Nope. You and this girl, it's starting to feel like Romeo and Juliet. So which ones are we, the Capulets or the Montagues?"

"Hell if I know. I flunked all that literature crap in high school."

***

Malee set the bin on the stainless steel counter next to the dishwashing machine. She clutched the folded note to her chest, and her eyes slid closed. She was terrified and excited at the same time as to what might be written on it. He'd come, here to her restaurant, and he'd done it just to pass her this note. She'd almost dropped the bin of dishes when she'd turned around and spotted him across the room. Her heart had plunged to her stomach. But she couldn't deny the thrill that seeing him again gave her.

She'd wanted to meet him, but she couldn't slip out that first night, and then with every night that went by, she was sure he'd eventually give up on her.

A tug on her sleeve had her eyes popping open. Shoving the note in her hip pocket, unread, she turned to see her sister signing to her frantically.

Did you see who came in for lunch?

Malee nodded.

Is he one of them?

Yes.

Which one?

The one with his back to the kitchen door.

Did he come to see you?

She pulled the note out. *He gave me this.*

Lawan pulled her by the arm into the broom closet, quietly closing the door and flipping on the light.

What does it say?

I haven't read it yet.

Well, read it. I won't tell anyone what it says. Hurry.

Reluctantly Malee pulled the paper from her pocket and carefully unfolded it.

Malee,

Meet me tonight.

I'll be at the gym after it closes.

I'll leave the light on above the front door for as long as I'm there.

I need to see you.

Please come.

Max

Lawan read it over Malee's shoulder, then looked at her and signed, *Will you go?*

Malee sucked her lips into her mouth. Did she dare?

Her sister persisted. *Do you want to see him?*

Malee wanted to see Max more than anything, but she'd been afraid. Finally, she nodded.

Lawan brushed a stray tendril back from Malee's

face and tilted her chin up to meet her gaze. Malee saw her sister's eyes had glazed over. Then Lawan smiled and hugged her. When she pulled back, she signed, *Do you want me to walk you there?*

Malee shook her head.

Okay, but I'm going to watch out the window and make sure you get there okay.

Malee laughed and rolled her eyes.

Her sister's look grew serious again. *He better be good to you.*

Malee gave her another quick hug and peeked out the closet door. No one was watching, so she quickly motioned Lawan to follow her.

Lawan put her arm out, stopping Malee. *Do you want me to slip him your answer when I bring them the check?*

Malee's eyes lit up and she nodded.

Lawan pulled a pen from her pocket and held it out to Malee, who snatched it and grabbed a paper napkin with the Thai Garden logo on it. She scribbled on it and tucked it into Lawan's apron pocket.

***

Max's knee bounced up and down. The plates on the table were empty, their lunch consumed, and all they needed was the check. He hadn't seen Malee come back out to the dining room since he'd passed her that note, and now he was worried that perhaps he'd overstepped. Maybe he'd built their relationship up in his head to be more than it really was. Perhaps she wasn't as interested in him as he was in her. He leaned his forearms on the table, his fingers interlaced.

The water glasses trembled with the rapid movement of his leg under the table.

"Dude, quit it," Liam said. "You're nervous as a cat."

The kitchen door swung open, and Max twisted his head to glance over his shoulder. Their waitress exited, her eyes on them, but before the door swung back he could see Malee standing in the kitchen. Their gazes locked for a split-second before his view of her was cut off. He tried to read her expression, but it was just too damn quick.

"May I get you anything else, gentlemen?" the waitress asked.

Liam answered for them. "No thanks, darlin'. Just the check."

She put it face down on the table and then her eyes connected with Max's as she pulled something from her pocket and held it out to him.

He slowly reached out and took it, and she walked back into the kitchen. His gaze followed her as the door that was all that separated him from Malee swung open again. This time she wasn't standing there.

He glanced back at the folded napkin the girl had slipped him. He opened it.

Yes, I'll come.
Wait for me.

He felt the fist constricting his heart ease, and he grinned.

"I take it she said yes."

Max lifted his eyes to Liam's teasing ones as he shoved the napkin in the breast pocket of his T-shirt. "Yup. Let's go."

They stood. Liam grabbed the check. "I got this one. You leave the tip."

Max dug in the hip pocket of his jeans and pulled out several folded bills. He plucked a twenty from among them and tossed it on the table. Malee's sister deserved it for delivering the note that had just made his day.

CHAPTER TEN

Max waited outside the gym, his hands thrust into his pockets, his shoulders hunched against the cold. He had a thermal shirt on under his short-sleeved black *Brothers Ink* T-shirt and a quilted flannel shirt over that, but he still felt the bite of the October night.

He could wait inside, out of the brisk wind, but he wanted to watch for Malee. It was almost eleven. He'd left the shop early tonight, purposefully scheduling his last appointment early enough to cut out by nine. That gave him enough time to come lock up the gym for Pops.

He glanced down the street. He'd give her until midnight before he gave up on her coming tonight. It was possible she wouldn't be able to sneak away, even if she'd wanted to, even if she'd said she would.

He leaned a shoulder against the corner of the doorway, his eyes on the distant darkness, and asked himself if he was crazy for trying to pursue this girl. On one hand he felt the deck was stacked against them. They came from two different worlds and, apparently, her family didn't approve of him. Being an O'Rourke in this town still held a trace of the old prejudices they'd come up against most of their lives. To some they were still the no-good hooligans half the town thought they were growing up — the disrespectable, disreputable bad boys who ran "that tattoo place".

Then there was the age difference. He was in his thirties. She was young. He didn't know how old, but she had to be in her early twenties, innocent and possibly naïve. Everything told him he should run for the hills.

But then there was that other hand. The one that told him they connected — on a level he'd never experienced. He felt it the first time he'd looked into her eyes and every time since then — when he'd first seen her staring up at the wall of art in Brothers Ink, a look of wonder on her face, and then when she'd turned her face toward him, and he'd been knocked upside the head with the aura that surrounded her…

He didn't know what the fuck it was, couldn't explain it if his life depended on it, but he knew it when he felt it. *Bam*! It hit him like a ton of bricks.

It was crazy, he knew, but that didn't make it any less true.

His eyes focused in on movement in the shadows a block down, and he straightened. The figure was slight and moving rapidly. It had to be her.

He stood in the circle of light from the bulb above the door. He wanted her to see him, to know he was here, waiting, just like he'd promised.

She wore jeans and a short hooded down jacket. The hood was pushed back, and her long glossy hair flowed in the wind, gleaming under the moonlight.

As she drew closer, he caught the smile on her face, and his broke out in an answering grin, the happiness at just seeing her bursting inside him. He couldn't help himself, when she got close enough he grabbed her face in his palms and pulled her close, his mouth descending on hers.

It was the best hello he could give her.

When they finally broke apart, he signed, *You came.*

She nodded. "You waited."

I promised I would.

"I was afraid I was too late."

He shook his head, and then reached out a hand and pulled her toward the door and out of the cold. He signed, *I'm glad you came.*

She tried to sign something to him, but he waved his hands. *I only know a few phrases. You have to use your voice.*

"What else did you learn?"

He signed the phrase he'd practiced the first day. *I missed you.*

She smiled. "I missed you, too."

I watch you walk by every Tuesday and Friday on your way to the market.

"You do?"

He nodded.

"I saw you that day you were across the street," she said.

I waited outside just to watch you come out.

"You did?"

He nodded again, the smile on his face near to bursting. He pulled her to him and kissed her once more. She opened her mouth when he probed, and she seemed just as eager as he was, but a few moments later she was pushing out of his arms, one hand planted firmly on his chest.

He looked down at her, his brow creasing in a confused frown. What had he done?

Her eyes searched his.

What's wrong, he signed.

"I didn't come here to…to have sex with you, Max."

He was so relieved it wasn't something else, he almost huffed out a laugh, but she wouldn't think it was funny, so he signed, *I know that. That's not why…* His hands stilled, he couldn't think of the symbols. There was so much more he wanted to say — more than the few words and phrases he'd learned. Finally he signed one he knew. *We need to talk.*

She nodded once and whispered, "Okay."

He pulled her to a couch against one of the brick walls. When she sat, she pulled a small backpack he hadn't noticed before off and dropped it to the floor. An artist's sketchpad poked out.

What is that? He pointed to it.

She pulled it out, her face bright with excitement. "My drawing book. I wanted to show you a picture I drew."

He bobbed his head enthusiastically and waggled his fingers to hand it over.

She flipped to a page and passed the book to him.

It was a picture of a hummingbird caught in mid-flight, its wings back, its body curved forward. The colors were vibrant, the detail amazing.

He mouthed the word, *Wow!* And then signed alphabetically, *Amazing!*

"You like it?"

I love it. It's very good.

Her face beamed with pride.

He made the motion of a pencil.

She nodded and pulled one out of her bag.

He turned to a blank page and pointed to it, asking silently if he could write on it. She nodded. He scribbled the things he wanted to say, but couldn't sign.

We have to work out a way to see each other. And no, I didn't ask you to come here for sex. I like you. I want to get to know you. Do you feel the same way, Malee?

He turned the pad for her to see and held his breath while her eyes traveled over the lines. When she reached the end, those beautiful dark eyes lifted to his, and she nodded.

He turned the pad back and wrote again.

Doesn't mean I don't still want to kiss you, because I do. But I'll be respectful. I won't do anything you don't want me to. You say, stop, I'll stop. We can just talk if you want. I want to know all about you. Okay?

He flipped the pad around.

She nodded again, enthusiastically. "I'd like that, too."

He wrote again.

Tell me about your drawings. Can I see others?

She nodded and motioned to the pad.

He thumbed through the pages. They were all good, one after another. *Incredibly* good. He looked up at her with big eyes and smiled, then flipped back to the page he'd been writing on to scribble another note.

You're an artist. They're all good. He paused and scratched out the word good and replaced it with the word *great!*

She blushed, but her eyes brightened from just those few words of praise, and it made him wonder if she received much encouragement regarding her art. He jotted another note.

Is this what you'd like to do for a living? Something with your art?

She shrugged.

No wonder you were so fascinated by the art on the wall at Brothers Ink.

She nodded. "All the colors were so beautiful. They inspired me."

Good. I'm glad. He hesitated with the pencil hovered over the paper, then scratched out another sentence. *Did you have any trouble getting out tonight?*

"I just had to wait until everyone went to sleep."

He began writing again, and she scooted closer to look over his shoulder so he wouldn't have to keep flipping the pad around.

Could you meet me here every week? Whatever time is good for you. Whatever day. I'll make it work. You could come to our shop if you want.

His eyes met hers earnestly.

She shook her head. "Not your shop. If someone saw me…"

He nodded. *After the gym closes, could you meet me here?*

She bit her lower lip and damned if he didn't want to kiss it. "Maybe. If I can sneak out."

He nodded, happiness flooding through him for the first time in a week. *When?*

"I don't know." She searched his eyes. "Maybe Wednesday nights."

He nodded. One night a week wasn't ideal, but he'd take it. He jotted another note. *The shop is closed on Sundays and Mondays now. Could we spend time together on one of those days? Can you ever go out?*

She bit her lip, thinking.

The pencil scratched across the paper. *You know I'd like to come to your door and pick you up, meet your parents, do this right.*

She shook her head frantically, a panicked look on her face. "No, you can't. My father would never allow me to see you."

Why? Because of the tattoo shop? Or because I'm not Thai?

"He hates your shop. He hates the people it

attracts."

And the other part?

She looked down, plucking at her sleeve. He tilted her chin up with a finger, searching her eyes.

"I think he would prefer I marry a Thai boy."

Max nodded. She was honest, he couldn't fault her for that, but it still saddened him to think he may never measure up, that he may never be the kind of man they thought she deserved. But, damned if it didn't make him want to try.

"I wish things were different," she whispered.

Me too, sweetheart, he scrawled and then looked away. She touched his sleeve, and his gaze fell to her delicate hand, resting on the soft flannel.

"I still want to meet you. I don't care if we have to sneak around. And maybe someday we won't have to."

He looked up into her eyes and signed one of the phrases he'd learned. *How old are you, Malee?*

"Twenty."

When will you be twenty-one? When is your birthday?

"November twentieth."

He nodded, studying her. She was so young, younger than he'd even thought. Jesus Christ, this whole thing was insane.

As if she read his mind, she said, "I'm not a child. Everyone treats me like one. Don't you treat me like one, too! Promise me."

He searched her eyes. God, he didn't want to disappoint her. He wondered if there would be any path that this would lead them down that didn't end in heartbreak for both of them. But somehow, he had to give it a shot. He signed, *Okay. I promise.*

"I should get home," she whispered.

He nodded and started to shove her drawing pad in her bag, but she stopped him with a hand. He looked up at her, and she took the pad, thumbed through it, stopping on one drawing. She tore it off and handed it to him.

"For you."

Taking it, his eyes dropped from her smiling face to the paper. The hummingbird. He met her gaze and signed, *Thank you.*

She shoved the pad in her bag and stood.

Can I drive you home?

"Okay. To the alley."

He nodded, grinning, and took her hand in his, watching as her eyes fell to their joined hands. He gave hers a squeeze, which caused her gaze to flick up to his. A smile burst across her face, and he gave her a wink. She returned the squeeze and winked back.

They walked to the front, and Max flipped off the lights and locked up. His truck was parked on the street, and he beeped it open, then held the door for her. When she was inside, he jogged around to his side and climbed in. He put the drawing in the glove box and started the engine while she buckled up.

He adjusted the heat and soon the truck was warm. Then he pulled from the curb. As he drove slowly down the street, wanting to stretch their time together, he reached out and took her hand in his. Threading their fingers together, he rested their joined hands on her thigh.

As he turned a corner and headed toward Main Street, he glanced over at her. She felt his gaze and turned her head. They both grinned.

He stopped at a red light at Main and glanced around. The town was quiet, the streets empty, nothing but a cold wind blowing scraps of paper and a few stray brown leaves down the street.

The light changed, and he drove across, a moment later pulling down the alley, until he was stopped in the same spot as the last time he'd dropped her off.

Putting the truck in park, he looked over at her and signed, *What do you do on the days the restaurant is closed?*

She shrugged. "Sometimes we prepare food or go shopping. Sometimes I read."

He pulled his phone out and tapped out a note, turning it for her to read. *If you can get away, I'd like to see you. You could put that light in your window to let me know.*

"Maybe."

His eyes searched the alley, and he noticed a pipe going up along the brick wall near the back door to their restaurant, and he had an idea.

You could leave me a note. You could tuck it between that pipe and the wall. I could check for it every day.

She nodded, brightening. "Okay."

He set his phone on the seat, and this time he didn't ask if he could kiss her goodnight. He just cupped her face, his fingers threading into her silken hair, and pulled her to him. She opened for him this time with no coaxing, and her hands moved to his shoulders.

Her kiss was just as sweet as he remembered. He could smell the fragrance of the soap she used, or maybe it was the shampoo she used. He wasn't sure. But its scent filled his nostrils, and he breathed deep. He broke off, remembering his pledge to go slow with her.

Stroking his thumb over her cheek, he studied her eyes. She would let him go further if he wanted, he could see that. And that was exactly why he needed to stop. She needed to be able to trust him to stop. He wanted her to trust him. It was important to him, he realized.

So he eased back, putting more space between them.

They smiled at each other, and then he lifted his chin toward the back of the restaurant, releasing her.

"Goodnight, Max," she said softly.

Goodnight, Malee, he signed. And then she slipped out of the truck, dashed across the side street and disappeared into the darkness. He watched until he saw the light that appeared when she unlocked the restaurant's rear door and slipped inside.

Then he cranked the engine and slowly pulled out.

***

Malee snuck up the dark stairs and crept through the quiet apartment. She slipped into the room she shared with Lawan. A small bedside lamp burned next to her sister's bed. Lawan lowered the book she was reading, and her eyes searched Malee's. She signed, *Are you okay?*

Yes. I'm fine. You waited up for me?

I was worried about you.

You don't have to worry. Not about Max.

You were out walking the streets at night. Of course I have to worry.

He drove me home.

Good.

Go to sleep.

Are you going to see him again?

I hope to, yes.

Was he nice to you? Did he behave?

Yes, Lawan. He was very nice. Now go to bed.

Her sister put her book aside, flicked out the light, and rolled over.

Malee changed into her pajamas, brushed her teeth, and crawled into bed. She stared out the window, down the street toward the gym. The light was off this time, but she could make out the building in the glow of the streetlamp.

She thought about Max's idea to write notes to each other. She would write him a letter. She smiled, thinking about tonight. He'd learned some actual sign

language for her. That melted her heart. And he'd been
so respectful of her. She had to admit, she'd had some
misgivings about meeting him, and then when he'd
kissed her, pulling her close, she'd been afraid her fears
would come true, that he was just interested in sex. But
he wasn't. He'd proved that. And everything he told
her, she believed.

He wanted to see her again. She'd have to come up
with some excuses, some reasons to be gone more. She
longed to have the freedom other girls had, but she
knew her parents were not like other girls'.

Malee closed her eyes and drifted off to sleep with
the image of Max smiling down into her upturned face.

CHAPTER ELEVEN

Malee was in the restaurant kitchen the next morning. It was early, and they hadn't opened for lunch yet. She was chopping vegetables, the steam in the kitchen already making her T-shirt damp. It didn't matter; her mind was a thousand miles away.

Okay, maybe just blocks away.

Kiet, who'd been peeling shrimp next to her, brushed off his hands and went to open the back door, talking to someone outside.

Malee frowned, wondering who it could be. They'd already gotten the seafood delivery this morning.

An older woman whirled in. She was dressed in a bright colored skirt, a flowered blouse, with scarves around her neck and a huge brimmed hat pushed down over the gray hair on her head. She pulled a pair of big designer sunglasses off and peered at Kiet.

It was Aunt Ratana! Malee hadn't seen her in years, but she remembered her father's oldest sister and her favorite of all her aunts.

Aunt Ratana had married a rich man, but he'd died a couple of years ago. They were from Thailand, but had lived in California since she was first married. She was the first in the family to come to America. Soon after, she'd worked to bring Malee's father over.

He was the youngest of the seven children, in his early sixties now, but Auntie Ratana, who was the oldest, was in her upper seventies. And her husband had been in his eighties.

Malee always loved when Aunt Ratana would come to visit. She was so vibrant, so full of life. She lived life to the fullest, always going, always doing. And now that her husband had died, Malee heard she'd been traveling all over the world. She had the money and freedom to do it, and a part of Malee envied her. To be able to do what she wanted, go where she wanted... Malee longed for that type of freedom.

Aunt Ratana hugged Kiet and then pulled back, holding his face in her palms. She studied him and said something to him. Malee tried to read her lips, but she didn't quite catch it all—something about being proud of him. Then her eyes moved past Kiet to Malee, and she clasped her face in surprise, her mouth forming a big O. The biggest grin formed on her face, stretching from ear to ear, and she clapped her hands and waved Malee over.

She signed, *Malee! Come here. Come see your Aunt Ratana!*

Malee dashed into her arms, surrounded by a big hug as a rich, exotic perfume enveloped her—a perfume she remembered from her childhood.

"Aunt Tan!" she called, using the nickname she'd given her aunt as a child.

Her aunt pushed back out of her arms so she could sign to her. *You have grown so big since I last saw you, Malee. And into such a beautiful woman, too!*

Malee's father came forward and hugged his sister. She patted his face and said something joyfully up into it. Then pulled back, turned to Malee, and signed, *I told him he is still my favorite little brother.*

Malee could see everyone shake with laughter, even if she couldn't hear it.

Her father said something to his sister. Aunt Tan poked his arm and gestured to Malee, then she signed, *Sign so she can understand you!*

That was one thing Malee loved about Aunt Tan. She always made sure she was included in any conversation — something her parents sometimes forgot to do.

Her father glanced to Malee, and then signed as he spoke to his sister. "Ratana, why didn't you tell me you were coming?"

"I thought I'd surprise you."

"I'll make up Kiet's room for you, Aunt Ratana," her mother said, signing along for Malee.

"No need. I already found a place."

"Found a place?"

"Yes, Brother. I plan to stay in Grand Junction for a while. I want to get to know my favorite nieces and nephew better."

Malee knew that Aunt Tan had never been able to have children of her own. Being the free spirit that she'd always been, Malee wondered if that hadn't worked out for the best for her aunt. She'd enjoyed a freedom that having children would never have allowed her.

But perhaps now, with her husband gone, she'd come to miss having children in her life. Malee didn't know, but she was glad to have her aunt come for a visit. Things around the restaurant were always livelier when she came.

"Where is this place you found?" her father asked.

"It's a furnished apartment over one of the stores just down the street. It's above the empty storefront next to the coffee shop. It's suitable for my needs."

Malee's heart skipped a beat. That meant it was right across from Brothers Ink. She knew the spot. It had a big bay window that overlooked Main Street.

"Do you need help getting the place cleaned up?" her mother asked.

"No, it's very clean, very lovely. But I do need some help unpacking. I'm having quite a few boxes shipped over."

"How long do you plan to stay?" Malee asked her.

"I don't know, dear. I've signed a six-month lease. So I'll be here until the spring. Then we'll see if I'll stay on. Perhaps the itch to travel again will hit me. But for right now, I've had enough of traveling. I'm ready to stay put for a while and get to know my nieces and nephew better," Aunt Tan said and signed.

"That's wonderful!" Lawan said, signing along for

Malee.

"I'm famished. How about you feed your Aunt Ratana, then maybe after the lunch rush, one of you can walk back and see my new place." She looked to Malee. "How about you, Malee?"

Malee nodded. "Oh yes, Aunt Tan. I'd love to."

She clapped her hands together under her chin and signed back as she spoke. "Good. Then it's all settled."

CHAPTER TWELVE

On Monday afternoon, when the shop was closed, Max taught an afterschool class for middle school boys at Pops' Gym. It was a beginner class that taught the basics of boxing and MMA, half aimed at getting them interested in signing up for the other classes—at least that's how Max had sold it to Pops—but really Max wanted to give the kids something to do to get them off the streets in the summer. It had been so well received he'd decided to offer another class during the fall.

Over the last few weeks, he'd begun noticing a skinny boy of about seven or eight years old hanging around. The boy would never come inside; he would just stare through the window and watch. Max had attempted to invite him in once, and the boy had run off when he'd opened the front door.

This afternoon, Max was trying a different approach. He left the front door propped open and ignored the boy, hoping his obvious curiosity would draw him inside. Max had turned up the music, trusting that would make him feel less noticed. It worked. Halfway through the class, the boy slipped inside to stand at the back.

Max pretended not to notice him until he decided

to show the class some techniques with the punching bag.

"Everyone gather around and sit in a circle." He pointed to the boy in the back. "You, there. Come hold the bag for me so I can demonstrate."

For a moment the skinny kid looked terrified, but Max just pretended not to notice while he got a pair of gloves. Honestly, he wasn't sure if the kid would come up to him or run out the door. Then the kid's scuffed hi-tops come into his peripheral vision.

Max extended his gloved hand, wrist up, and asked nonchalantly, "Can you close up that Velcro for me, kid?"

The boy hurried to comply, pulling them tight around Max's wrists.

Max grinned at the boy and extended his knuckles toward the kid. "Great job. Give me a fist bump."

The boy's face lit up under Max's small praise, his smile bursting ear-to-ear as he bumped his frail fists to Max's huge gloves.

"Think you can steady the bag for me?"

The boy shrugged.

"It's simple." Max pointed to a spot on the floor. "I just need you to stand here, brace your shoulder against the bag, and hold it in place for me. Can you do that?"

The boy nodded enthusiastically as Max took him by the shoulders and moved him into position.

"Perfect."

He turned to the class and gave the boys some pointers on how to stand, how to throw a jab, and other techniques.

When he was finished, he turned to the boys. "That's all for today. Next class maybe you'll each have a turn hitting the bag. Let's have a round of applause for my assistant."

The boy grinned shyly as they clapped.

"Class dismissed."

The boys all scrambled off the mat. Some of their parents were waiting for them. Max turned to his new assistant. "Could you put these gloves in that box over there?"

He nodded.

Max extended his wrist. "Give me a hand getting 'em off?"

The boy reached to pull the Velcro loose.

"What's your name, son?"

"Ben," he replied softly.

Max extended his hand. "Pleased to meet you, Ben. You can call me Coach Max."

They shook, the boy's frail hand looking ridiculously small in Max's big mitt.

"Well, Ben, you're the best assistant I've ever had. I sure wish you could stick around and help me some more. I've got to sweep this big ol' floor all by myself. I might be here all night."

Ben thrust his chest out proudly. "I could sweep. I'm a good sweeper."

"You are? That's awesome! Come on. I've got this push broom. Think you can handle it?"

"I can handle it," he assured Max with his chin up.

Max led him over to the wall and got the broom. The boy eagerly pushed it around the floor at racecar speed. Max grinned, not sure how much actual good it was doing, but happy he'd finally drawn the kid in.

When he was done, Max asked him if he could come back next Monday and be his assistant again. The boy excitedly agreed.

"You live close by, Ben?"

He nodded.

"Do you want me to call your mom or dad and have them come pick you up?"

He shook his head, his smile disappearing.

"Do they know where you are?"

The boy hesitated.

"Is your mom home?"

He shook his head.

"Where is she? In town shopping?"

"Momma's gone."

Max wasn't sure if he meant she was dead or on a trip, so he didn't question it. He just nodded. "I see. And where's Daddy?"

"Daddy's at the bar."

That had Max's chin coming up an inch. "Oh. Is the bar near here?"

"It's the one with the green frog."

There was only one bar around that had a frog in

the front window—a green neon frog. Otto's Pub, a tiny dive bar two blocks down on Colorado Ave.

"Do you need to call him?"

The boy shook his head.

"Do you need a ride home?" Max knew it was probably not a good idea to be driving a child anywhere without his parents' permission, but he hated to have the kid wandering the streets after dark. And this time of year, dark came just after six o'clock.

"I have a key." Ben pulled the red yarn string it hung by from under his shirt as if that made him responsible.

"Can I walk you home? Just to make sure you get there?"

Ben shrugged. "I guess so."

Max moved to some hooks on the wall and grabbed a hooded sweatshirt jacket that had Fourth Street Gym imprinted across the chest. He glanced over at Ben as he slipped it on, noticing the boy didn't even have a decent coat. "Hey, Ben, seeing as how you're gonna be my assistant and all, you really need to wear one of these jackets. Come on."

Max led him to the office and dug around on a shelf. He knew Pops had an extra one somewhere that he'd gotten for one of his grandkids who'd come to visit from Florida last summer. He found it and pulled it out. It was brown like his, but a small.

He held it out. "Try this on for size."

The boy turned and slipped his slim arms into it. It

hung off his shoulders and down to his knees as he turned with a huge smile, modeling it. Max held out his hand for a high five. "Looks fantastic!"

The boy smacked his hand, and Max led him outside. He paused to turn out the lights and lock up, his eyes automatically straying down the street toward Malee's bedroom window.

There was no light on.

He turned and held his arm out. "Lead the way, my good man."

Ben marched off, his chin in the air for all the world, as if he were dressed in a tuxedo.

Max chuckled, flipped his hood up, and jammed his hands in his pocket. A moment later the boy mimicked his actions, flipping his own hood up and tucking his hands in the low hanging pockets. Max reached over and folded back the edge of the too-big hood so the boy could see. They exchanged a grin and walked down the street.

They walked two blocks down Fourth Street, in the opposite direction of Main. When they reached Pitkin Avenue, the boy turned right and led him down two blocks to a less-than-desirable side of town. The boy stopped in front of a small run-down house. The gray paint was peeling, and the tiny yard was nothing but dirt. The house next to it was boarded up, a rusted BEWARE OF DOG sign hanging lopsided by one corner on the chain-link fence. The house on the other side was a drab mud color, but the tiny porch had a rocker and a broom leaned against the wall next to the door. Faded floral curtains hung in the windows. It was run down, but at least the place appeared to be kept tidy.

Max glanced back at Ben's house. It had no fence, but it should have had a condemned sign on it, in his opinion. The roof looked like it leaked, and one of the windowpanes had been broken at some point and now was repaired with nothing more than a piece of cardboard and duct tape. A navy blue bed sheet hung in the front window as curtains.

"Is anyone home, Ben?"

The boy shook his head.

"No brothers or sisters?"

He shook his head again.

Max glanced down the street. "You have any family around? Aunts? Uncles? Grandparents?"

He lifted his bony shoulders in a shrug. Then he turned and inserted the key. *Hell of a lot of good the lock did*, Max thought. He or anyone could have booted in that flimsy piece-of-shit door without half trying. Hell, he could just punch his fist through the cardboard and climb in.

Max stood on the walk, not at all feeling good about leaving this child here alone. He glanced down the street, wondering if he should call the police or child services, or if he should find Ben's dad and beat the shit out of him.

"You wanna come in?"

Max's head swung back. Christ, how many people

did this kid invite into his home? Max hesitated. But maybe Ben was afraid of the dark house. Maybe Max should go in just to make sure there wasn't anyone inside. Feeling uneasy about the whole situation, Max nodded. "Yeah, sure. Just to make sure you're safe."

Ben flipped the light on, and Max followed him. The inside wasn't much better. Ratty couch. Ancient TV that Ben immediately flipped on. An old game system hooked up, so at least the kid had that. Must be his only form of entertainment while he waited around for his alcoholic father to come back from Otto's.

Max knew he was making all sorts of snap judgments, but he was having a hard time coming up with any explanation for this boy's current living conditions. Yeah, he knew some people had a hard go of it, struggling to make ends meet, but then why the hell would his father be at a bar drinking away what little money the family had while his son wandered the streets?

"Think I could get a glass of water, Ben?" Max asked, more because he wanted an excuse to see the kitchen than anything else.

"Sure, come on." Ben led the way.

The floors creaked under Max's weight as they moved down a hall to the kitchen at the back. It was as ancient as the house. An old chipped porcelain sink and drain board perched atop dingy pale green cabinets on one wall, an old stove squeezed next to it, and on another wall, an old refrigerator with a box of kid's cereal on top.

"The glasses are in there." Ben pointed to an upper cabinet and started to climb up on the sink to get one, but Max stopped him.

"I got it, son." He reached up and opened the cabinet, half afraid what he might find. In the back of the cabinet, he spotted a bottle of whiskey, an inch of amber liquor remaining. It was tucked behind some mismatched dishes, a couple chipped coffee mugs, and some glasses that looked like they'd been swiped out of a bar.

Max took one down and leaned to fill it at the tap. He glanced over as Ben opened the fridge and stood looking inside for something to eat. Max could see there was not much there. A bottle of ketchup, four cans of beer, a gallon of milk that looked like it was down to its last glassful, and on the second shelf, a half empty pack of hot dogs.

Ben stared forlornly at the contents.

This was just too much for Max to handle. He couldn't bring himself to leave this boy here with barely any food.

"Hey, Ben. You want to share a pizza with me?"

Ben's eyes got big as he swung around. "A pizza?"

"Yeah." Max rubbed his stomach. "I'm starved. I was just thinking about ordering one."

Ben nodded his head. "I love pizza. We don't have it much, though."

I bet, Max thought, pulling his phone out. "You like

pepperoni?"

Ben's head bobbed in excitement.

Max called the local place and ordered two large pizzas and a six-pack of colas. When he hung up, he looked at Ben and asked, "So, you got any good video games?"

Two hours later, they were full of pizza, the leftovers tucked away in the fridge, Max having purposely ordered more than they could eat so the kid would have some for tomorrow. Max had wrapped it in a piece of tin foil he'd found in a drawer and hidden it down in the vegetable crisper. He'd put his finger to his lips, and told Ben. "Shh. Don't tell anyone. It's your secret stash for tomorrow."

Ben had grinned and nodded.

Max had discarded the empty boxes in the garbage can outside.

Now they were on their third video game; it was almost ten and Ben's father still wasn't home.

Max stared toward the window, wondering how he should handle this. Should he wait around for the man and give him a piece of his mind? Would the guy turn the tables on him and call the police, saying he was the intruder or worse, accuse him of being some kind of child molester?

If Max confronted him, would Ben's father forbid him from ever coming to the gym again? Right now that may be the only safe place this kid had to go. Max might have a chance at being a positive influence for

Ben. If he played this wrong, he might be cut out of the boy's life and any chance of that would be gone.

If he called the police, where would Ben end up? Would he be put in the care of the state? Could he be doing the boy more harm than good by reporting this?

And what did he really know?

The phone on the kitchen wall rang. Ben went to answer it. When he came back, he said, "That's my dad. He's on his way home."

Max nodded and stood. "Good. I guess I should be going, then. You gonna be okay?"

Ben nodded. "Thanks for the pizza, Coach Max."

He ruffled Ben's hair. "You're welcome, Ben. I'll see you for the class next Monday, right?"

"You bet."

Max headed to the door. "You ever want to stop by the gym, it'd be okay."

"Okay." Ben's face brightened.

"I have another job. I work at the tattoo shop on Main Street. You know where it is?"

"The one where the motorcycles park?"

"That's the place. You ever need anything, or just want someone to talk to, you can come by and see me anytime you want, okay?"

Ben's eyes got big. "Okay."

Then Max pulled his wallet out and took out a business card with his cell phone number. "You hang onto that. Call me if you ever need me."

Ben nodded, looking at it.

Max opened the door, but paused to turn back. "You lock up, now, okay?"

"I will."

"Goodnight, Ben."

"Goodnight, Coach Max."

He waited until the boy had locked up before he stepped off the stoop. As he headed down the sidewalk in the brisk October night, he wondered if he was doing the right thing. He'd only gotten a few feet when a voice from the neighbor's porch called to him.

"What business you got with that boy?"

It was the voice of an old woman. Max stopped in his tracks, his eyes searching the dark porch. The rocker creaked, and he spotted an elderly woman sitting in it. A flashlight beam hit him in the face, and he lifted his arm, shielding his eyes from the blinding light. "Ma'am?"

"Who are you? You aren't that boy's father." Her voice was accusatory. She dropped the beam to the ground, and he could see again.

"He was hanging around the Fourth Street Gym. I wanted to make sure he got home safe."

The beam hit the logo on his sweat jacket. "Fourth Street Gym, huh? That where he's been going?"

"Yes, ma'am. Do you know the boy's father?"

"Useless piece of garbage is what he is."

Max walked closer. "I'm Maxwell O'Rourke."

Her chin came up. "O'Rourke?"

He'd heard the censure before in townspeople's

voices when they said his name like that. He was an O'Rourke. No matter that he'd never been in any serious trouble before. He was one of those wild parentless O'Rourke boys, and they all knew no good ever came from them.

"You one of Betsy's boys?"

Max cocked his head to the side, frowning. "You knew my mother?"

"Yup. Knew both your parents. Used to come in our store all the time."

"Your store?"

"My husband ran Larsen's Hardware. I'm Ingrid Larsen."

Max leaned forward and shook her hand. "Nice to meet you, Mrs. Larsen."

She looked over to Ben's house. "I keep an eye on the boy. Saw the pizza delivery. Take it you fed him."

"Yes ma'am. There's hardly any food in the place. He said his ma was gone and his dad was at the bar. What's the story on the kid?"

"His mother died a couple years ago. The father's been a drunk ever since. Lives off some bogus disability claim and whatever he gets from social security for Ben."

"So he drinks away most of it?"

"That'd be my guess."

"Jesus Christ," Max murmured half under his breath.

"I try to make sure he eats. Share what I can. I had

some soup on the stove. I was going to ask him to come over and have some. You want a bowl?"

Max wasn't hungry, but he thought the woman might be a source of more information on Ben, so he accepted. "If you don't mind sharing, sure."

She was slow getting up out of the chair that rocked as she stood. She wore a faded floral housedress with a full smock apron over it, her silver hair pulled back in a neat bun.

He followed her inside, the aroma of something delicious cooking on the stove wafted through the house to him. The front door opened into a small living room. The furniture was old and had seen better days, but the place was clean and tidy. She led him through to the kitchen in the back.

"Sit down, Maxwell." She indicated a mint green, chrome and Formica dinette set straight out of the 1950's. He took a seat while she moved to the stove and began ladling up two bowls of soup.

"Can I help?" he asked.

"No, dear. I've got it." She carried over a steaming bowl and set it before him, placing a spoon down next to it. Then she set a plate with some rolls in the center of the table and returned for another trip with her own bowl. She sat across from him.

"It smells delicious, ma'am. Thank you."

"It's homemade turkey noodle."

He spooned a helping and tasted it. It was wonderful. "Mmm. This is great."

"Thank you. The boy likes it."

"Do you feed him often?"

"Most nights."

Now that they were in the light, he got a look at her face. She must have been a beautiful woman in her youth. Her eyes were a pretty blue, and her silver hair still held a few wisps of blonde around her face.

"So you owned the old hardware store, the one on Main Street?"

She nodded. "Forty-seven years."

"I remember it, vaguely. You had some die cast metal cars on a shelf in the front, right?"

She smiled at his recollection. "By the cash register. Some of the young boys in town collected them."

He nodded. "I was too old, but I remember Liam and Rory being into those."

"Your father used to bring them in with him when he needed something."

Max stared into his bowl. "That was a long time ago."

Her wrinkled hand moved across the table and covered his. "I'm sorry about the accident."

He looked up and saw only sincerity in her eyes. No pity. He used to hate when the town folk would look at them with pity. "Thank you."

Her hand slid away, and they both went back to silently eating. She tore a roll in half and dunked it in her bowl.

Max wondered if this was what her dinners usually

consisted of — some soup and bread. He paused with his spoon halfway to his mouth. "How long has the store been closed now?"

"Going on eleven years. Just after my Gunderson passed away."

"So you're a widow?"

She nodded.

"No children?"

She shook her head, a trace of sadness in her eyes. "We weren't blessed with children."

"And now you have Ben to look after."

Her face brightened a little. "Yes. Now I have little Ben, and he has me."

"I'm glad he has you. He needs someone."

"What he needs is a good man to look up to. One to set an example." She set her spoon down and looked him dead in the eye. "Are you that man, Maxwell O'Rourke?"

Max dropped his eyes to his bowl, moving his spoon in a slow circle in the soup, considering her question. "I don't know if I'm anyone's good example, but I want to help the boy. He needs looking after."

"That he does."

"You remember me from back then, all the trouble I got into?"

"I remember. I also remember who turned you around."

Max glanced up into her knowing eyes. "Pops."

She nodded. "Pops. Maybe you can be for that boy

what Pops was for you."

He looked away, his eyes stopping on the slow drip coming from the old faucet as he remembered how his life had changed the day Pops had taken him under his wing. Could he be that for this boy?

He'd been yearning for something more fulfilling for a while now. Although he loved tattooing, and knew it could be healing for so many clients to have their grief expressed in a visible way, he felt there was room in his life for more. Brothers Ink would always be his work. It was the family business, but he enjoyed the time he spent at the gym teaching the young kids. Perhaps helping Ben wouldn't be such a hardship.

He looked back at Mrs. Larsen. "I'll help him any way I can. I'm at the gym on Monday nights to teach a class, and sometimes I'm up there to close up the place. I told Ben he's welcome anytime. I kind of made him my assistant for the class. Hoped it would get him off the street. He's been hanging around outside with his nose pressed to the glass. Every time I tried to talk to him, he'd run off. Tonight was the first time I was able to coax him inside. Had him helping out a little. Told him he could be my assistant from now on."

"Good. The boy needs a place to go."

"I gave him my card and phone number. Told him he could call me if he needed anything." Max reached into his wallet for another one. He slid it across the table to her. "I want you to have it, too. You or the boy need anything, just call."

She nodded.

"I guess I should be going." He stood and carried his bowl to the sink. "Thank you for the soup."

"You're welcome. It was nice to have the company."

He hesitated. "Mrs. Larsen, I don't know how to say this without sounding…"

When his voice trailed off, she prodded, "Just say whatever's on your mind."

"You're on a fixed income. Things must be tight, yet you share what you have with the boy." He nodded to the table. "And with me just now. Would you let me help you out with a little grocery money, so you can continue making sure the boy eats?"

She gathered her bowl and carried it to the sink. Setting it in the basin her hands clenched on the rim as she considered his offer.

Max studied her stooped back and boney hands, hoping he hadn't offended her.

"I should refuse. But I can't let my pride stand in the way of that poor boy getting enough food to eat." She turned to face him. "So, I'll take you up on your offer and thank you for it."

Max nodded, a smile bursting on his face with his relief. He reached for his wallet and pulled out three twenties, holding them out to her. "I'll stop by with more every week."

She reached up and took them, tucking the bills in her apron pocket.

He turned and headed toward the front door, and she followed behind him. With his hand on the doorknob, he turned. "Thanks again for sharing your meal with me. I'm glad we got a chance to talk. Take care."

"You, too."

"You've got my number now. Think you could give me a call tomorrow night, just to let me know Ben's okay?"

She nodded. "I will. I promise."

"Well, goodnight, then."

He moved out the door, pausing on the porch, his eyes moving to Ben's house. The place was quiet, so he stepped off and headed up the street.

At the corner he glanced back, wondering if Ben's dad had shown up when suddenly he sensed movements in the darkness toward Main Street. It was a man approaching. Max pulled out his phone and pretended to take a call as he stood and watched. The guy walked right past him, barely glancing up, but it was enough for Max to get a good look at him and smell the alcohol on his breath. The man moved down the street and up to Ben's house. He swayed slightly on his feet as he unlocked the door.

When he disappeared inside, Max moved closer, trying to listen for any yelling. When he heard none, he flipped his hood up and headed home, the man's face embedded in his memory, filed away in case Max ever had to drag the bum out of Otto's some night.

Max walked the four blocks back to Pops where he'd left his truck parked. As he approached, he glanced up the street toward Main. In his concern for Ben, and getting him home safe, he'd forgotten to check for a note from Malee.

He got in his truck and drove the few short blocks. Pulling to the curb of the side street, near the back alley that led to Thai Garden, he put the vehicle in park. Leaving the engine idling, he got out and jogged up the alley. All was quiet as he moved to the pipe to look for a note. He spotted a piece of notebook paper that had been folded up into a little square. He pulled it out and jogged back to his truck, climbed in, and sat in the warmth, his cold fingers unfolding the paper. He flipped on the overhead light and read it.

Dear Max,

I missed you today. But something wonderful happened. My favorite aunt came to visit and has rented an apartment across the street from your shop. It's above the empty storefront next to the coffee shop.

Tomorrow I am going over there to help her unpack. Perhaps I'll catch a glimpse of you out the window.

I miss you.

Malee

Max grinned. She missed him. That thought had a feeling like warm honey spreading through him. He leaned and dug through the glove box, coming up with a pen and pad of paper that he'd stashed in there for just this occasion. He quickly jotted down a response, tore the sheet off, folded it, and jumped out of the truck. Jogging back up the alley, he hid the note before driving home, happy for the chance to maybe see her tomorrow.

CHAPTER THIRTEEN

Malee slipped out of bed at the crack of dawn to check to see if her note was still there. She tiptoed across the kitchen, and opened the door to the stairs slowly, cringing at every creak it made. Then she dashed barefoot down the wooden stairs. The restaurant and kitchen were dark, with only the glowing exit sign over the back door to light her way. She unlocked the bolt, opened the door that led to the alley, and peered outside, her eyes landing on the pipe. Her note was gone, and in its place was a folded piece of tan paper. She leaned out the door, her arm stretching until her fingers nabbed the note. She quietly closed the door and flipped the light switch for the bulb in the stairwell. She sat with her butt perched on the wooden step, her bare feet on the linoleum, and unfolded the paper. Smoothing it out lovingly, her eyes took in his scrawling handwriting, a script she was coming to love.

Any glimpse of you, I'll take, so I'll be watching for you.
I miss you, too, baby.
So much.
I'm happy your favorite aunt has come to visit, but I'm

not sure how this is a good thing for us. Will she be just another set of eyes watching your every move like a hawk?

Something happened to me tonight, too. I found a young boy hanging around the gym. I've seen him before, but he never comes inside. He always runs off. Tonight his curiosity finally drew him inside. I think I made a connection. This kid really needs help, and it makes me feel good to think that maybe I can help him.

I'll try to catch a glimpse of you when you're at your aunt's new place. Wave if you see me standing at the window. I won't wave back, because I don't want your aunt to see, but know in my heart, I'm waving back. Maybe we can have a signal. I'll pull on my ear to let you know how much I miss you.

And lady, knowing you might be right across the street will mess with my concentration tomorrow! I know I'll keep going to the window and checking to see if you're there.

I'll wait for you at the gym tomorrow night…if you can make it.

Max

Malee read the note twice. He'd called her baby. She smiled, her heart soaring. He missed her, too! And he was just as excited to tell her about his day as she had been to tell him about hers. She couldn't wait until it was time to go to Aunt Tan's apartment. She'd get to see him today. She was as excited as if it were Christmas morning.

***

At noon, Malee was waiting with Aunt Tan as the movers carried up the last of her Aunt's things. The apartment was furnished, but she'd shipped a dozen boxes and several smaller pieces like artwork, a hand-carved teak hope chest, an oriental rug, and a carved four-panel dressing screen.

The apartment itself was quite lovely, with gleaming polished floors, fresh paint, and an updated kitchen and bathroom. But perhaps Malee's favorite feature was the big bay window that protruded out the front of the living room, giving a wonderful view of the street and the mountains in the distance.

While her aunt was settling up with the movers and signing their paperwork, Malee moved to the window to look across the street to Max's shop. There were three motorcycles parked in the spaces in front. The blue neon sign read, *Brothers Ink*. Max wasn't at the window, but she could see him sitting on a stool, bent over the arm of a man sitting in one of the tattoo chairs. He looked intent on his craft. She admired what he did, being able to create something so beautiful, using skin for his canvas. It fascinated her. As if he felt her eyes, he glanced toward the window. A moment later, he said something to his customer, set his tattoo machine down, and stood. He approached the plate glass, and suddenly he was looking right at her.

She lifted her hand in a small wave.

A big grin spread across his face, and he tugged on his ear.

She couldn't help the answering smile as her face glowed with happiness, and she returned the gesture.

The apartment door closed, and her aunt called her name. She turned her head, then looked back at Max and gave another tiny wave before retreating from the window.

***

Max stood in the shop window, the soaring happiness at just seeing her, at knowing she was just across the street, moved through his system like a shot of adrenaline. But at the same time, he couldn't help but wonder if her aunt would be a help or a hindrance to their budding relationship.

He moved back to his client and took up his tattoo machine. It buzzed as he clicked it on.

***

Two hours later, Malee and her aunt had her clothes hung in the closet and her dishes unpacked and stored in the kitchen cabinets. They'd just unpacked a tea set.

Aunt Tan signed, *How about some tea, dear?*

Malee nodded, and her aunt pointed to a small wooden box.

There's tea in there. Could you make us some?

"Of course," Malee said. "Go sit down and rest, I'll bring it out."

Aunt Tan moved slowly toward the couch, and Malee could see her age was starting to catch up with her. No matter how vibrant her aunt was, there was no stopping the aging process. Malee noticed, for the first time, that her aunt was much frailer than she'd realized. She turned back and began preparing them both some tea.

A few minutes later, she carried it in on a tray to the living room, setting it down on the coffee table.

Her aunt patted the couch cushion next to her, and Malee sat while Aunt Tan poured the tea like a queen holding court. After they each drank a cup, Aunt Tan set her cup down and signed, *So, what have you been up to Malee? Tell me everything.*

Malee set her cup down and shrugged. "I work in the restaurant. I read. I've been doing a little drawing."

How wonderful. You have to show me some of your drawings.

"I'll bring them next time I visit."

Her aunt nodded. *What else is going on in your young life? Is there a boy?*

Malee bit her lip, and her aunt pressed her.

There is! You must tell me everything, dear. Is he handsome?

Malee couldn't stop the smile that burst across her face as she nodded.

Well, come now; tell me about him.

"He's very kind to me. He's even trying to learn sign, just for me."

He must really like you, dear.

"I think so."

Where did you meet him?

"I delivered food to his business. I'm not supposed to, but I snuck it out."

Why on earth can't you make a delivery?

"Father doesn't want me to. He doesn't want me to leave the restaurant."

Why not? Are you afraid?

She shook her head. "No! I'm not afraid. I want more freedom. I long for it. But Papa is so protective of me."

I see. Perhaps we can do something about that. Perhaps I could help.

"Will you talk to him about it?"

I have an even better idea. I'll ask him if you can stay here with me a few nights a week.

Malee's mouth dropped open. "Really?"

If you would like that, I could tell him I need someone to help me. Someone so I won't be alone so much. Would you like to stay here with me? I have an extra bedroom. I would love to have you.

"I would love that, Aunt Tan!"

Good. It's settled then.

"But what about Papa?"

I'll handle him. Don't worry, dear. Now, tell me more about this boy. Has he met your father yet? Malee flushed and looked down, plucking at the hem of her shirt. Her aunt reached over and tilted her chin up to see the sadness in her eyes. *What is it, dear? Why are you sad? Doesn't the boy want to meet your family?*

"It's not that. He does want to meet Papa. He wants

to be able to come and pick me up and take me out on a proper date like normal people do, but we can't do that."

Her aunt frowned. *Why ever not?*

"Because Papa wouldn't approve of him".

But why?

Malee looked away.

Aunt Tan reached over and squeezed her forearm.

Malee stood and took her aunt's hand and tugged her to her feet, then led her to the bay window and pointed across the street at Brothers Ink. "He's one of the brothers who own the tattoo shop."

Aunt Tan's eyes moved to the storefront and the motorcycles parked at the curb. *I see. So you've been seeing him behind your father's back?*

Suddenly, Malee put her face in her hands and burst into tears.

Aunt Tan put her arms around her, gathering her close in a hug and patting her back while Malee's body shook with sobs. Finally her aunt drew back to look up into her face, tugging her hands away. Then she signed, *It is not the end of the world, Malee. If he is a good man, if he cares about you...*

"He does! I know he does."

Then things will work out. If he is the one, then he is the one. Love comes in all shapes and sizes.

"But Papa wants me to marry a Thai boy. Lawan said so."

Aunt Tan waved her hands as if to dismiss that

idea. *You cannot force the heart to go where it will not go. It will lead, and all you can do is follow.*

"But Papa…"

You cannot live your life for your father. You cannot live your life for anyone but yourself. Do you understand, Malee? Because this is most important.

She nodded, her eyes searching her aunt's. "But what will I do, Aunt Tan?"

You will come stay here with me part of the time. And you will bring that boy to meet me.

"He isn't really a boy, Aunt Tan."

Her aunt grinned. *I expect not. Just promise me you will be careful and listen to the voice in your head. It will tell you if something isn't right. Agreed?*

"Yes, Aunt Tan."

She pulled Malee in for another hug. *Now, let's finish our tea, and you can tell me all about him.*

***

That night Max waited at the gym, the light above the red door burned brightly in the fog as midnight approached. He sat on a bench inside, his elbows on his knees, running his hands over his head as impatience and worry filled him. He stood and began to pace. The light was in her window. He's seen it, her sign that she was coming, that she intended to meet him. But as the hours dragged on, he wondered if maybe she hadn't been able to sneak out, that maybe she'd fallen asleep.

He'd wanted to see her so badly tonight, too. He'd been itching to take her in his arms since earlier that afternoon when they'd smiled at each other through the window. He'd been bouncing with excitement all day. But it was getting late. Perhaps he should just drive by the alley, see if she left a note…

The door opened, and he whirled.

Malee pushed the hood of a blue rain slicker back, her eyes searching the dimly lit cavernous space, until they landed on him. And then they were both moving toward each other to meet halfway across the room, flying into each other's arms.

He clutched her to him, breathing in her scent, and then took her head in his hands, his mouth coming down on hers. And the long wait had been worth it as she met his kiss with an eagerness of her own, melding against him, clutching at the fabric of his charcoal gray thermal shirt where it stretched between his shoulders.

His hands pushed the slicker off her shoulders until it fell to the floor.

One of his hands slid down and around to the small of her back, pressing her soft curves closer against him. He only hoped he wasn't being too forward, but he knew his actions conveyed his sexual desire, frustrations, and an age old drive to possess that was imbedded in every red-blooded man in his sexual prime.

His worries were silenced as she responded with just as much desire, her response as primal as his.

It made it just that much harder to reel himself in with a steely control he made himself assert.

His hand slid down over her perfectly shaped ass for just a moment before he broke the kiss and put a few inches of space between them. He pressed his forehead to hers, sucking in air.

Her sweet answering pants brushed across his chin, and he wanted nothing more than to drink from those lips again, but he forced himself to refrain. He put a hand between them and signed, *I was afraid you weren't coming.*

"I had to wait. My father was up late. I had to sneak down the fire escape."

His eyes pinned hers with a look that told her he wasn't too happy with that. *Don't do anything dangerous. I don't want you to get hurt.*

"I won't."

Promise me, Malee. No more fire escapes.

She tugged on his hand, and he let her pull him to the bench where they sat beside each other.

"I have something to tell you."

He searched her eyes. *Something good, I hope?*

She nodded, smiling. "Maybe I won't need to sneak out the fire escape again."

Good. Is that what you had to tell me? He frowned.

She shook her head. "I'm going to be staying with my aunt a few nights a week."

He pulled back an inch. *Across the street from the shop?*

She nodded. "It's good. Don't look so worried."

But…

"I told her about you."

He stood suddenly, running his hands over his head as he took a step, then whirled back to her to sign. *What did she say?*

"She wants to meet you."

Does she know what I do?

She nodded.

Does she approve of me? Of us?

"She wants to judge you for herself."

What did you tell her about me?

"I told her you are kind to me, that you are a good man, and that you make me happy."

He smiled. *I make you happy?*

She nodded, but then seemed filled with uncertainty. She stood and approached him. "And do I make you happy?"

He took her face in his hands and stared into her eyes. Finally, he released her to sign. *Yes. You make me very happy.* He pointed to the stupid grin on his face. *Can't you tell?*

She laughed.

Do that again.

"What?"

Laugh. It's a beautiful sound. His eyes moved over her face. *You're beautiful. Did I tell you that?*

She shook her head.

He took her hand and sat on the bench, then pulled her to him, grabbing her around the waist until she was sitting on his lap, facing him, her knees around his hips. *So beautiful.*

He kissed her. When he pulled back this time, he signed, *When do I get to meet her?*

"Tomorrow?"

He nodded. *Okay. I want to kiss you again. I want to more than kiss you. I know it's wrong, but I can't help it. I think about you all day, wanting just to see you. Do you feel the same way?*

She nodded and ran a finger lightly across his eyebrow, down the side of his face, across his cheekbone, skirting the top of his beard, and down to his mouth to stroke his lips. She stared at them a long moment as if they hypnotized her, and then she bent her head and replaced her fingertip with her lips.

When her mouth came down on his, he let her take the lead, promising himself he'd keep a tight leash on his urges and go at her pace. His head tilted back as she ate at his mouth. Her hands roamed over his face, his neck, and his shoulders.

The kiss was part sweet and part seduction in a way he was finding Malee was so good at, whether she realized it herself or not.

His arms tightened involuntarily around her small waist, and he felt her pelvis thrust against him. Hell, she probably didn't even realize she done it, but his body was answering, his cock hardening beneath her. Her breasts pressed against his chest, and he longed to touch them. He broke the kiss, unable to help himself as his head dipped, his mouth brushing kisses along the cleavage peeking out above the scoop neck of her soft gray T-shirt. Her nipples hardened, the nubs clearly visible through the paper-thin fabric of her shirt and bra.

Her head fell back, and her arms tightened around his head, pulling him closer. He ran his hands up her rib cage on either side, longing to cup her small breasts in his big hands and brush his thumbs over those erect nipples.

He hesitated, and her head came down, their eyes meeting. Her hands slid from his head to cup each side of his powerful neck. He watched her expression as he slowly, firmly smoothed his palms up, taking the soft globes in his hands. Her mouth parted, and he squeezed. Her eyes slid shut, and her head fell back again as he brushed the nipples again and again. His mouth found the soft skin of her throat, just under her ear. He sucked, nipped, and licked until her body writhed against him. He wrapped his arms around her, one hand smoothing up her back, his fingers threading into the hair at her nape while the other slid low to cup her ass. His mouth followed the graceful curve of her neck, returning to her cleavage, his nose pushing aside the fabric of her tee and his tongue following the lace edge of her bra. The hand at her ass reached up to pull the neck of the shirt down, and his mouth closed over that taunting nipple right through the fabric of her bra.

She bucked against him, and the moan that escaped from her mouth made his blood rush like a heat wave through his veins, and his heart beat so strongly he was sure she could feel the pulse pounding in his neck beneath her palms.

God, he wanted more. He wanted to lay her out on the bench, the mat, anywhere. And that's when he knew he had to stop. Because if she let him have more, he'd take it. He'd take it all.

He pulled back, his lungs drawing in deep bellowing breaths. Her head came down, and their eyes met. His jaw clenched, and her hand slid up to cup his cheek. She knew. She saw the control he was exerting for her, and she smiled, pressing her forehead to his.

He laughed, and she did, too.

It was the tension release they both needed.

He hugged her, stood, setting her on her feet, and signed, *I'll drive you home, okay?*

"So soon?"

It's after midnight, baby.

She grinned. "I like when you call me that."

Baby?

She nodded.

He leaned down and kissed the tip of her nose, then bent and retrieved her slicker, holding it out while she slipped her arms in. Then he led her out to his truck, holding the door for her as she climbed in.

When they arrived at the alley and he put the truck in park, they both moved into each other's arms with no hesitation. The kiss was hot and could have led to more, but they both knew they were playing with fire.

Things were escalating. He knew it, even if she didn't.

He broke off to sign. *Goodnight, sweetheart.*

She gave him a bright smile. "Goodnight, Max."

As she exited from the cab of the pickup and dashed up the alley, he watched her go. He hoped things went well tomorrow with her aunt. It would give her some much-needed freedom, and perhaps this sneaking around could end.

CHAPTER FOURTEEN

Max crossed the street, carrying the small white pastry box, and entered the nondescript brown and glass door. It creaked as he slowly shut it. He glanced around at the tiny ground floor entry. His eyes took in the old black and white tile and the two bronze mailboxes in the wall of the hundred-year-old building. He climbed the steep staircase to the second floor and knocked on the door on the left with the shiny brass number one attached.

Malee opened it, a bright smile on her face. She pulled him inside, giving him a quick peck on the lips before turning to an elderly woman who sat in an armchair. "Aunt Tan, this is Maxwell O'Rourke. Max, this is my Aunt Tan."

The woman rose and moved toward him, her hand extended, a smile on her face. "It's good to meet you, Maxwell."

Max shook her hand, returning her smile. "I'm glad to meet you, Mrs.…."

She waved her hand, dismissing his formality. "Call me Aunt Tan, please."

He nodded and extended the white box. "Aunt Tan, Malee told me these were your favorites."

Aunt Tan took the box tied with white string and gave Malee a mischievous look. "She did? Well, we must have some." She gestured to a small dining table covered with a lace cloth. "Please, sit."

They moved to the table, and Aunt Tan set the box down and signed to Malee as she spoke. "Please, dear. Bring us some plates, and we will enjoy these while we talk."

Max watched her retreat to the small kitchen while he pulled a chair out for her aunt, who smiled up at him.

"Why thank you, dear."

He sat next to her. "Malee was so excited when she told me you'd come to town."

"Malee is very special to me."

"She's very special to me, too," Max replied, wanting to make that clear. He didn't want to waste time beating around the bush. "I want you to know I'd never do anything to hurt her."

"That is good to know. Her father is a traditional man, set in his ways, but he loves his daughter. He wants the best for her."

"So do I."

"But that doesn't mean he always knows what is right. What you do for a living—he would not approve."

Max looked down at the table and slid his palm over the lace. "I suppose he wouldn't."

She reached over a hand and laid it on his forearm.

"I have nothing against what you do, dear. I am just trying to explain. My brother's way of thinking isn't always right."

"But he is her father."

She let go of him. "Yes, his is, and he is protective of her, perhaps overly so. Malee is a young woman now. She must have the freedom to experience all that life has to offer. My brother cannot keep her locked away because he is afraid she will get hurt."

"I understand his fears. Sometimes the world can be a cruel place."

Her eyes met his. "Yes, that is true."

"But I want you to know I'd never hurt her… or allow *anyone* to hurt her."

She nodded. "That is good to know, because I'm going to trust you with her today. I expect you to treat her with respect."

"Yes, ma'am."

She waved her hand. "Pfft. Ma'am! Don't call me that. It makes me feel old."

For a moment, Maxwell thought he had offended her, until she turned her twinkling eyes to him and grinned.

They both chuckled.

"Understood," Max agreed.

Malee returned and set a plate in front of each of them. Her eyes immediately shot to Max's, the questions plainly written on her face. She wanted to know what she'd missed and if they were getting along. Max smiled and gave her a wink. She exhaled, her relief clear as her eyes dropped to her aunt's happy expression. "Coffee?"

They both nodded, and she disappeared into the kitchen again.

Aunt Tan studied Maxwell until finally he asked, "What's wrong?"

"Nothing. I was just thinking what beautiful children the two of you would have."

His brows rose, but he knew her game, and that little tidbit wasn't about to scare him off. He grinned. "I think you're right."

She chuckled, reached over, and pinched his cheek.

***

An hour later, Max had Malee by the hand and was leading her across the street toward his shop. They were sneaking away for a rare day together, and he didn't plan to waste a moment of it. He had so much he wanted to show her. But first, they needed to make a quick getaway. Not that anyone would probably notice, but her brother did make deliveries, and he could come up the street at any moment. He paused next to his bike, and she gave him a questioning look as he pulled a helmet out of his leather saddlebag and held it out to her.

"We're taking the bike?"

He nodded. *Unless you don't want to. You're not afraid are you?*

She shook her head, giving him a look that almost

dared him to say that again. He couldn't help but grin back at her.

"Where are we going?"

I have a lot I want to show you.

She took the helmet and fastened it while he did the same. When she was through, he tilted her chin up and signed, *Hold on tight, okay?*

She nodded, her eyes sparkling with excitement.

***

The motorcycle was parked rear wheel to the curb. Malee stood back as Maxwell threw his leg over, lifted the big bike off its kickstand, and fired it up. Then he jerked his head to the side, motioning for her to climb on.

She did, wrapping her arms tight around him. A moment later, he twisted the throttle and pulled out. They drove slowly through town, pausing at light after light, and it gave her time to get used to the feel of the powerful bike beneath her.

She couldn't hear the roar of the pipes, but she could feel the vibrations. When they were finally out of town and on the open road, Max let the engine loose, and the bike surged forward. Malee tightened her hold, and Max turned his head to the side for a moment, showing her the curve of his grin as he glanced back at her.

She gave him an answering smile filled with her excitement. The wind washed over her, whipping her face with the cool afternoon air. She could feel the temperature change as they moved from long hot stretches of sun-drenched pavement to dips in the hills where the cold air settled.

Malee loved everything about the ride, from the exhilaration of speeding along the open road to the freedom she felt in leaving the town, the restaurant, and all her responsibilities behind her. She was free to spend an entire day with Maxwell, and she intended to enjoy every moment of it.

Too soon, Max was slowing down to make the turn into a drive. She held on tight, enjoying the opportunity to be pressed close to his body and have her arms wrapped around him.

They bumped up a long gravel and dirt drive toward a big farmhouse. There was a large three-car garage set back a ways. Set off to the side was the framework of a new home under construction, although she couldn't see any laborers currently working on it.

Max brought the bike to a stop and cut the engine. She hopped off, looking around as he dropped the kickstand and stood. She asked him, "Where are we?"

This is my family home. I live here with my brothers.

"You're building something?"

He followed her gaze. *My older brother, Jameson, is building a new house for him and his wife, Ava. She's pregnant with their first child. Come on. I'll introduce you to her. She's a sweetheart.*

He took her hand and led her up the stairs onto the

back porch and inside. The door led into a big country kitchen. Max tugged her along through to another big room with a dining table on one side and a living room on the other. There was a huge stone fireplace anchoring the wall in the living room.

Max moved to the staircase in the middle and hollered something up that she couldn't hear. She assumed he was calling for his sister-in-law. He waited a moment, listening, before moving to the window, pulling the lace curtain aside and peering out. He turned back to her. *Her car is gone. I guess she's out somewhere.*

Malee nodded.

He led her back into the kitchen and opened the fridge, studying the contents. Then he looked at her with a grin. *Are you up for a picnic?*

She shrugged and smiled back. "Sure."

***

Twenty minutes later, they were back on the bike with saddlebags stuffed full of supplies. Maxwell rode down a dirt back road that led deep into the family property and up to a bluff. Finally, they parked and dismounted. Malee took in the spectacular view as Max grabbed the blanket he'd stuffed in his saddlebag along with a bag of picnic items.

They were high up, overlooking his family's property with the town in the distance and the whole valley spread out before her. It was breathtaking.

Max shook the blanket out on the ground under a

nearby tree, and they both sat. He dug in the paper grocery bag and pulled out cheese and crackers, apples and grapes, and lastly, a bottle of wine and two plastic cups.

Malee grabbed up an apple and munched on it while he used a corkscrew on the bottle, poured some wine in a cup, and passed it to her. She grinned. "I'm not twenty-one."

He chuckled and signed back, *Close enough. Your birthday is next week.*

Her mouth dropped open. "You remembered."

Of course I did. I already know what I'm getting you.

"You don't have to get me anything."

He clicked his plastic cup to hers, ignoring her protest, and they both drank. He lay back on his elbow, his booted feet crossed at the ankles, and took in the view.

Malee sat next to him with her feet tucked under her. She sipped her drink and admired the view as well. The wind blew over her, catching her hair and whipping it back.

He patted the spot next him, so she set her cup aside and lay down beside him. They both stared up at the blue sky.

She sighed. "It's beautiful here."

It is, isn't it? Max replied.

"Do you come here often?"

Not often. Sometimes. When I need to think. He turned his head to smile over at her. *It's a good place to reflect and contemplate life.*

She nodded. "I would imagine so."

Or when I have a problem or something is bothering me, I come up here. It's quiet, peaceful. It helps me remember what's important.

She nodded.

He gestured to the view. *How can you look out at that view and not feel it?*

"When did you first come up here?"

My brothers and I used to come up here as kids just to goof off. But when I was fifteen, I started sneaking up here alone.

"Why?"

It was just after my parents were killed in a car accident. I used to come up here to work through my grief and to feel closer to them, some days to try to figure out my life, and I'm not gonna lie, some days just to curse God for taking them.

"I'm so sorry."

He turned his head to look at her. He didn't tell her any of the usual things people might say to brush aside an expression of sympathy they weren't comfortable with like, 'I'm okay now' or 'it was a long time ago.' Instead, he just signed, *Thank you.*

"When was the last time you came up here?"

The day after you came to the gym.

That took her by surprise. "Why?"

He looked right into her eyes, and Malee felt like he looked right into her soul. *To thank God for putting you in my path. Because you changed everything.*

"I did?"

He nodded, turned back to the view, and changed the subject.

They talked for hours, telling each other all their hopes and dreams. They talked about everything; no topic was off limits. They were both completely open with each other.

Malee told Max about her frustrations working at the restaurant. She told him about how much she loved and wanted to please her father, but he was over-protective and that made her feel stifled. She tried to express to Max how isolating being deaf could be, and how sometimes she felt cut out of conversations.

She liked that Max just paid attention to what she was conveying to him, and that he didn't interrupt her by suggesting solutions or trying to solve her problems. He just gave her his undivided attention and let her vent. For the first time, with anyone other than her sister, she felt free to express her feelings; that she could tell Max anything, and it was a wonderful experience.

Max told Malee all about the tattoo shop. He told her what it was like to give someone a tattoo, especially when that tattoo held real meaning for the client. He told her how it felt to give that person a way to express their love, their accomplishments, and sometimes even their grief. He told her about loving the creative outlet it gave him. He also told her about wanting more, wanting to make a real difference in people's lives in a meaningful way other than through his art.

He told her about how helping the kids at the gym was really becoming important to him, and all about the boy he'd met, how Ben had touched his heart.

He asked what she thought about that, and if he'd handled the situation right. She loved that it mattered to him what she thought. How long had it been since anyone wanted her approval or opinion?

They even talked about the future, and how many kids they each wanted. Surprisingly, they both wanted a houseful.

They laughed over that one.

Were you born deaf? Max finally broached the topic.

She shook her head. "When I was five years old, I got sick. My parents didn't have much money and waited to take me to the doctor." She shrugged. "They think it may have been an infection that went untreated too long."

He studied her face. *Maybe your father feels guilty about that. Maybe that's why he's so protective of you now.*

She nodded. "Maybe you're right. I hadn't thought of that."

Malee sat up and reached for some grapes. Max tilted his head back, his mouth open. She chuckled, popped a grape into his mouth, and couldn't resist bending her head down to kiss him.

When she pulled back, he signed, *I like your aunt.*

"I'm glad. I think she likes you, too."

If she didn't, she wouldn't have let you come with me

today.

Malee looked out over the view. "It's nice to be away, to not have to worry about getting caught."

He grinned up at her and teased her. *I think you like the sneaking around. You find it exciting.*

She laughed and admitted it with a nod. "I suppose I do. And you? Do you find it exciting?"

He chuckled and pulled her down on top of him. *I find everything about you exciting.*

She laughed down into his face.

He rolled until she was under him. They stared at each other, the laughter dying off as desire took hold. He dipped his head and kissed her. She slipped her hands up to cup his face, pulling him back for kiss after kiss until kisses weren't enough. His hand moved between them, his fingers going for the buttons down her shirt, popping them free one after another, until he reached the bottom, pulling her shirt wide. His mouth moved down her throat to follow the slope of her breast while his warm palm slid over her ribs.

Her small hands smoothed over his broad shoulders, the fabric beneath her fingers warmed by the sun beating down. She closed her eyes and drowned in the sensation of his beard brushing over her skin. They shot back wide-open when his fingers were at the fastening of her jeans. Should she stop him? Did she want to?

He popped the button open and drew the zipper down. A moment later his warm palm was gliding inside, smoothing over her belly as his fingers slid into her panties. Those long fingers caressed gently in slow circles before dipping to find her wet.

She'd never been touched there before, and she gasped in a breath.

That brought Max's head up, his eyes connecting with hers, the heat in his dark brown eyes plain in their molten depths. He was breathing heavier now, his body tense, poised over her. But there was a question in his expression. He wouldn't go further without her permission.

As badly as she wanted to, and oh how she wanted to, she just couldn't let herself give that permission. She wanted him, needed him, like she'd never experienced before, but she had to be sure she was it for him, not just for now, but for always.

"Max," she breathed his name.

He dipped his head to kiss her lips, just a soft touch. Then he was pulling his hand free and lifting off her a bit to pull the edges of her shirt together.

"I'm sorry," she said.

It's okay, Malee. You're not ready. I can wait. Someday you'll know.

"What will I know?" She frowned up at him.

How much I care for you, and that I'd never hurt you.

She searched his eyes and had to ask the question. "Do you love me, Max?"

He grinned down at her. *Yes, Malee. I love you.*

Her mouth parted as he stood and pulled her to her

feet.

I'm not just saying that to get sex, either. I want you to understand that.

I think I love you, too, Max. This time she signed it rather than spoke it, perhaps because she was afraid to say the words out loud. Her signs were rushed, jerky.

His eyes studied her hands a long time, as if he wanted to make sure he understood them right, then they lifted to her face, and he slowly signed. *Just think?*

She shook her head. *No. I know I love you.*

Say it. Please.

"I love you, Max."

A bright grin split across his face.

"You look happy."

I am happy. He glanced around, then back at her. *I think we need to commemorate this moment.*

She looked at him quizzically as he walked over to the trunk of the tree, then pulled a folding knife from his pocket and opened the blade. He stuck the point in the bark and made a big heart shape, going over it again and again. Then he carved in the center Malee + Max.

It took him awhile. When he was finished, he put the knife away and stepped back to admire it. *Do you like it?*

"I love it. No one's ever carved my name in a tree before."

I hope not. He grinned.

She stared at the heart a long time, touched by its

meaning and that he'd done that for her. Then she threw herself in his arms. He caught her to him as they both tumbled to the ground, laughing and kissing.

Finally, when they both caught their breaths, he signed to her, *This is our spot now.*

She looked up at the tree. Our spot. She liked that. She liked that a lot.

***

Max pulled the motorcycle in the space in front of Brothers Ink. The sun had set, and the temperature was dropping as they'd made their way back into town. Max had promised Aunt Tan he'd have Malee back before dark, and he wanted to keep that promise. The last streaks of purple and blue painted the western sky as he glanced down Main. He took Malee's hand, and they jogged across the street, darting inside the glass door that led up to Aunt Tan's apartment.

Their feet pounded up the steps. Just before she was about to slide her key in the lock, he grabbed her hand, stopping her. She looked up with wide questioning eyes before he grinned, took her head in his hands, and kissed her one last time without any prying eyes on them. It would have to last them until the next time she could manage to slip away.

When finally he released her and they went inside, Aunt Tan was sitting on the couch, watching the news. She looked up when they entered, smiling and laughing.

You two look happy. Did you have a good time, Malee?

Malee turned and gazed into Max's face, her smile bright as she replied, "I had a wonderful time."

CHAPTER FIFTEEN

They began to meet at the gym every Wednesday night, and now they added Mondays. But the days in between, they had to settle for catching a glimpse of each other or stolen moments when they could find them. And they had their notes. Max had never been good at expressing his feelings, but somehow with Malee it was easy. He found even writing letters, something he'd not done much of in his life, didn't seem hard. The words just flowed onto the paper.

They'd found a new spot for their notes, too. Since she was staying most nights right across the street, he only had to go to the entryway to her aunt's apartment and tuck them in the edge of the brass mailbox. Every morning before work, and every evening after they closed up the shop, he'd dash across the street to see if she'd left one for him in the same spot.

This morning she'd left him one.

My aunt and I will be going to the Fall Farmers Market around three o'clock. Maybe I'll run into you?

He smiled at her blatant hint. *Damn right she would.* Grand Junction was experiencing an unseasonably warm snap, and the sun was shining bright. The temperature was in the sixties.

During the summer months there was a farmers market every Thursday afternoon, lasting into the evening. It was a Grand Junction favorite, attracting thousands of shoppers each week with a four-block street festival showcasing Colorado produce, baked goods, crafts, jewelry, and more. Grand Valley orchards and farmers brought in sweet cherries, apricots, raspberries, pears, plums, and peaches. There was a stage set up for local bands. There were homemade jams and fresh-baked bread and all kinds of treats to be nibbled on while browsing handmade soaps, beautiful arts, and crafts.

Last year, due to popular demand, the town had added a couple of fall dates to the schedule. Sweet corn and plump pumpkins sold by the truckload, so they'd kept it going this year.

Maxwell stood at the window, watching for her.

When finally he saw her and her aunt strolling down the street, headed that way, he left the shop and followed. The streets were crowded, the gorgeous weather bringing out many shoppers. He made his way down the sidewalk, weaving in and out of the crowd. There were stands set up with vendors displaying all sorts of goods. Max kept his eyes on Malee, determined not to lose her in the crowd.

He followed them at a distance, watching as her face lit up with excitement when she saw some arts and crafts booths. She loved the handmade silver jewelry; she also loved the hand-painted scarves for sale at another booth. The vendor was giving a demonstration, and Malee seemed fascinated. He loved to see her enthusiasm and delight.

When the demonstration was over and they'd moved on, Max positioned himself down the row so as to make it appear they hadn't planned this little outing. Although, one look at Aunt Tan's face, and he knew the jig was up. She was totally on to them.

Hello, Malee.

"Hello, Max."

They were stopped in front of a vendor selling apple cider. He nodded to it. *Can I get you ladies some?*

Aunt Tan smiled and answered for both of them. *That would be lovely.*

He paid and led them over to a bench. They sat and watched people go by. Max put his cup between his knees so he had free use of his hands to sign. *They have a lot of beautiful crafts here.*

Malee was excited to tell him about the vendor she'd just seen. "Yes, some beautiful things! I just saw a woman who does watercolor on silk. I was fascinated. It inspired me to maybe give it a try. It would be fun to go to fairs and sell something."

Or perhaps even a shop, Max suggested.

"Well, that would cost money."

Max nodded. *It would be something to strive for. Maybe one day.*

"Maybe one day."

Max reached down on the bench between them and took Malee's hand in his, where no one could see. She smiled up at him, and somehow it was enough just being close to her and being able to touch her, even if it was something as small as handholding. Somehow it got him through his day.

CHAPTER SIXTEEN

When Malee and Aunt Tan returned to her apartment, Aunt Tan patted the seat beside her on the sofa. *Come sit.*

Malee sat, giving her Aunt a questioning look, wondering if she was going to say something about her not-so-secret meeting with Max. But that wasn't at all what her aunt wanted to talk to her about.

I saw how interested you were in the hand-painted silk.

Malee nodded. "Yes. It was beautiful."

Her aunt pointed to her carved wooden chest. *Bring me the item at the bottom. The one wrapped in rice paper.*

Malee moved to the chest, raised the lid, and dug through the items carefully. She brought the item back to the sofa. It was long and rolled up, but soft, like there was something fabric inside the wrappings.

Aunt Tan carefully untied the silk ribbon and unwrapped the rice paper. When it was unrolled and the item lifted from the wrappings, it revealed a hand-painted silk parasol with a bamboo frame.

Aunt Tan opened it and twirled it. It was stunning. She passed it to Malee. *I painted this when I was a girl. It is a tradition that goes back generations.*

Malee's mouth fell open.

I could show you how to paint on silk if you'd like, dear.

Malee closed the parasol and set it down carefully. "Oh, yes. Please."

Aunt Tan smiled broadly. *Perhaps the elders still have a few skills worth passing down, huh?*

Malee nodded and smiled brightly, her eagerness apparent. "When can we start?"

Aunt Tan threw her head back and laughed, clapping her hands together. *We'll start tomorrow with a trip to the fabric store. I'll help you pick out just the right silks. They must be of good quality.*

"Okay."

You can paint anything — scarves, sarongs, parasols, kimonos, even something to be framed and hung on the wall. But you must decide, so we will know how much silk to buy. Okay?

Malee nodded. "I'm so excited. I think I'll be up all night sketching some designs. Thank you, Aunt Tan. This means a great deal to me."

Aunt Tan wagged her hands, motioning Malee into her waiting arms and giving her a big hug. When she pushed back to look into Malee's face, she signed, *I'm so happy to share this with you. From the drawings you've shown me, I know you will have a great talent for it.*

Malee's eyes glazed over at her kind words, and Aunt Tan pulled her in for another hug.

CHAPTER SEVENTEEN

This year Malee's birthday fell on a Monday. The restaurant was closed, and her family held a birthday party for her there. Her Aunt Tan came, of course, as well as relatives on her mother's side that drove in from Denver: Uncle Rama, Aunt Nin and her three cousins, who were around her age. Together with herself, Lawan, and Kiet, the young adults filled one table, giggling and talking, while their elders laughed and gossiped at another.

After they ate dinner, they put on music and Chula, her oldest cousin showed them some crazy dance he'd put up on Youtube that was getting lots of hits. They pushed tables out of the way and all did the dance in a line. Malee couldn't hear the music he'd pulled up on his smartphone, but she could feel the beat with the stomp of their feet vibrating on the floor.

Malee enjoyed her time, but she kept sneaking looks at the clock. She had told Max about the party in the note she'd left for him yesterday.

He'd written her one back, saying he understood she had to spend it with her family, but asked if she could sneak out and meet him later, after his class was over and her party was finished. He told her to leave the lamp in her window if she could sneak out the back. He would wait for her in the alley.

After everyone left, Malee snuck down the stairs, tiptoeing as quietly as she could. She threw on her jacket and peered out the back door. Max's truck was parked in their usual spot. It was dark, and she couldn't see his face, but he must have seen her, because he flashed his headlights.

She slipped out the door and dashed through the alley and across the side street. A moment later she was hopping into the warm cab of his truck.

They flew into each other's arms, kissing as if they hadn't seen each other in months rather than days.

When they finally came up for air, he grinned down at her, pulling back to sign, *How's my birthday girl?*

"Good. Thank you. We danced and had cake."

Can you slip away with me for an hour?

She nodded. "Lawan said she'd cover for me."

Max grinned and put the truck in gear.

"Where are we going?"

You'll see.

They drove through town, Max finally pulling into the parking lot of a small Italian place called Nino's. When he put the truck in park, she turned to him. "Max, I already had dinner."

That's okay. We don't have to eat.

She looked down at her jeans. "But I'm not dressed up."

You look beautiful to me. His eyes swept over the sequined tank she wore with her jeans and leather jacket.

He climbed out of the truck, came around to her door, and gave her a hand down from the big truck that sat so high up with its lift kit. He led her inside.

The place was tiny, no bigger than the Pizza Hut down the street. But it had charm going for it. There was a dining room through an arched doorway to the right. Glancing in, Malee saw little square tables set with white linen and candles. Max led her through a doorway on the left to the bar. The place was dimly lit, with tiny colored lights strung everywhere. Malee had the impression the place always had them up and not just for the approaching holidays.

Max led her to two stools at the end and pulled one out for her. She settled on it, giving him a questioning look.

He took the stool next to her. *You're twenty-one. You have to go out for a drink. It's the rule.*

She gave him a big grin. "I wouldn't want to break the rules."

The bartender came over and put two coasters down on the bar. Luckily for Malee, he didn't even ask for her ID, because she realized she didn't have her purse. Perhaps it was because she was with Max, and he was older, and the bartender assumed she had to be older, too, if they were together.

Max turned to her and signed, *What'll you have?*

She shrugged, having no clue what to even order.

Max grinned and turned to the bartender and ordered for both of them.

When the bartender left to make their drinks, Max swiveled toward her and grabbed her knees, spinning her to face him.

I ordered you a Pina Colada. It's sweet and not too strong. You'll like it.

"What did you get?"

A cola.

She frowned.

I'm driving. I'm your designated driver for the evening, my lady.

A moment later, the bartender brought their drinks. Max lifted his glass and clinked it to hers. His was a small rocks glass, while hers was a more elaborate stemmed goblet with a straw, which she put in her mouth and sipped. She noticed Max's eyes on her mouth.

Do you like it?

She nodded. It was delicious. After another couple of sips, she set her glass down.

Max leaned forward and kissed her, just a sweet brush of his lips. Then he leaned back and signed, *I have something for you.*

She grinned. "You do?"

He nodded, grinning back and pulled a small box from inside his coat pocket. It was about the size of a box of checks, and tied with a sparkly red ribbon. She pulled it off and stuffed it in her pocket to save as a keepsake. Then she tore open the silver paper.

Her mouth fell open and she stared down at the gift. It was a smart phone. Her eyes flew up to Max's to find him grinning back at her.

I added you to my plan. Now we can text back and forth.

Her eyes teared up at the expensive present. He looked so happy, too. But she knew she couldn't accept it. She shook her head and held it back out to him.

The smile on his face fell, and that tore at her heart.

"I can't," she murmured the words.

Baby, why not?

She shook her head, tears spilling down her cheeks at how thoughtful his gift was and how much it must have cost. "It's too much."

He opened the box, pulled out the phone and closed her hands around it. Then he signed, *I already programed my phone number in it and set you up with some cool apps.*

She stared down at it, reaching up to wipe the wetness from her cheeks with one hand.

He pulled out his phone and typed out a text.

A moment later her phone lit up with his incoming message. He showed her how to open it.

She read her very first text.

No one has to know.
The phone is set on silent.
You just have to check it now and then for a

message from me.
Or you can put it on vibrate.
Baby, please take it.
We'll be able to talk anytime, day or night.

She looked up at the imploring look on his face, and then she leaned forward and wrapped her arms around his neck, hugging him tight and sobbing.

His arms tightened protectively and reassuringly around her, and she felt him shushing her, the soft puffs of his breath at her ear.

She held him a long time.

Finally, she pulled back, and he cupped her face, his thumbs brushing the tear tracks away. Then he smiled down at her, pressing his forehead to hers. He kissed her again, and then pulled back to sign, *I have something else for you.*

She held up the phone. "This is already too much."

Too bad. You're getting this, too. He pulled something from his pocket. It was a small velvet jewelry box.

She took it and opened the lid. It was a necklace with a silver heart shaped pendent. There was an engraving in the center. *I love you.*

She put a hand to her mouth and broke down in sobs again.

I saw you admiring the silver jewelry from that crafter the other day. I had her engrave it for me. He took the necklace from the box, and his hands lifted to clasp it behind her neck.

She reached up to touch it. "It's beautiful. Thank you."

He grinned down into her face. *Happy birthday, sweetheart.*

After she stopped crying and they were on their second drink, Max took her cell phone and held it at arm's length, then cuddled her close and snapped a selfie of the two of them smiling at the camera.

She watched as he looked down at the phone, his thumb moving over the screen.

"What are you doing?"

He grinned up at her. *I sent it to my phone. I'm going to put it as my screen saver.*

"Put it on my phone, too."

He turned the phone to show her that he'd already done so.

She took it, smiling down at the photo of the two of them. They both looked happy. It was a great shot. Now she could pull out her phone and look at his gorgeous face whenever she wanted.

***

After Max dropped her off and Malee was back home in her warm bed with her cell phone in her hand, it lit up with an incoming message from Max.

Safe in bed?

Yes.

I'm glad I got to see you tonight.

                             Thank you for the presents.

Isn't this easier than passing notes?
We can talk all the time now.

                                Yes. But I like your notes.

Then maybe I'll keep writing you those, too.

                                  I love my necklace.

And I love you.
Happy birthday, baby.
Now get some sleep.

                                  I love you, Max.
                                        Goodnight.

Goodnight, baby.

***

Now that they had an easier way to communicate, they texted each other all the time. Malee kept her phone in her pocket all day while she worked at the restaurant, checking it often and slipping in the back to find a corner or closet to text him. Those nights she stayed with her aunt, she would sneak time with Max.

Mostly it was on the weekend. The nights she stayed at home, she would have to find an opportunity to sneak away, but when she couldn't, they texted.

One night Max asked her a question.

Will you be staying at your aunt's Friday?

I think so. Why?

My brother, Rory's band is playing.
I want to take you to see them.
I know you can't hear them,
but I think you'll have a good time.

It sounds like fun.

Only one problem.

What's that?

They're playing in Telluride.
It's a couple hours away.
We might not get back until midnight or later.

Oh.

Charlotte Justice is playing a practice gig for an upcoming tour.
Rory's band is opening for her.

She's pretty famous.
I guess they met her on the road somewhere.
They became friends, and she wants them to open the show.
He's so excited about it.

> *I'll bet he is.*
> *It sounds wonderful.*

Do you think your aunt will let you go with me?
Liam will be coming with us, too.
We'll take my truck.

> *I can ask her when I go over there tomorrow.*

I could come over, and we could ask her together.
That way she can ask me any questions she has,
and I can put her worries to rest.

> *Okay.*
> *That would be great.*
> *I think she would appreciate*
> *you respecting her enough*
> *to come and ask her.*

You know I'd ask your father if you want me to.

> *No! He'd never let me go.*

All right.

I'll see you tomorrow.

I love you.

I love you, too, baby.
Goodnight.

CHAPTER EIGHTEEN

The day of the concert, Max picked Malee up at her aunt's door like a gentleman. She already had her coat on and was waiting when he knocked. He barely had a chance to tell her aunt that he would bring her straight back home after the concert before Malee was kissing her goodbye and hustling him out the door.

His big black crew-cab truck was parked in front of Brothers Ink, and he held her hand as they dashed across the street. But instead of leading her to his pickup, he pulled her toward the door to the shop, signing, *Just for a minute.*

She let him pull her inside the business she had only been in once since the day she'd delivered them food and had first laid eyes on Max. The sun had gone down, and she immediately noticed the place had a different vibe after dark. The neon *Brothers Ink* sign against the exposed brick wall washed the entry in a soft blue. There was a pretty blonde lady behind the reception counter. She looked up when they entered, a big smile forming on her face.

Maxwell signed to Malee. *This is Ava, my sister-in-law. Ava this is Malee.*

She came around the counter and surprised her

with a hug. Malee's eyes connected with Maxwell's over her shoulder.

Grinning, he signed, *She's a hugger.*

When Ava pushed back out of her arms, she turned to say something to Max, but Malee couldn't read her lips; she was excited and talking too fast.

Max translated for her. *She's happy to finally meet you. She told me you're beautiful. I told her, I know.* He winked.

Ava pulled her in for another hug, and Max signed over her shoulder. *Told you.*

When she finally let go, Malee said, "Hello, Ava. I'm happy to meet you, too."

Ava looked to Max and said something.

She wants us to come to the house for dinner one night.

"That would be nice," Malee said.

Maxwell signed, *Liam is coming with us. It will be just a minute. Let me go find him, okay?*

Malee nodded.

Maxwell moved to take her coat off, and she let him slide it down her arms. He tossed it on one of the leather sofas.

Ava pointed at what she had on underneath. She was wearing a silk kimono that she had made out of a hand-painted silk piece she'd created just for tonight. It was a mix of blues and greens with dragonflies on it. It was loosely belted at the waist over a sparkly tank top. She'd worn it with a pair of jeans and a cute pair of boots.

Malee wasn't great at lip reading, but she could tell what Ava had said even before Maxwell translated for her.

She said, 'Oh my God, I love that!'

Ava's face beamed with the compliment. "Thank you. I made it."

Ava's mouth dropped open. "You made that?"

Malee nodded.

Maxwell beamed with pride for her as he told Ava and signed along for Malee, "She hand-painted the silk. Isn't it beautiful?"

"It's amazing! I want one! Do you sell them?"

Max translated.

Malee shook her head bashfully. "I've just started learning. I've only done a few things."

"You're very talented! Maxwell, tell her she's talented." She slapped Maxwell on the arm.

He signed the words to her, but that time Malee had read Ava's lips. "Thank you."

She said something else, and Maxwell signed, *She says you should sell your pieces. Says she knows several people who would buy something this beautiful.*

Malee blushed again.

A man she recognized as Maxwell's oldest brother, Jameson, walked up. He pulled his wife to him in a side hug and kissed her cheek, his palm running over her pregnant belly. He whispered something in her ear that made her smile and slap him on the chest. Then Jameson turned to Malee with a smile.

Maxwell signed, *Malee, this is my brother, Jameson. Jameson, Malee.*

Jameson extended his hand, and she shook it.

He said something to Max, who signed to her, *He says to tell you that you're too pretty to be with his little brother.* Max looked at Jameson, continuing to sign. *Who are you calling little?*

Jameson laughed.

Maxwell's brother Liam walked up. Malee remembered him from that first day. He winked at her and signed, *Hello, Malee*, then gave her a hug. *I see you haven't dumped my big brother yet.*

She grinned at his joke and shook her head.

When you do, I'm available… and more fun, and much better looking.

Maxwell elbowed him in the solar plexus, and then signed while giving Liam a death stare. *Keep that up and you'll be walking home tonight, Liam.*

Liam chuckled and rolled his eyes so Malee could see what he thought of that threat.

We'd better get going, Max signed.

***

It was a two and a half hour drive down for the show. Max drove, and Liam sat in the back. It was nice to spend some time with one of Maxwell's brothers and get to know him better. It also put Malee at ease to know she would have someone else who knew sign language.

Malee found that, just like Max, Liam was easy to

talk to, and he made her feel comfortable, like she fit right in with the O'Rourke family — like her and Maxwell being together made sense and wasn't an odd fit at all.

He included her in all the conversation, too, not talking around her like she wasn't there. He told her some childhood stories about Maxwell that — judging by Max's body language and the death glare he gave Liam in the rearview mirror — made him uncomfortable. Liam just snickered.

And then there was the time we ran out of dish detergent, and Max thought he could just squirt a ton of dish soap in the machine instead.

Max glared at him. *Hey, it was an honest mistake. They're both for dishes, aren't they?*

Liam looked at Malee. *You should have seen Jameson's face when he walked in, and there were suds all over the kitchen floor.*

Malee burst out laughing.

And then when Jamie opened the door to the dishwasher, they poured out everywhere. You should have seen him chasing Maxwell around the house, both of them slipping and sliding as they ran, Jamie threatening that when he caught Max, he was going to beat his ass.

Max rolled his eyes and signed to Malee, *Ask him to tell you about the time he and Rory decided to snowboard behind Jameson's pickup truck like water-skiers.*

Hey, that was a blast.

Yeah, until you ripped his bumper off.

Wasn't my fault. Rory tied it up wrong.

Max looked at Malee, grinning, and signed, *Right. Let's blame Rory.*

Liam tapped her on the shoulder. *Always blame the brother who's not around.*

She was laughing so hard her eyes were watering.

The time flew by and soon they arrived in Telluride. Mountains on all sides surrounded the town. There was a full autumn moon that lit up the low hanging puffy clouds, and the dark silhouette of the mountain range contrasted against it. The snowy mountain caps illuminated by the moon were visible at the precipice.

The town had an old western feel to it that Malee found lovely.

They parked in a city lot and walked a couple of blocks to the venue, a large nightclub that often booked smaller bands. Along the way, they passed quaint shops in the turn-of-the-century buildings.

As they walked up a side street, Max pointed down an alley. Malee could see a tour bus parked behind the club. Charlotte Justice's name was emblazoned on the side, and there were security guards keeping fans back.

Malee's eyes lit up. She found it all so exciting, and not just going to the concert, but being on a trip out of town with the two handsome O'Rourke brothers. The last time she'd been out of Grand Junction was to Denver to see a specialist about her hearing. That had been when she was twelve.

When they got to the front of the nightclub, Liam pulled his phone out and made a call. When he hung up, he signed, *Rory says to come around back. He'll meet us by the tour bus.*

Max frowned. *The tour bus?*

That's what the boy said. Liam shrugged.

Max took Malee's hand, and they followed behind Liam. When they were almost to the security team, Rory came forward with some lanyards containing backstage passes and handed them each one.

Malee looked to Max, her mouth open with excitement as he draped one over her head and around her neck.

He grinned down at her, his finger coming up to close her mouth, before his head dipped to give her a peck on the lips. He turned back to his little brother and signed, *Rory, this is Malee. Malee, my rock star brother, Rory.*

Rory smiled and shook her hand. Then he turned and led them toward the bus, saying something over his shoulder to Max, who translated for her.

He says Charlotte invited them on the bus before the show.

Malee tugged on his arm, her eyes huge. "You mean we're going to meet her?"

Guess so.

Rory led them onto the big tour bus. They climbed the stairs, passed the driver's seat, and stepped behind a set of curtains. The interior was complete luxury, all done up in a girly rocker chick style. There were suede couches on either side, and a glossy wood floor warmed up with a beautiful carpet. It was dimly lit and decorated in a very bohemian style.

Charlotte Justice was sitting on one couch, with an electric guitar in her hand. She was strumming chords while another musician sat across from her trading riffs with her. Both their fingers moved rapidly over the strings, but Malee couldn't hear the notes they played. There were a couple of other musicians lounging around.

The singer looked up when they entered, and smiled, putting her guitar aside.

Rory introduced them. "Charlotte, these are my brothers, Liam, Max and his girl, Malee. She's deaf."

Liam translated.

Charlotte shook hands with each of them. When she got to Malee, her eyes moved over the kimono in awe. She said something excitedly, and Malee had to look to Liam for translation.

She says she loves your kimono. She has a new album coming out called Dragonfly.

Malee nodded. "It's nice to meet you."

Max's eyes were filled with pride. "She hand-painted this. She's very talented."

The girl's mouth fell open, and she said something to him.

Liam translated. *She wants to know if you sell them. She wants one for an interview she's doing.*

Malee shrugged it off and held it out. "Here, Ms. Justice, you can have this one."

"Are you serious?"

Malee nodded.

"Let me pay you for it. I insist."

Malee waved her hands in the air. "No. No."

"She can be quite stubborn." Max chuckled.

"Well, I'll be sure to tell everyone who made it for me. You better have a website up. The orders may pour in."

Max didn't want Malee to get her hopes up, so he left that part out. Instead, he signed, *She says you should definitely sell them. And that we should get you a website set up.*

Malee grinned. "Maybe."

"No maybe about it. I know a bunch of other female musicians who would adore something like this. Do you do skirts and scarves as well? The girls in my fan club would go crazy for it, especially when they see me wearing it."

Max translated, and Malee replied, "I could."

Soon it was time for Rory's band to take the stage, and they all climbed out of the tour bus and headed inside. Their passes got them seats on stage, just behind the curtains.

Malee was fascinated by everything, even though she couldn't hear the music, she could feel it vibrating up through the wooden floor, and she enjoyed watching the lights and the way the band moved around the stage.

When Rory went to the front of the stage to sing lead on one of the songs, Malee could feel the energy in the place change, and she noticed the females in the audience going crazy. She couldn't blame them; Rory was very good looking.

Their set lasted about forty-five minutes. When they finished, the band moved to the front of the stage to stand in a line with their arms around each other and took a bow. As the crowd roared with applause, stomping their feet, even Malee could feel the vibrations. When the band came backstage, they were all pumped with excitement. Malee was happy that everything had gone well for them.

Charlotte Justice walked up with her electric guitar and stopped to give Malee a hug, thanking her again for the gift, which she was now wearing.

"Ms. Justice, could I get a picture of you in the kimono with Malee?" Max asked.

She smiled brightly and wrapped her arm around Malee's shoulder. "Of course!"

After Max snapped a couple, she gave Malee another hug and then walked out on stage. The spotlight hit her, and she waved to the crowd that erupted in thunderous applause. She began playing, her hands flying over the guitar strings and her long hair flowing down her back.

Malee had to admit, the kimono looked great on stage.

Max held the phone up for Malee to see the great shot he'd gotten of the two of them. She smiled, and then pointed to Charlotte Justice out on stage. "Max, take one of her on stage wearing it."

Great idea, babe!

He took a few, then he texted the photos to Malee.

They stayed for a few songs, but then Max thought they'd better hit the road, knowing the long drive they had ahead of them.

As they headed out the door into the chill night air, Max took his leather jacket off and wrapped it around Malee's small shoulders. It hung down to her thighs, but she hugged it around her, breathing in his scent. They held hands all the way back to the truck.

Malee glanced around the town one final time as they drove out. It had been so exciting to get away. She pressed her hand to the glass, watching the quaint town pass by, and wondered what it would look like in the daytime. She would love to come back and go in all the shops.

As if Max could read her mind, he squeezed her leg. She turned to look at him. He lifted his chin to the view beyond her passenger window and signed, *Maybe we can come back sometime during the day.*

She nodded, perking up. It was something to look forward to, and actually, it didn't matter where they went, as long as she got to spend more time with Max.

***

An hour into their long drive back, Max glanced

over to see Malee angled in her seat toward him, her head resting against the headrest. She was sound asleep, her face angelic, her hair cascading over her shoulder, and a wave of protectiveness washed over him.

He adjusted in his seat, shifting toward her and draped his left wrist over the steering wheel. It freed his right hand to reach over and lace his fingers with hers. Her drowsy eyes looked up at him, and she smiled briefly, before her lids drifted back down. He brought her hand to his mouth and brushed her knuckles with his lips.

Then he settled in his seat, his eyes on the road, and took them home, a contentedness he hadn't felt in a long time filling him.

***

The cessation of motion roused Malee from her slumber. The truck was pulled to the curb, and she found herself slumped against the door. She straightened slowly, blinking her eyes to the blue neon sign. *Brothers Ink.*

They were home.

A wave of sadness and regret consumed her. She'd had time with Max, and she'd squandered it sleeping.

Liam climbed out of the backseat, and Max rolled down his driver's window, the chilly night air seeping in as they said goodbye.

Liam bent and waved goodbye to Malee, then he climbed in his vehicle and backed out.

Max rolled the window up, but he made no move to shut the truck off. He turned toward her, and as if he'd been dying for his brother to get out and give them some privacy, he pulled Malee into his arms, his mouth coming down on hers.

She was just as eager for his kisses, and her arms twined around his neck, pulling him as close as the console dividing them allowed.

Max pulled back and glared down at the offending item, then signed, *Come on.*

She frowned, watching as he shut the engine off and climbed out. A moment later, he was around the truck and helping her out her door. Then he opened the back door and motioned her in. She climbed in and found the bench seat fairly roomy. He slid in behind her, shutting the door and locking them into a warm dim cocoon.

Malee was grateful Max had sprung for the dark tinted windows. The dashboard clock read just after 1:00. Although it was late, and the streets were deserted this time of night, Malee still was glad no one would be able to see them.

Max wasted no time pulling her into his arms. This time there were no barriers between them, and he made full use of the bench seat, falling to his back against the door and taking her with him.

She sprawled over his hard body, and his arms pulled her tiny waist up against him. She could feel the bulge in his jeans as his mouth sought out hers. He kissed her passionately. One hand reached up, his fingers threading through her long dark hair. It cascaded forward over both of them.

Soon his mouth was dipping, his lips and tongue trailing along the edge of her sparkly scooped-neck tank. His other hand moved over her ass to her upper thigh and pulled her against him. She couldn't help rocking her hips, and she felt the groan rumble up from his throat.

They were so in tune with each other that it no longer took them much foreplay to get to the hot-and-heavy stage. It was starting to be like this every time they snuck time to be together. The necking and petting was getting more serious, falling into that danger zone they both knew was becoming harder and harder to pull back from. The more time they spent together like this, the less they were inclined to put on the brakes, taking it a little bit further each time, both knowing they were pushing their limits.

Malee could tell it was especially hard on Max. He was a grown man, not used to being celibate, and she saw the toll it was taking on him to pull back each time, which he always did. It was as if he knew that exact breaking point. He hovered near it, but he never crossed it.

Malee knew his pain; she felt the torment, too. The longing, the urges, and the primal need that was inherent in all humans to procreate. It was as imbedded and essential to her as it was to him. Well, maybe not exactly equal. She knew that drive had a powerful effect on him, maybe more so than her. But, anytime she was in his arms—hell, anytime she was within ten feet of him—she felt that pull.

Max broke their kiss, breathing hard, and his hand came up to sign, *It's never enough time with you. I always want more.*

"I know, Max," she murmured the words softly.

You know I don't want to disrespect you, but goddamn I want you, girl.

"I want you, too."

That had him sitting up, taking her with him. It was like her words had thrown ice water on him.

She frowned at him. "What is it?"

We need to stop.

"No."

Yes!

"Why?"

Because if we don't stop now, I won't stop at all. He searched her pleading eyes. *Don't look at me like that, Malee. Don't tempt me into something like that. I don't want you regretting anything we do together. Especially that.*

"Who says I'll regret it?"

He stared at her a moment, as if he was weighing the temptation she was holding out to him. Then his fist closed around the door handle, and he practically vaulted out of the vehicle. He stood in the cold night air and signed to her, *Come on, baby. I need to get you back to your aunt.*

"Do we have to?"

You know we do. Come on. It's getting late, and she's probably waiting up for you. I promised her, remember?

She nodded, disappointment written all over her face.

I told her I'd have you home by one, and it's past that now, Malee.

"I know."

Then don't give me a hard time about this.

That pissed her off, and she jumped angrily from the truck.

He tried to take her hand as they walked across the street, but she yanked it back. When they got inside the alcove, Max grabbed her, stopping her from climbing the stairs.

You know I'm right.

She looked away.

Malee, don't ruin the night by giving me a hard time about this. You know I want you. More than you even know. I'm trying to do the right thing here.

She signed angrily, forgetting her words, *Maybe I don't want you to do the right thing.*

A muscle in his jaw ticked, and then it was like something inside him broke free. He took her face in his hands, backed her to the brass mailboxes and kissed her. It was passionate and aggressive and controlling, and she loved every minute of it. Finally, he pulled back and pressed his forehead to hers, breathing hard and fighting to regain his control.

After a tense moment, he eased back. *Meet me tomorrow night at the gym.*

She looked up into his eyes. Was he giving in? Was he asking her to meet him so they could finally consummate their love?

She nodded, both excited and suddenly scared. "Okay. I'll be there."

You better not be sorry, Malee.

"I won't be, Max."

He walked her up the stairs. When they entered, Aunt Tan was asleep in the chair by the window, softly snoring. Max grinned at Malee, put his finger to his lips, and tiptoed toward her. Squatting down in front of Aunt Tan, he gently touched her arm.

Aunt Tan's eyes fluttered open and looked into his face.

He smiled back at her. "Wake up, Sleeping Beauty."

She put her hand to her chest in surprise, her eyes darting from him to Malee standing by the door. "Oh, you're home. I must have dozed off."

"I told you I'd bring her home safe."

She patted his cheek. "Thank you. Now help me up."

Max pulled her to her feet, and she grabbed her cane. She shuffled toward Malee and paused, hooking her cane over her forearm to sign to her. *Did you have a good time, dear?*

Malee's eyes connected with Max. "I had a

wonderful time."

Well, I'm off to bed, come give me a hug.

Malee hugged her aunt, her eyes meeting Max's over her aunt's shoulder.

After her aunt had gone to bed, Max took Malee's hands in his and brushed her lips with a kiss. He released her and signed. *Thanks for coming with me tonight.*

"Thanks for taking me. I had a wonderful time."

Me, too. I love you.

"I love you, too."

Goodnight, sweetheart.

"Goodnight, Max."

He moved to the door and kissed her again. *Get some sleep.*

CHAPTER NINETEEN

The next night, just like they planned, Max waited for Malee at the gym. She was fifteen minutes late. He paced back and forth, wondering if she'd changed her mind. He was just pulling his phone out to text her when the door opened. His head swiveled toward it.

Relief flooded through him momentarily as she walked in, but one look at her, and Max could tell she was nervous. She walked slowly toward him. He met her halfway and took her face in his hands, tilting it up as his lips descended on hers. The kiss was part passionate and part playful, meant to put her at ease. Releasing her, he searched her eyes. *How was your day?*

Her eyes moved to the sofa. Was she wondering if they were going to have sex on that worn out old thing? He reached up and turned her face back to his.

You aren't really thinking I'd take you on the dirty couch your first time are you?

She looked up at him with relieved eyes. "It's not my dream, but where we are doesn't matter. It doesn't have to be some fairy tale. I just want to be with you."

Do you mean that?

"Yes."

I want to ask you something, and I want an honest

answer. All right?

"Okay."

Can you see us together?

She frowned, confused. "We are together."

No, I mean could you see a life with me? The two of us having a family of our own?

She smiled. "Yes. I love you."

I lied.

"What?"

I've got two questions for you. He dropped to one knee and pulled out a velvet covered ring box, popping it open. A diamond solitaire sparkled up at her. *Will you marry me?*

Her hands flew to her face. "Are you serious?"

I'm on one knee, baby. Do I look serious?

She nodded, tears in her eyes.

I want to hear you say it.

"Yes!" she shouted.

He slipped the ring on her finger and stood. She jumped in his arms, holding him tight and burying her face in his neck.

He caught her to him, wrapping his arms around her.

After a few moments, he set her down and pulled her arms from around him so he could sign to her. *I want to do this right. I want to ask your father for permission to marry you.*

He watched the happiness slide right off her face, and her head turned toward the door, an uneasy look filling her eyes.

He grabbed her chin and turned her back. *What's wrong? Tell me.*

"Max..." she trailed off, like she didn't know what to say.

What?

"Can't we wait? Let this be just between us for now?"

Are you going to marry me?

"Yes."

Then he's got to know sometime. You're wearing my ring. He's gonna see it.

She looked down at it, twisting it around her finger, like she hadn't thought of that.

Max straightened, his chin coming back, and he signed with a little irritation showing, *Unless you're planning on taking it off and hiding it.*

She looked up at him imploring. "No. It's just.... You don't understand."

Make me understand, Malee.

"He's the head of the family. It's not easy. He doesn't even know about you. This will all be a shock to him."

He'll get over it. I'll be polite. I'll talk to him.

"He won't be happy with me."

It doesn't matter. I'm happy with you.

"It does matter, Max. He's my father."

And I'll be your husband. You won't be under his control any longer. You won't have to obey everything he says.

"It's not obedience, Max. Don't you see? It's respect."

He nodded. *I know you respect your father. And I'll have the utmost respect for him, too. Don't worry, Malee. Everything will be fine. All right?*

She looked down and nodded, giving in.

He tilted her chin up with a finger. *Hey. I love you. I promise, it'll all be fine.*

She nodded.

Come on. Let's go.

"Now? Tonight?"

Yes. He paused when he saw her panicked face. *Malee, it won't do any good to wait. There won't ever be a perfect time to drop this on him. Let's just do it and get it over with.*

She tried one last stalling tactic, gazing toward the old couch. "But, I thought we were going to have sex."

He was on to her, though. *After we get this taken care of. After they all know I'm serious about you. I'll take you to the best hotel in town.*

He took her hand, kissing the back of it, and pulled her outside toward his truck, where he tucked her in the passenger seat. He had no intention of sneaking around anymore. He was over and done with that. She had his ring on her finger, and they had their future ahead of them.

***

This time he pulled to a spot on the street in front

of the restaurant. It was closed but there were lights still on. Max could see through the tinted windows at night. He tapped Malee on the knee and signed, *Are they in the restaurant?*

She nodded. "When they finish cleaning the kitchen and preparing for the next day, they like to sit together and drink Oliang."

What's that?

"Thai iced coffee. It's my father's favorite."

Good. Then maybe he's in a good mood. He unbuckled his seatbelt and climbed out of the cab. He came around the hood and opened her door, helping her down. She grabbed at his coat, and he paused, looking down at her. She was wedged between the truck and him. She glanced over his shoulder toward the entrance.

"Are you sure you want to do this?"

He grabbed her hands in his and brought them to his mouth for a kiss. They were ice cold and trembling. *Malee, it's going to be okay.*

They walked to the front entrance. It was locked, so Malee knocked on the glass. She cupped her hand around her eyes to peer inside then she waved to her parents.

Her mother got up and came to let them in. Her eyes skated past her daughter to the big man with her.

Malee, are you okay? Who is this?

"I'm fine. We need to talk to the two of you."

Her father approached. *What is the meaning of this?*

Where have you been? His eyes swept over her coat and then Max. *Malee, you were supposed to be upstairs. Who is this man?*

"Papa, Mama, this is Maxwell. Max, this is my father and mother."

He extended his hand. "How do you do, sir. Ma'am."

Her mother bowed her head slightly, but her father was slow to take his hand. Max was glad the coat covered his tattoos. No sense making this any harder than it already was.

"Do you have a last name, Maxwell?" her father asked him.

Max signed as he spoke, so that Malee was included in the conversation. "My name is Maxwell O'Rourke, sir."

He watched the man draw up like he'd just insulted him. So Max went ahead and told him what he already knew. "My brothers and I own Brothers Ink, just down the street."

"Yes, I know of it." Her father's chin lifted in the air. "What are you doing with my daughter?"

"I met her a while ago. She delivered our lunch order one day."

Her father signed something frantically to Malee about that, but it was so fast, he couldn't catch what it was.

Max signed to her, *What did he say?*

"He is mad I took a delivery. He said I know I'm

not supposed to."

The fact that Max was signing with his daughter made the man even more upset.

"Why are you here?"

"I've gotten to know your daughter, sir, and —"

"Know my daughter?" he snapped. "When?"

"I've been seeing her. We've gotten to know each other, and I've come to care for her very much."

This made the man livid, but he tried to hold his temper.

Malee's mother started chattering to her husband in Thai, but the man held his hand up, and she immediately fell silent.

Max took the chance to explain. "We're in love, and I've asked her to marry me. I know this must be a shock to you, and I'm sorry about that."

"Marry her?"

Maxwell nodded. "Yes, sir. I love her, and she loves me."

Her father lifted his chin. "She will not marry you. She will not see you again. Do you understand?"

"No, sir. I don't. She's a grown woman."

"She is my daughter. This is a proper household. Malee would not go against her father's wishes, nor would she marry a man her father does not approve of."

"And why don't you approve of me?"

"You are not suitable."

"Why not?"

"There are many reasons. You are not Thai. You are too old, and most of all, you run a disreputable business that invites dishonorable men and shameful women. How can a man like you be worthy of my daughter?"

"I may not be Thai, and I'll admit, I'm older than she is. But we run an honest business. And our clientele come in for tattoos for all sorts of honorable reasons. Because they're grieving over losing a child, to honor a parent who has passed too soon, to celebrate their love, or just to express themselves. But none of that matters. The only reason you should be concerned with is that I make her happy, and I promise you, sir, I will spend the rest of my life trying to make her happy. That's the most important reason of all for you to give your blessing."

"I know who you are. You and your brothers are all troublemakers. Bad troublemakers come around your shop. That's no place for my daughter. No life for her. Working in your shop?" He lifted his chin. "You take advantage of her."

"I've never taken advantage of her, sir. I've treated her with nothing but respect."

"Malee will marry a good Thai boy! Malee would never disgrace or shame her family by marrying you. I forbid it."

"Sir—"

Malee's father stepped between them, pushing Malee behind him. "I will never give my blessing.

Thank you for bringing my daughter home. Now, please leave, and do not come back here again."

Max looked to Malee who had stayed silent this whole time. Her eyes were filled with tears. She tugged her father around. "Papa, please. I love him, and he loves me."

He signed back with angry motions, *Malee, I am the head of this household, and I forbid this. Do you understand? This man will give you nothing but a bad reputation. Him and his brothers, they are not good people.*

Malee, come on. Let's go. Max held out his hand, fully expecting her to take it. But she didn't. She hesitated. He stood there, waiting, and he felt a flicker of cold dread slither up his spine. It moved through his body and wrapped its tentacles around his heart. And the longer his hand was extended in the empty air, the more and more constricted it felt. *Malee, take my hand.*

I forbid it, Malee. Go upstairs to your room.

Baby, all you have to do is take my hand and walk out the door with me. Everything will be all right. I promise.

Malee, if you do, I will disown you. You will be cut off from your family. Is that what you want?

A tear ran down her cheek, and she shook her head, and another band squeezed around Max's heart.

Malee, I thought you wanted to marry me.

"I do."

Then come with me.

"I can't. Don't you see?"

His hand dropped, and with it he felt his heart

shatter. *Yeah, I guess I do.*

He backed up a step, his eyes on her sobbing face. This wasn't how this was supposed to go. They were supposed to be happy. This was supposed to be the happiest night of their lives.

His eyes swept over her one last time, and then he turned and walked out the door. He walked through the brisk night air, feeling just as cold on the inside. He yanked his door open and vaulted up into his truck, slamming the door. The truck roared to life, and he jammed it into gear. He couldn't get out of there fast enough. His chest felt tight, like he couldn't breathe. He didn't know where he was going. He didn't care. He just drove aimlessly out into the country.

His phone chimed. He pulled it out and glanced at the text.

I'm so sorry.

He threw it down in the console.

It chimed several more times.

Max?

Please, talk to me.

He ignored them all. Finally, he shut the phone off.

CHAPTER TWENTY

Malee stared out her window down the street toward the gym, like she had for the past week. She watched for any sign of Max. He'd been avoiding going there, just like he'd been ignoring her texts.

If he didn't show up tonight, she'd decided she would have to go to his shop. There would be no way around it. The thought of talking to him at his shop — a place that still intimidated her — was terrifying. It wouldn't be private. There would be customers and his brothers and a million ways for him to turn her away... or worse, break her heart in front of a roomful of people. But she'd do it if she had to, if that's what it came to.

She looked up at the sky. Sleet was falling in a thin, cold sheet. The night sky was a ghostly gray overcast, lit by the lights of Grand Junction. Her eyes dropped to Main Street. Strings of white bulbs were strung across it for the approaching holidays, but they did nothing to lift her spirits. A car drove down the street, its tires kicking up a wet spray.

She saw the light two blocks down Fourth Street when it flipped on — the one over the red door. It shone with a foggy halo around it, beckoning to her. She knew who was there, even if he'd parked in back.

If he were only there to lock up, it wouldn't take him long. She might make it to him before he pulled out if she ran all the way.

***

He had already locked up and climbed into his truck when Malee came to a heaving stop, right in front of his headlights. With her eyes blinded by the beams, she couldn't see him, not until he stepped around the door and into the beam of light with her. He was just a dark silhouette, his face in shadow. But she saw his hands gesture in the light.

What are you doing here?

She took a step toward him, telling herself to be brave. "I saw the light from my bedroom window. I knew it was you. I need to tell you something."

There's nothing left to say. We're through. He looked off in the distance, as if he were dismissing her.

She stood there indecisively, willing him to look at her. Regret and fear boiled up inside of her. He can't really mean that. God, what had she done?

"Max, please, I was scared. He's my father. How can I disobey him? I wanted to go with you, but—"

Don't! he interrupted her, his face emotionless. *It's okay. I understand. I know all that. I should have known better. Maybe he's right. Maybe we don't belong together. Maybe I'm not what you need.* He made an impatient movement, as if to get her to go home.

But she hesitated. "Please, Max. Can't we go back

to how things were? We can still see each other. I could—"

He cut in impatiently, gesturing over her. *No, Malee. I can't go back to the way things were. If we can't move forward, then there's nothing for us anymore. I don't want to sneak around anymore. If this continued, we couldn't tell anyone or go anywhere; it would have to be secret; it would be like living a lie. And that would eat at me. I'd start to wonder if maybe you didn't want to be seen with me, that maybe I'm really not good enough in your eyes either. Don't you see? I can't do that, Malee. Not even for you. I'm done.*

"Max, please. There has to be a way—"

There was a way, Malee. If you had taken my hand. That's all I needed. If you'd had the courage to walk across that room and put your hand in mine and put your faith in me… Girl, I would have walked through fire for you.

Tears rolled down her cheeks. "Max, please—"

When it was clear she wasn't leaving, he did. He climbed in his truck and pulled out.

She stood in the empty parking spot for a long time, staring out at the dark street, remembering things—the first time he'd kissed her, how happy she'd been when he'd asked her to marry, the hurt and despair in his face when he'd walked out of her parents' restaurant. He thought he'd been measured by her father and come up far short. But worse than that, he thought she'd let him down.

Well, hadn't she?

Tonight he confirmed her worse fears when he told her he was done with her. His words echoed around her head until she thought she'd drop to her knees with the pain. How would she ever survive this?

She stared unseeing and thought of other things, too. The touch of his gentle hands, the tenderness of his kiss…

She buried her face in her hands, whimpering to herself like a hurt animal. She'd destroyed his love. She'd destroyed *them*.

CHAPTER TWENTY-ONE

As the weeks went by, Max learned all over again how to live life without Malee. He forced himself not to stand at the door and watch her walk by on Tuesdays and Fridays. He didn't leave any more notes or check for any either. He no longer left the light on at the gym.

His heart was breaking and probably hers, too, but he knew he had to be strong. The things he'd said to her were true — he couldn't continue on how they had been.

One unseasonably balmy day, just before the Thanksgiving weekend, Max was headed out to bring Ava some ice cream while Jameson finished up a tattoo. Her cravings were running his brother ragged, and Max was happy to fill in.

He pulled on his leather jacket and headed for his bike parked out on the street. Halfway across the sidewalk, he saw her.

Malee was walking hurriedly up the opposite side of the street, her hair whipping behind her in the brisk autumn wind.

He knew the exact moment she saw him, too. She

stopped abruptly, looking right at him. *Why don't you look away?* he wanted to demand, and he stared back at her across the hundred feet that separated them.

It killed him to do it, but he forced himself to be the one to break their eye contact. He turned to his bike and pulled the helmet from where it dangled off the handlebars. He didn't look back, but he took his time strapping it on, hoping maybe she'd cross the street and come to him.

He pulled out his sunglasses and slid them on, then his gloves. When he could drag the moment out no longer, he flung his leg over the bike, lifted it off its kickstand, and fired it up.

Surreptitiously, as he glanced down the street before pulling away from the curb, his eyes scanned the spot she'd been standing in. She was gone. His eyes flicked up the street, but there was no sign of her. And he felt the hurt of losing her all over again.

When would the pain stop? When would he finally get over her?

He'd been kidding himself when he'd thought he could be her man. She was too sweet, too innocent for the likes of him. To prove his point, he twisted the throttle, and the thunder of his drag pipes echoed off the buildings as he roared down the street.

***

Two days later, an envelope addressed to him was delivered to the shop. He stood at the front counter, staring at it a long time before finally turning it over and opening it. He unfolded the single sheet of paper, and something wrapped in a Thai Garden napkin fell into his hand. His eyes scanned slowly over Malee's feminine script.

> *Max —*
> *I know I let you down*
> *and I'm so sorry*
> *But I want you to know*
> *I'll never stop loving you*
> *Not until the day I die*
> *— Malee*

He unwrapped the napkin, and the solitaire fell into his palm. He held it up between his thumb and finger, watching the refracted light sparkle through it as he remembered how full of happiness and hope for the future he'd been the day he'd stood in the jewelry store and purchased it.

His eyes moved to the storefront window and the street beyond to the spot where he'd seen her standing the other day. Then he took a deep breath, shoved it in his hip pocket, and went back to work.

CHAPTER TWENTY-TWO

Max dropped down into a chair in front of Jameson's desk. "You wanted to see me?"

Jameson looked up from his sketchpad as Maxwell's eyes strayed to the window behind him and the bright afternoon sun. He was in a mood today, and would rather be anywhere but in the shop. His thoughts strayed to the bluff and the day he'd taken Malee up there. It seemed so long ago now.

Jameson tossed his pencil down, drawing Max's attention from the window. "Yeah. I wanted to talk to you. What's the deal with you and the girl?"

Max frowned. "The deal? There is no deal."

"Come on, man. Don't make me pull teeth here. You've never talked about it. What happened?"

"Maybe I don't want to talk about it. Ever think of that?"

"Max, it wasn't so long ago that roles were reversed here, and it was you talkin' to me."

Max remembered it well. His brother had been screwing everything up with Ava, and Max had talked to him. Seems it was easier on the other side of the conversation. "Yeah, well, maybe I should have stayed out of it."

"I think you know I'm glad you didn't, even though at the time I didn't like it. Tables are turned now, so spill."

Max blew out a frustrated breath and crossed his leg, resting his booted ankle on his knee. He tapped the leather nervously with his hand. "She's not the kind of girl who belongs with me."

Jameson spoke sharply. "You want to tell me what that's supposed to mean?"

"Come on, Jamie. She's a nice girl from a good family."

"And your family's not? That what you're sayin'? She tell you that?"

"No, but her family's not the kind that's gonna want her mixed up with one of us."

"One of us?"

"O'Rourke brothers. Not with the reputation we've got around this town."

"Brother, any girl who's not willing to take you for who you are, for the good man you are, she's not worth having."

"It's not her. It's her family, her father mostly. He thinks this shop is trouble, attracts the wrong clientele."

Jameson leaned back in his chair, his hand stroking his mouth, contemplating Max's words. "Thai Garden. Was he one of those businesses that wanted us shut down?"

"Yup."

Jameson dropped his hand and growled, "Fucking hell. I'm sorry, Max. What can I do?"

Max shrugged. "There's nothing you can do."

"I could go talk to the man."

"You might want to think that one through. The Thai don't like anger or confrontation. We're Irish. How's that gonna go?"

The corner of Jameson's mouth pulled up. "I see your point. What about you? Have you tried talking to him?"

"Yes."

"And?"

"It didn't go too well." Max stood, shaking his head. "Nothing I say is going to matter, and Malee — she just doesn't have it in her to stand up to her father or to go against her family's wishes. She has too much respect for them. That's their way. How am I gonna get around that?"

"I'm sorry, brother."

Max nodded. "Are we done here?"

"Yeah."

Max turned to go, but Jameson stopped him.

"Max? Just remember, I'm here for you if you ever want to talk."

Max nodded. "Thanks."

"You gonna be okay?"

Max's eyes strayed to the window and the blue sky before dropping back to meet Jameson's. "Yeah. I just need time."

***

On Friday night after the shop closed, Liam and Rory cajoled Max into going out for a couple of drinks, insisting they couldn't take his brooding anymore. They were determined to shake him from the depression he'd fallen into since his breakup with Malee.

Max, on the other hand, was certain adding alcohol wouldn't magically do the trick, but he went along with them just to get them off his back about it.

The three of them walked into the small dance club two doors down the street. It was open late and served their purposes. Usually they'd argue over where to go. Maxwell preferring the brewery, Liam, the dive bars, and Rory varying between the pickup spots or wherever had the best music on any given night. Tonight, Maxwell didn't care enough to fight about it.

The pounding dance vibe hit him as they entered.

The three of them turned heads wherever they went; it was something Maxwell had always been aware of, but tonight the female attention that followed them as they prowled through the crowd was especially palpable.

Usually it was Rory, with his rock-star good looks that drew the women, but tonight Max noticed a majority of the attention was aimed at him. Perhaps it was the brooding, stay the hell away look he gave them that sucked them in. He was well aware of the bad-boy appeal some women had a thing for. God, he hoped none of them were brave enough to hit on him tonight. He wasn't in the mood.

The three of them squeezed in at the bar and ordered drinks.

"Remind me again why the fuck we're here," Maxwell growled as Liam passed him a Scotch.

"To get you laid." Liam grinned back.

Max's eyes scanned the club. "Right. We're not exactly the business suit/dance club crowd."

"Don't sell yourself short, bro. Women love that whole bad-boy, 'don't-fucking-mess-with-me-or-I'll-punch-you-in-the-throat' vibe you've got goin' on tonight."

"Don't tempt me."

Liam chuckled. "Well, a bar fight wouldn't be my first choice, but if getting you laid isn't in the cards, maybe a good knock-down brawl will get you out of this funk you're in."

"I'm not in a funk."

"Right. Keep tellin' yourself that." Liam clinked his glass to Max's.

Rory was already striking up a conversation with a brunette at the bar. Max scanned the room. This was so *not* his scene. He had ten years on every girl in the place. The irony of that hit him. Malee had just turned twenty-one. Hell, how could he have ever thought that could have worked? But he had. And it was because she was different. She was innocent and naïve, yes, but there was a certain maturity in her, too.

Christ! He needed to stop thinking about her. As his eyes connected with a curvaceous blonde headed his way, he thought maybe his brothers were right. Maybe another woman would wash Malee from his mind.

"Hello, big boy. I'm Serena." She stood in front of him, staring up into his face with a self-assurance he hadn't seen in a long time. She was bold and brash and about as opposite from Malee as a girl could get. His eyes skimmed down over the tight mini-dress made of some type of sparkly pink spandex. It showed off her long legs, tits, and ass. And none of it did anything for him.

She could never mean a thing to him. He'd never be in danger of losing his heart to this girl. Maybe that's why he bought her a drink.

An hour later, he was out on the sidewalk with her. They'd come out for some air, and now he had his back to the brick wall with her plastered to his chest. She was all over him.

As her kisses moved from his mouth down his throat and his hands drifted down over her ass, he thought about taking her to bed. If he did, it would mean nothing. She would just be an outlet for the months of sexual frustration that he'd built up. But even as his hands molded over her shapely bottom, he knew he couldn't do it.

Correction — *wouldn't* do it.

She just wasn't Malee.

Sure, he could take what this girl offered, but tomorrow he'd know he'd used her, and that didn't sit right with him. And somewhere in the back of his mind he realized he still held hope that somehow Malee would come back to him. And as small a chance — and perhaps as foolish — as it was, he just wasn't ready to extinguish that last flame of hope that burned inside him.

About the time he realized her lips had clamped onto his neck, she was already sucking. He pushed her away, shoving her off him, but it was too late. The damage was done. He knew what she'd just done had left a mark.

"Goddamn it, quit," he snapped as she tried to push back into his arms.

Her eyes blazed up into his. "What's the matter? It's just a little hickey. You're skin's covered in ink, and you're afraid of a little mark?"

She moved back toward him, her mouth latching on again. He caught both her wrists in his, pushing her off him.

"Serena. Knock it off."

Her brows shot up. "Oh, so you remember my name. Well, that's something."

"Let me drive you home," he offered, wanting nothing more than to get the hell away from her. The last thing he wanted was to stand here on Main Street and argue with her.

He was struggling to keep her off him when his

eyes strayed to a figure skulking past the club, staggering drunk. He'd know that face anywhere, even though he'd only seen it once. Ben's father.

All the anger simmering beneath the surface tonight exploded out of him. He pushed past Serena and confronted the man. "Hey, you!"

The man lurched to a stop, his watery eyes meeting Max's. "You talkin' to me, asshole?"

"Yeah, *asshole*. I'm talking to you."

"Fuck off," the man snapped and moved to stagger on.

Max grabbed a fistful of his jacket and whirled him around, pushing him up against the lamppost. "Who's watching your kid?"

"Whadya know about my kid? Get yer damn hands off me." He staggered as he shoved back, and then took Max completely off guard when he threw a punch at him, slamming into Max's jaw with a powerful blow.

Max's head snapped back, and then his eyes flared as they focused back on Ben's derelict father. "You son of a bitch." He punched him back, sending him crashing to the ground.

It was then that Serena screamed, and two big burly bouncers came charging out of the club. Max was pushed up against the wall, his face to the brick, but before he could explain, he heard the whoop-whoop of a siren. A squad car came racing up the street. The next thing he knew he was bent over the hood of the squad, his arms wrenched back, and his hands cuffed behind him.

Ben's father was also cuffed, but left to sit on the curb as the cop realized the man was too drunk to stand. The officer's radio crackled as he called for backup before he even got their stories.

Liam and Rory piled out of the bar.

Liam took one look at Max and grinned at him. "I see you went for option number two."

Max glared at him. "'Let's go have a beer,' you said. 'It'll be fun,' you said."

"Hey, we wanted to get you laid, not arrested," Rory put in.

Liam folded his arms and chuckled. "Big brother decided on another method of getting his frustrations out."

"Just shut up, all of you," the cop growled. Max recognized him. Officer Hewitt, a cop who knew him and his brothers all too well. "Ain't you O'Rourke boys getting a little too old for this bullshit?"

Liam looked at Rory. "He just called you old."

"Nope. Pretty sure he was referring to you."

Max rolled his eyes, wishing he'd just gone home to bed.

The second squad pulled up, and a moment later, he was yanked up and off the hood of the car to an erect position. As he was whirled around, he noticed a car driving slowly down this side of the street. It passed not three feet from him, the eyes of every occupant on him. The driver was an Asian man. Max's eyes flicked to the passenger, and he sucked in his breath in a sharp hiss.

Christ! Could his luck get any worse tonight?

There was a stricken look on Malee's face, her wide eyes taking in the silver cuffs that clipped his wrist together, and as luck would have it, the mark on his neck. Then those eyes flicked to the blonde in the sparkly mini-dress standing nearby.

Malee wasn't stupid. She added it all up in an instant.

Max's eyes slid shut, and he turned his head, unable to stand the devastation written on her face.

Fucking hell.

And right there on the curb that night, he felt that tiny flame of hope sputter out for good.

***

Malee's father dropped her off at Aunt Tan's apartment. They'd worked especially late at the restaurant tonight. Papa knew they were due for a monthly health inspection soon, and as he always did, he made them do a thorough cleaning in preparation. She was bone tired as she climbed the steep stairs, but worse than that, a horrible depression and sadness had settled over her at what she'd just witnessed.

It all felt so overwhelming; everything that had happened since that night Max had asked her to marry him seemed to push them further apart.

When she opened the door and stepped inside, her aunt was sitting in a chair by the window, the lights from the squad cars still flashing outside.

Malee dropped her bag on the dining table and walked into the front living room, her hands signing the words. *Did you see? That's Maxwell down there.*

Her aunt nodded. *I saw it all.*

Malee couldn't believe what she'd seen as her father had driven past. When they'd come upon the police cars, she'd perked up in her seat, looking to see what was happening. She noticed the man sitting on the curb with his hands cuffed, the bouncers, and the sexy blonde in pink. But it was the other man who'd stopped her gaze cold. His back had been to her, standing rigidly, his chin in the air. His face was bruised, his lip bleeding, but she recognized him instantly. Her eyes had traveled down his muscular arms with their scrolling ink, down to the silver handcuffs that pulled back those powerful arms and clipped his wrists together tightly. His fingers flexed several times, as if he longed to wrap them around someone's throat. And she couldn't help but remember the way those same hands and long fingers had touched her so gently, so tenderly.

Almost as if he'd sensed her stare, he'd glanced up and toward her father's car to catch her openmouthed. And for just a split second something flashed between them, and it was as if the squad car with its flashing lights, the bar, and the whole damn street had faded away until it was just the two of them staring at each other. That brief moment was over all too soon, and he turned away. Was it shame or distain for her that caused him to turn?

Malee moved to stand next to her aunt and stare out the window. It looked like they were releasing Max,and hauling the other man to his feet.

What happened? Malee signed. *Maxwell's face was bruised and his lip split. Was he fighting?*

Her aunt shook her head. *He didn't start it. The other man hit him first.*

Why?

I don't know.

As they watched, one of the officers pointed to the second man and asked Max a question. He responded with a shake of his head. A moment later they were releasing the other man as well. Perhaps they'd asked Max if he wanted to press charges.

Malee's eyes strayed to the woman in pink. *Did you see that woman?*

Aunt Tan nodded.

Was she with him?

I don't know. He seemed to keep pushing her away from him. Maybe she was drunk.

Malee's jaw tightened, and her signing was abrupt and jerky in motion, revealing her anger. *He had a mark on his neck.*

Her aunt looked up at her with sad eyes. *Malee, I don't think it's what it looked like. He didn't look happy with her.*

She stared unseeing out the window. *I guess he's*

moved on already.

Her aunt tugged on her shirt hem, drawing her attention. *You don't know that.*

She turned from the window. *It doesn't matter anymore. I'm going to bed.*

Malee?

But she didn't stop. She moved to her room, threw herself on the bed, and cried into the pillow — long, gut-wrenching sobs that emanated from her soul.

CHAPTER TWENTY-THREE

It was late when Max got back to the old farmhouse. Liam and Rory offered to go with him, but he insisted they stay. He'd told his brothers he was done for the night and just wanted to be alone.

The pine floors creaked as he walked across the kitchen, through the dining room, and to the living room. Ava was asleep on the couch, an afghan thrown over her.

A fire burned low in the stone fireplace. Max had brought in firewood earlier. It sat in a stack by the hearth. It was wood he and his brothers had cut and stacked by the side of the house at the beginning of fall.

He pulled on the big gloves that lay by the hearth, opened the fire screen and quietly set a few more split logs on top. The red coals of a log burned down to embers broke and shattered into a hundred flaming pieces, sending up a crackling, hissing sound.

He took the poker and adjusted the new logs until the flames flared up, licking over the fresh wood. When he set the poker down and tossed the gloves back to the stone hearth, he heard movement on the couch.

Twisting his head, he saw Ava sit up, tucking her feet under her and stretching her arms over her head. His eyes moved over her now large belly.

"Sorry if I woke you," he said.

She yawned. "I guess I dozed off waiting for Jameson. What time is it?"

He glanced at the clock on the mantel. "After eleven." Headlights flashed across the windows as a truck pulled in. "That's probably him now."

Max stood watching the fire, one palm resting on the mantel, his long-sleeve thermal shirt and plaid flannel pushed up to his elbows, revealing his muscular, tattooed forearm.

"Are you okay, Max?" Ava's voice was quiet.

"No. I don't think I am."

"You haven't wanted to talk about your breakup. But, Max, it's been weeks. Will you tell me now what happened between you?"

He hesitated a long moment, staring at the fire, before quietly confessing, "I asked her to marry me, Ava."

"Oh Max, I had no idea. What did she say?"

Max shook his head, his eyes still on the flames, not sure he could even form the words.

"Please, Max. Tell me what happened."

"We went to tell her parents. I wanted their blessing, you know? Her father forbade her from marrying me. Said if she walked out that door, she no longer had a family."

"I'm so sorry. What did she do?"

"I held my hand out to her. I expected her to choose me. She didn't."

"Oh, Max," Ava whispered.

"I've waited for weeks for her to come to her senses."

"Have you talked at all?"

"She came to see me. Wanted to continue as we'd been, sneaking around behind her father's back." He turned to look at Ava then, his hand dropping from the mantel. "I can't do that." He shook his head. "Not anymore. That night, when she didn't come with me, when I had to walk out of there alone... something broke inside me. I can't go backward. And if she doesn't want to move forward with me, what is there? What do we have left? There's nothing."

"Max, I'm so sorry. Maybe if you give her time, she'll realize..."

He shook his head. "No. I don't think so. Not after tonight. I think I just need to give up that dream. I need to move on. Decide what's next for me."

Jameson walked in. He bent to kiss Ava and then straightened. He must have felt the vibe in the room, seen the concern on his wife's face. His eyes moved to Max.

"What's goin' on? Everything okay?"

Ava reached up to slip her hand in her husband's, but her tear-filled eyes were on Max.

"Brother, you okay?" Jameson tried again.

"No." Max shook his head. "But I will be. I'm thinking of going up to the bluff."

"When?" Jameson asked.

"Tonight. Now. I just need to get away and think. It's a good place to do that."

"Tonight?" Ava asked. "But it's so late."

Jameson studied his brother, and then his eyes dropped to her. "He'll be okay."

"But it's so cold."

"I'll put on a warmer coat," Max said.

"You should take one of the down sleeping bags if you're planning on staying up there all night," Jameson suggested. "I'll go get one for you."

Ava pushed aside the afghan and stood. "I'll make you a thermos of coffee."

Max went outside to his pickup and stood for a few minutes, bracing his hands on the cold metal edge of the truck bed.

The dirt road stretched before him, deserted and black; far in the distance, past the trees, he could see where the land began to lift up to the ridge, up to his and Malee's spot.

The screen door behind him creaked, and the sound of boots on the porch steps carried to him. Jameson tossed a sleeping bag in the bed. Max turned as Ava passed him a thermos.

"Thank you, sweetheart." He gave her a hug.

Jameson handed him a flask. "Here's something to put in it."

Max grinned as he took it. Then Jameson pulled him in for a hug and a couple of pounds on his back. "Stay warm, bro."

With that, he climbed in the cab and headed off. A dirt trail led out of the back of their property and up toward the bluff, up to the place he and his brothers had gone many times as boys, up to the place he now thought of as he and Malee's special spot.

He parked near the tree he'd carved their initials in, dropped the tailgate, and hopped up on it. His legs swung as he uncapped the flask and took a hit. The stars sparkled overhead, and the lights of town glittered in the cold, crystal-clear night.

He took a deep breath, filling his lungs with the clean mountain air and letting it out slowly as he reflected on everything that had transpired.

When he'd first met Malee, he'd worried that perhaps he wasn't good enough for her. Now it dawned on him that he felt that way about a lot of things throughout his life. He'd always felt his ink wasn't as good as his brothers. He'd worried he wasn't good enough to fight MMA. Recently, he'd let feelings of the like hold him back from buying the gym from Pops, thinking that maybe he wouldn't be able to run it.

Ava's words came back to him from that day at the shop months ago; she'd told him not to let anyone tell him he wasn't good enough to have what he wanted. He'd brushed her words off at the time. Now they sunk in.

Goddamn it, she was right. He had to stop thinking that way and letting those negative thoughts stand in the way of getting what he wanted.

He'd worked at Brothers Ink since he was barely out of high school. It probably wouldn't have been his choice, but it was a way Jameson felt he could support the family after their parents' death, so naturally Max had gone along with it. And for the most part it was a fun job.

No, it more than a job; it was the family business, and he knew in his heart, that no matter what problems there sometimes were between he and his brothers, he would never leave the business. It would always be home to him.

But lately, he'd wondered if there wasn't something more—something with a deeper meaning, more fulfilling to his soul. Oh, he knew he helped people with his art; he knew he helped heal people who were suffering loss over grief or illness or any of a myriad of life's trials. But helping the kids at the gym? That filled his soul in a different way, a way he needed.

So, was that his future then? Did he have to face the fact that it was time to let go of the dream he'd had of a life with Malee, of building a family with her? Was it time to look to a new dream? Perhaps taking over Fourth Street Gym was the new dream he needed right now. It was something to look forward to, something to give him meaning and direction, because if he just stagnated now, he'd spiral down into a deep depression.

He loved Malee; he'd *always* love Malee, but he'd come to realize that wasn't enough to save a relationship. She had to want it just as much as he did for it to work.

He glanced over at the tree, the heart barely distinguishable in the moonlight. He'd had visions of them making a life together, having children, creating a family all their own. But sometimes dreams didn't work out the way you want them to; sometimes you have to let them go.

It tore at his heart, as he took another sip off the flask, closed his eyes, and let that one go.

CHAPTER TWENTY-FOUR

Maxwell climbed from the warmth of the sleeping bag he'd spread out in the bed of his truck and jumped to the ground. He stretched, taking in the horizon. It was dawn, and the sky was just beginning to lighten with the approaching sunrise. He took in a deep breath of the chilly air, watched his foggy breath as he exhaled, and looked down over the sleepy town spread out before him with a renewed purpose in life.. He needed to have something to move forward toward, and he'd decided what that was.

He rolled up the sleeping bag, slammed the tailgate closed, and slid behind the wheel to head back to the farmhouse.

A few minutes later, he jogged up the back porch stairs and entered through the kitchen. The thought of a hot cup of coffee had him bee-lining for the coffee maker to start a pot.

While it brewed, he headed quietly to the desk next to the stairs and dug through the drawer where he kept his bank statements, tax returns, and bills. He gathered them up and returned to the kitchen to pour himself a steaming mug of coffee and then spread his finances out on the kitchen table.

He went over his savings, income, and expenses as he sipped his coffee, scratching out figures on a yellow legal pad. When he looked up from it in frowning concentration, he saw Ava leaning against the door jam in her fuzzy robe, studying him. He set his mug down. "Sorry, honey. Did I wake you?"

As if on cue, she yawned, then smiled and moved to the coffeemaker. "No, it was the smell of this brewing that drew me down the stairs." She poured a cup and moved to stand behind him, resting her free hand on his shoulder as she peered over it to the paperwork spread over the table. "What's all this?"

He twisted his head to look up at her. "I've been thinking about something for a long time, and I think I can swing it."

"What's that?"

"I'm gonna buy the Fourth Street Gym."

Her brows rose. "Pops' place?"

He nodded.

"Well, I know you love working with the kids…"

"I do."

"But what about the shop?"

"I'll still work there. Brothers Ink is the family business. I'll always work there. But Pops is going to close his place up and move to Florida. Without it, the young kids will have no place to go."

"Why is he closing down?"

"His wife is getting worse. He wants to be closer to family."

"Oh, I'm sorry to hear that."

"The kids need that place. I've been going over my finances, and I think I can swing it."

"But if you're at Brothers Ink, who will run the gym?"

"I'll hire someone. The place practically runs itself. I know I can do this. I *need* to do this, Ava."

Her blue eyes sparkled down at him. "Believing in yourself is half the battle, Max. And I believe you can do this, too. And I have no doubt about you being the perfect person for those kids. Kids seem to like you." She stroked her hand down his cheek. "You're going to make an amazing uncle."

He twisted in his seat, put one arm around her waist, and patted her belly with the other hand. "You pick a name for this little angel yet?"

"Lila Rose."

He spoke to her belly. "Well, Lila Rose, you're going to have an awesome mommy."

"You hittin' on my woman?" a masculine voice said from the doorway.

Max turned to see Jameson scratching his bare chest, his pajama bottoms hanging low on his hips, and a bad case of bedhead. He squinted with sleepy eyes toward the two of them.

Max grinned at his brother and tugged Ava closer. "Yup. That's exactly what I'm doing."

Jameson moved to the coffee pot without another word.

Ava and Max exchanged a look, Ava rolling her eyes.

"Well, you're a romantic bastard, Jamie. Aren't you gonna come fight me for her?"

Jameson yawned as he poured himself a cup. "Maybe later."

"Did I wake you when I got out of bed?" Ava asked her husband.

He turned and leaned back against the counter, raising the mug to his mouth. "I suddenly had the whole bed. I didn't know what to do with myself."

She put her hand on her hip. "Are you saying your wife is a big fat cow who takes up the entire bed?"

Jameson realized he'd just stepped in a pile of it, and Max burst out laughing at his brother's sudden unease.

"Baby, did I say that? No! I just meant I missed your beautiful sexy body pressed up against me." He took a sip and continued, "I love hanging off the edge of the bed. Really."

Ava grabbed a dishtowel off the counter and swatted him with it. "Jameson O'Rourke, you apologize to me right now."

He pulled the cup down from his mouth, fending off the towel with the other forearm. "I thought that's what I just did."

Max laughed harder. "Jamie, you don't know shit

about women."

"You shut up," Jameson growled, grabbed the towel with his free hand, and tugged his wife to him, hooking his forearm around her waist. He gazed down into her face. "Settle down, woman. You know I love you."

She smiled up at him. "You'd better."

He kissed her, and then peered down into her mug. "You're not supposed to be drinking that."

She winced. "I know. But it's *so hard!*"

Jameson grinned and tightened his arm. "Come here, my little caffeine addict, and I'll show you what's hard."

She giggled as he tickled her, and she almost spilled the mug.

"Hey, take it upstairs, you two," Max growled with a grin.

Jameson wrestled the mug from his wife's hand and dumped it out in the sink, then he looped his arm around her shoulders and pulled her with him to the table, peering down at the paperwork. "What's all this?"

Ava smiled up at him, taking pleasure in spilling the beans. "He's buying Pops' Gym."

Jameson's brows shot up, his eyes pinning his brother's. "You're what?"

"Don't look so worried, Jamie. I'm not putting in my notice. Just... expanding the family holdings."

"Pops' Gym, huh?" He nodded, contemplating.

"It's a good investment. You need some capital, let me know, I'll go in on it with you."

Maxwell looked up at his brother. "I appreciate it. And I may have to take you up on it, but I'd like to try and swing it on my own if I can."

"Understood. Just remember the offer stands if you need it."

Maxwell swore he saw a new respect shining in his brother's eyes. He glanced from Jameson to Ava, who was hugging her husband's waist and looking up adoringly at him.

Max was happy his brother had found someone so right for him. They could rail and rib each other, and then a moment later be cuddled together like now, just the two of them against the world.

Max had thought he'd found that with Malee. At the reminder, a new wave of loneliness hit him.

He turned back to his paperwork and gathered it up, swallowing down the emotion. He'd survive and somehow he'd get over the hurt. But right now he needed to get a shower and make a trip to see a banker about a loan.

CHAPTER TWENTY-FIVE

Malee climbed out of bed and walked through the apartment to her aunt's tiny kitchen. She poured herself a steaming cup of coffee and glanced at the clock. It was almost 11:00 a.m. She'd gotten very little sleep the night before and was glad her aunt had let her sleep in. She yawned, and then caught her reflection in the dining room mirror. Her eyes were still red and puffy from all the crying she'd done last night. It had been such a shock to see Max in handcuffs. But more than anything, it had hurt to see Max standing next to that blonde in front of that dance club with a hickey on his neck. It meant he was moving on, and she wasn't ready for that.

Malee closed her eyes and told herself to stop thinking about it, because if she didn't put it from her mind, she was going to start crying all over again. Taking a deep breath, she carried her mug into the living room, where she found her aunt sitting on the sofa and watching the local news on television. Aunt Tan had the captioning on so she could follow along, but Malee was barely paying any attention to it as she sipped her coffee.

How are you feeling this morning?

Malee knew her aunt saw the sadness in her eyes; still she tried to smile and signed, *Okay.*

Aunt Tan reached over and patted her leg. *Everything will work itself out, my dear. Just wait and see.*

Malee tried to smile, but she didn't feel very optimistic about it. She stared down into her coffee mug.

A moment later, her aunt was tapping her frantically on the leg and pointing to the television. Malee looked up at it curiously, wondering what on earth could suddenly have her aunt so excited.

There on the screen was Charlotte Justice being interviewed by some entertainment host. Malee's mouth fell open. The beautiful rock musician was wearing Malee's kimono for the interview!

She glanced to her aunt who was excitedly pointing at the screen and grinning from ear to ear.

Malee read the captioning. The host was asking Charlotte about an upcoming concert tour and a stop she'd be making in Denver. They talked about her new album that dropped today. A graphic of the album cover flashed on the screen behind them. The host said, "The title of your new album is Dragonfly, and I couldn't help but notice the beautiful dragonfly design on your kimono, Ms. Justice."

"Please, call me Charlotte." She looked down at the kimono and stroked her hand over it, lovingly. "Yes, it's hand-painted silk by a local artist in Grand Junction named Malee. It's extraordinary, isn't it? The craftsmanship is exquisite. She gifted this to me for the Dragonfly Tour. It's my new good luck charm."

"Well, luck aside, I'm sure your tour will be a huge success. I'm hearing the first portion has already sold out."

The rest of the interview was a blur. Malee could only stare in a trance until her aunt shook her. *Malee! She told everyone your name!*

Malee could only stare at her, shell-shocked.

Quick, bring me my laptop!

Malee frowned at her. "Why?"

We have to get you a website quickly, even if it's only with your name and email address.

"You really think so? You think people will contact me?"

Yes! Yes! Quickly now! We have to hurry.

An hour later they had the most basic of websites set up. She uploaded a photo she'd taken of a hummingbird she'd drawn as her background logo with the words *Designs by Malee* over it, along with several shots of her standing with Charlotte Justice in the kimono, and the rock star wearing it on stage in Telluride. They added an invitation for parties interested in her designs to contact her through her email.

A few minutes after the website went live, she began to get emails. All afternoon inquiries from all over poured in. Charlotte Justice's fan club got wind of it. Soon there were pictures of Charlotte from the interview, wearing the dragonfly kimono popping up all over the Internet.

Malee and Aunt Tan read over the emails as they poured in.

Malee, they want your designs! Do you know what this means?

She shook her head.

You're in business! We're going to have to figure out some pricing. We're going to have to get you set up with some supplies and a workspace. Oh, my, there's so much to be done!

"Maybe I could set up a card table."

No, no, no. You'll need much more space. There are hundreds of emails coming in.

"Papa has no room, there's nowhere."

Aunt Tan grabbed her hand, her eyes getting big. *The empty storefront downstairs!*

"Aunt Tan, I have no money for that."

Aunt Tan's eyes sparkled. *But I do.*

Malee stared at her unbelievably. "You'd do that for me? You'd loan me the money to rent a space?"

Of course, dear. We'll call the realtor right away. Then we'll go price some wholesale silk, get you some more paints, tables, whatever you need. Aunt Tan clasped her hands together, her face beaming. *Oh, my dear, I haven't been this excited about something in years.*

"Do you really think we can do it, Aunt Tan?"

We? You*! I'll help you all I can, Malee, but this is your business.*

Malee's head was spinning. She had a business! A real business!

CHAPTER TWENTY-SIX

Liam chuckled as he pulled a frozen burrito out of the break room microwave and carried it to the table, sitting down across from Max. "You should have seen him, Max. Ava was standing there pointing at different spots on the tree, and poor Jamie was hanging the ornaments wherever she directed. Then she'd tap her lip, study it, and make him move it. I could tell he wanted to chuck the whole box in the garbage. He'd glare at me while I tried not to bust out laughing, and then he'd move the damn thing."

Max grinned, crumpled up his fast food wrapper and leaned back in his chair, folding his arms. "You should have seen him the other day when she pointed at the tree she wanted him to cut down. He looked at me like, *is she kidding?* The thing was two feet taller than our ceilings."

"Did you laugh?"

"The man was holding a chainsaw. What do you think?"

Liam almost snorted his bite of burrito out his nose. He grabbed a napkin and wiped his face as he choked it down. Then his watery eyes moved over Max who was staring blankly at the tabletop instead of making a crack about it like he usually would. And the reason was obvious. His brother was still struggling with his breakup with Malee. It had been weeks now. "How're you doing?"

"I'm fine."

"No, you're not. Have you talked to her?"

That brought Max's eyes up. "No, I haven't talked to her. That's done. I'm over it."

"Like hell you are."

"Liam, quit."

"It may be done, but you ain't over shit, Max. Sweet, beautiful girls like her—ones you feel you have a real connection with—they don't come along every day."

"No, they don't. But ending it wasn't my choice."

"You sure about that?"

"What the fuck is that supposed to mean? I asked her to marry me, Liam. She chose her family instead. End of story."

"I'm just sayin', you could've pushed harder."

"You don't know fucking shit about it, so keep your opinion to yourself, okay?" Max stood, crushed the can, and flung it in the waste can before heading back up to his station.

Liam watched his brother's retreating back. He wished there was some way he could help him get over this. So far, nothing had worked. They'd tried talking to him, getting him drunk, even tried getting him laid. None of it had worked; their brother wanted no part of it.

Liam let out a huff and pushed his plate away. If Max continued to be the bear he was being, Christmas was going to suck this year.

***

Max walked out of the break room and rolled his shoulders, trying to shake off the comments his brother had made. He knew his brothers meant well with their attempts to help him, but he just wanted to be left alone.

Halfway across the room, he saw her.

Malee.

She was standing in the lobby, her eyes searching the shop for him. It stopped him dead in his tracks. Stiff and taut, he stood for a moment, watching her.

He knew the exact moment she saw him, too. She froze, looking right at him, their eyes meeting across the space.

Confused, he hesitated, waiting. *Why are you here?* he wanted to demand as he stared back at her across the few feet that separated them. But he didn't say a word.

She began to walk toward him.

His legs finally remembered how to walk, and he moved, ignoring her approach as he headed to his station. He'd be damned if he'd even acknowledge she was there.

His name on her lips stopped him abruptly. She rarely spoke. He stood stiffly, caught between his chair and Rory's.

"Max."

Her voice was closer this time.

He turned his head. She was standing right beside his chair now, so close he could smell that honeysuckle scent of hers, could have reached out and touched her, could have laid his fingers over the pulse beating in her throat and felt her breath as she dragged it into her lungs.

They looked at one another.

He tried not to show any emotion, to keep his face like a stone.

She took another tentative step closer.

His eyes flicked to her décolletage. The silver heart pendant he'd given her still hung around her neck, the engraved words *I Love You* taunting him. Why did she still wear it?

What are you doing here, he signed at last. *Isn't this place off limits to you?* His gestures were choppy and his stance unfriendly and distant. He was as rude as he could make himself be. Why were her eyes so wide, so imploring?

"I wanted to ask you something."

What?

She looked over his shoulder and pointed. He twisted to look. The damn drawing she'd given him. It was taped to the wall by his station. He'd never taken it down. Now he wished he had. He hated that she saw he still kept it, like it meant something to him, like she still had a hold on him. She did, but he didn't need to advertise the fact. The drawing had always brightened his day. Now it's telling presence pissed him off.

You want it back? Here. He yanked it down and held it out to her, deliberately cold, as he tried to harden his heart.

She shook her head. "I don't want it back."

Then what?

"I want you to tattoo that on me."

He couldn't have been more surprised if she'd grown two heads. *What?*

"It's my symbol."

And then it dawned on him, and his eyes flicked toward the window and her shop across the street. He'd seen a company installing a sign above the storefront the other day — Designs by Malee, with her hummingbird next to the company name.

He shoved the paper back at her. *Find someone else to do it. I can't.*

"Please, Max. I want you to do it. It has to be you."

Why?

"Because you're the one who made this all possible." When he hesitated, she pushed. "Please. I could come back whenever you have time."

He glanced over and saw Liam — who'd returned to his own station — give him a look. Maybe it was because he'd just spent his break trying to convince his brother that he was over her. And maybe he needed to prove that to himself. So he gestured to his chair. But he couldn't help asking one question. *You sure you really want this? You won't be sorry tomorrow?*

"You told me all those times we were together that you believed in me. You made me believe in myself. And now my art is selling, and I have a shop. This tattoo represents all that. No, Max, I won't be sorry."

He searched her eyes a long moment, then nodded curtly, determined not to let the effect her words had on him show. *Fine. You want it done, then we do it right now. I've got another appointment in a few hours, and I'm booked up all week.*

It took a while for him to draw up a stencil, but soon she was in his chair, her skin cleaned and he was doing the transfer. She wanted it on her shoulder. When he got it in place, he handed her a mirror so she could check the placement.

***

Good?

Malee nodded at Max's short question, and he grabbed the mirror out of her hands. She tried not to let his abruptness hurt her feelings, but it did. And deep down a part of her knew she deserved it.

He positioned her and pulled his rolling tray over. While he fiddled with his equipment and inks, she glanced across the aisle to Liam. He met her eyes briefly, but didn't smile at her. She supposed they all hated her now. She'd hurt their brother. Naturally, they would rally around him.

The only one who had smiled at her had been the girl at the reception counter, but she was not the one Malee had been introduced to the night of the concert. She was not his sister-in-law, Ava. Perhaps this girl had been hired to fill in. Ava must be due soon. Perhaps she'd already had the baby.

Malee's eyes drifted to Max's bent head, and she wondered what other changes had occurred in his life since she'd last seen him. Somehow the thought that she'd missed out on pieces of his life, no matter how small, twisted the knife in the wound she already carried.

He glanced up and signed, *Ready?*

She nodded, and he reached down and flipped on the machine.

He laid one hand on her skin and warmth flooded through her body at just that simple touch. Then he brought the hand with the tattoo machine up and the needle to her skin. She felt it prick and then the vibration as the needle moved. She couldn't hear the buzz of the machine, but she noticed a million other things, like the smell of the ink and the cleanser he'd used on her, the cold of the vinyl under her, and the heat of his body as he leaned over her.

For a moment, she watched the needle bounce and his other black-gloved hand wipe the excess ink away with a cloth, before she had to turn her head away.

***

Max might have been halfway through the design when it really began to hit him exactly what he was doing. He was laying ink on the woman he loved.

She had come to him. The thought shook him.

Maybe it was just about the tattoo. Maybe it was nothing more. He better not dare let himself think it was anything more.

Still, somehow knowing his ink would live on her skin all the days of her life did something to him. It touched him deep down in a part he'd thought he'd locked away.

He took his time. He wanted to do it right. He wanted it to be some of his best work. He meant to make sure she didn't have any regrets for this day. He only had a few hours with her, to be near her, to touch her.

And if this was no more than a tattoo, at least she'd have it to remember him by.

***

Business continued around them, customers coming and going. Malee was conscious of none of it as Max worked except his body so close beside her. She didn't dare look at him more than once or twice; she'd give her feelings away if she did.

When she did dare glance at his eyes that were intent on his work, a hot rush of sweet pain shot through her. And when her eyes would drop to his gloved hands with his long agile fingers and pronounced knuckles, she remember how she had caressed them, kissed them in the darkness those nights in his truck and at the gym.

Her eyes moved over his head; he was letting the shaved hair grow out and she longed to run her hands over it, to see if it was as soft as she imagined. Her gaze traveled down along the beard that still framed his strong jaw and beautiful mouth. How many times had those lips been on her skin?

He glanced up, his eyes dropping to her lips as if he'd read her mind. When his gaze dropped, she felt bereft. Perhaps she was wrong to come, wrong to ask him to do this for her. Was she just torturing herself, torturing them both with things they couldn't have?

Time passed and eventually he shut off his machine, wiping the design clean one final time. Then he set the items down and held up the mirror. She met his eyes. Was that nervousness she saw? Was he worried she wouldn't like his work?

Her gaze dropped to the reflection, and it took her breath. Her face lit up with her excitement. She loved it. Just like she knew she would.

She looked at Max. His eyes were on the design, but when he lifted his gaze to hers and saw her happiness, he couldn't stop the responding smile that gave her a flash of his white teeth. Oh, how she had missed that smile. It changed his entire dark face, and the effect that had on her was powerful. She tore her gaze away, shivering a little, and whispered, "It's beautiful."

A few minutes later as she was leaving, he stopped her with a hand on her arm. When she looked at him, he signed one phrase and then turned back to clean up his workstation.

Congratulations on your shop, Malee. I wish you all the best. Really.

CHAPTER TWENTY-SEVEN

Lawan grabbed Malee's arm as she bussed a table and yanked her around, frantically signing to her. *They're here!*

Who is here?

Kai and San'ya. Uncle Rama just drove them down from Denver. They're in the back talking to Father.

Malee's eyes slid past her sister to the door to the kitchen. As the long winter gave way to spring, this had been her worst fear. She had known somewhere in the back of her mind that her father had planned something like this; Lawan had told her as much months ago, but now that it was real, she felt sick to her stomach.

Malee wanted to be a good daughter — the obedient, respectful, helpful daughter her father expected of her. And she tried every day to be that. Even though her business was doing very well, and her silks were selling, Malee still worked long hours, making time to help out at the restaurant, especially at busy times. She still did everything her father asked of her.

But this? To actually let her father try to arrange a

match for her? She didn't think she could go along with it.

Have you seen them?

Lawan nodded. *Kai is tall and good looking. He smiled at me.*

Oh God, her sister sounded smitten already.

And San'ya?

Her sister looked away. *He is…*

He's what, Lawan? Tell me.

He's older, Malee.

How old?

I think he is almost our father's age. I heard them talking. He is a widower who lost his wife several years ago. They have no children. He wants children.

And I'm supposed to be his second wife and give him these children?

Lawan shrugged. *I don't know what Papa is thinking. Perhaps he is a good man.*

What does he look like, Lawan?

Lawan hesitated.

Tell me, sister.

He is short and bald, with bad teeth.

Malee shoved the gray tub of dishes at Lawan and dashed out the front door. She ran all the way to Aunt Tan's, stumbling up the stairs, her vision blurred by the tears she tried to hold back.

She burst in the apartment, surprising her aunt who was sitting on the sofa.

Malee, what a nice surprise —

Aunt Tan barely had time to sign the phrase before Malee collapsed at her feet, her head falling onto her aunt's lap.

She felt her aunt stroking her head and patting her back.

Finally, when her sobs subsided, Aunt Tan tapped her shoulder, and Malee looked up.

My dear sweet child, what is wrong?

Malee was so upset, she couldn't form words, so she signed, *The Thai boy father wants to marry me to...*

Yes?

He's an old man, Aunt Tan. Lawan said he is father's age. He's an old, short, bald man with bad teeth.

What?

It's true.

I will talk to your father. This nonsense must stop.

Malee felt anger replace her despair. She slashed the air violently with her signs. *Is that all father thinks I am worth? That no normal boy my age would want me because I can't hear? Does he think I have no value?*

I'm sure that's not it.

I think that is exactly it.

Malee, then you must decide.

She wiped the last of her tears away. *Decide what?*

Decide the life you want.

She stared at her aunt blankly.

If it's Max you want... you have to want him for him, not because he's an escape from your father. Malee, your life is not your father's. How you will spend it and whom you will spend it with is for you to decide. You must live this life for yourself — no one else — if you are to truly find the freedom you so desperately want.

The tears came again, and Malee fought them back. *I ruined everything with Max. He doesn't want anything to do with me anymore.*

That's not true. If that man loved you, then he will listen to you if you go to him and tell him you made a mistake.

I'm afraid he's moved on.

Bring me that pretty little box, the one where you keep those notes he wrote you.

Aunt Tan.

My child, please, do as I ask.

Malee got up and went to her room. She picked up the decorative tin box on the nightstand and brought it back to her aunt.

Aunt Tan patted the cushion next to her, and Malee sat.

Open it, my dear.

Malee pulled off the lid. Inside was a stack of neatly folded notes.

Only you know if the man who wrote those notes is the man who deserves you. Only you know if he is the man you want.

It's too late.

Malee, there is still a chance. But don't wait too long, my child. Go to him. Now. Right now.

Malee closed the box and stood. *I need to think.*

Aunt Tan took her hand and squeezed it. *I love you,*

Malee.

I love you, too, Aunt Tan.

Could you help me to bed, dear? I think I'll lie down and take a nap. I feel tired today.

Are you okay?

I'm fine, dear. Just tired.

After Malee helped her Aunt to bed and covered her with an afghan, she bent and kissed her on the forehead.

Aunt Tan grabbed her arm as she straightened. *Malee, you must go to him.*

I'm afraid, Aunt Tan.

He's loves you. He's waiting for you to go to him and admit you were wrong.

I'm not sure he is waiting.

Where's your backbone?

Aunt Tan it's not so simple.

Yes, Malee, it is. It's very simple. Go to him. Promise me.

Okay, I promise. Now get some rest, Aunt Tan.

Her aunt's eyes closed, and Malee slipped quietly out of the room. She shrugged into a jacket that hung by the door, and as she was about to turn the knob to leave, her eyes fell on the tin box she'd set on the sofa. She went over and picked it up, carrying it with her as she exited the building.

Standing on the sidewalk just outside the door, she stared across the street at Brothers Ink. Then she gazed down toward Thai Garden. She couldn't go back there.

Not now. And she just wasn't ready to face Max yet. She needed to think.

Her eyes lifted to the mountains on the horizon at the end of the street, and she knew where she would go.

CHAPTER TWENTY-EIGHT

Malee texted her sister from the alley behind Thai Garden.

A moment later, the back door opened and her sister's head poked out. When she spotted Malee, she slipped outside, hurrying over to her.

Where did you run off to?

Aunt Tan's.

Are you coming inside?

Malee shook her head. *Can I borrow your car?*

Of course, but where are you going?

I need to think. I'm going to drive up to the ridge, to the spot Max took me — our spot.

Lawan looked to the sky. *Don't stay up there too long, Malee. Please. Be home before the sun goes down.*

I will.

Lawan dug the keys out of her hip pocket and then pulled her in for a hug.

***

Twenty minutes later, Malee parked her car on the side of the dirt road and picked the tin box up off the seat. She carried it with her as she walked to their spot. Her eyes lifted to the top branches of the tall tree. They swayed in the wind. She set her palm on the heart Max had carved into the bark, and her fingers moved over the letters. *Malee + Max.*

They'd been so happy that day.

Turning to look out over the valley, she let her hand drop. It really was quite beautiful up here. She looked toward the ridge, to the grassy spot where they'd had their picnic.

Sitting on the cold grass beneath the tree and leaning back against it, she opened the box and read every note and letter. Some were sweet, some were silly, and some were urgently imploring her to meet him. But they all had one thing in common—they were the letters of a man in love with a girl. She folded them back up, always careful to keep them in the order in which she received them, then returned them to the box and set it aside.

Her eyes lifted to the horizon, and she scanned the view as memories flooded through her from the first time he'd brought her up here. She remembered how they'd lain on a blanket, and she'd fed him grapes, how they'd laughed and told each other all their hopes and dreams, and how they'd told each other those three little words: I love you.

There was a chill in the air as the wind whipped over her, and she pulled her jacket more tightly around herself.

She thought of what had set this ball in motion today to bring her to this spot. The actions of her father, whether there were good intensions behind them or not, were wrong. Could he truly not see that? Could he not understand how it made her feel? Like she was some kind of damaged goods who had to be bartered off to some old widower? She loved her father, but today she was as angry as she had ever been. She wasn't sure she could even bring herself to talk to him now, not with respect, because inside her there was none of that—just rebellion, anger, and resentment.

Why did she keep trying to please him and do things his way? He never even stopped to consider her feelings. There were things she wanted. She had hopes and dreams just like everyone else. She was no different. Couldn't he see that?

Up here, she could almost forget all of it.

It felt so good—so good—to be away and free like this. The March wind brushed against her face, carrying the scent of nature. Malee breathed in the fresh, clean air and turned her face up to the rays of the early spring sun, closing her eyes to the brightness.

Her father wanted her to marry a good Thai, but even if he found someone her own age, it wouldn't matter. None of them would ever make her twist and turn in the darkness of her room, remembering the feel of his lips, the caress of his hands.

Not like Max had.

He'd listened to her, believed in her, wanted to protect her. He'd set her free. He'd given her freedom to talk, to pour out her problems, even to dare to dream.

He'd opened her world up to new experiences. He was freedom from all the expectations and limitations. He was all that she craved alone at night in her bedroom. He made her heart beat in her throat and her hands long to touch him. He was everything to her. And damn it, she wasn't going to let him go.

A shadow crossed her face, and she opened her eyes to see a dove fly overhead, white against the blue sky. It circled and dipped, almost as if to signal her.

She put her hand up to shade her eyes as she watched it, and right then everything her aunt said made sense to her. It wasn't complicated; it was simple. Max and her, they loved each other, and nothing else mattered.

Those realizations hit Malee hard, and the sense of freedom it gave her was suddenly so exuberant, so bright, that she laughed. The dove flew toward the sun until she couldn't see it anymore.

Her hand dropped.

Max. He's the one I love, she thought. *He's where I belong*.

She wanted to live the life she wanted, for herself, not for anyone else, and she was going to, in spite of her parents.

It wouldn't be easy going against them, but she had no choice. And she realized something else, too. She was going to have to take responsibility for her own happiness, and to protect it fiercely from anyone who tried to take it from her.

She saw the big house across the valley — the O'Rourke's property.

Today was as good a day as any to beg for forgiveness and maybe start a new life.

She stood, brushed her hands off, and felt the vibration in her pocket, her cell phone notifying her of an incoming text.

She pulled it out and opened the message from Lawan.

Come quick. It's Aunt Tan.

CHAPTER TWENTY-NINE

Max rolled his truck to a slow stop on the shoulder of the cemetery road, parking behind a line of other cars. He climbed out and reached in the back to pull his suit jacket out, then shrugged it on. A large crowd of mourners, some coming in from all over the country, gathered around the green tent that covered the flower-laden casket. Max moved to stand in the back during the quiet graveside service that didn't last long. It was a blustery overcast day, as depressing as the event itself.

Malee sat with her family in the front row. Once Max locked eyes on her, he couldn't tear his gaze away. She had her head down, her long black hair falling in a sheet to shield her face as her aunt was quietly laid to rest. She wore a black wool coat that made her look thin and frail as she stood at the end of the service and laid a flower on the casket.

Max was sorry to hear of the sweet lady's passing. He could still remember the shock of it when Liam had come home that night and told him of the paramedic unit that had been parked in front of the building across the street.

Max had been home, helping Jamie finish up

construction on the house he was building, while Liam held down the fort at Brothers Ink.

Max had later heard Malee's aunt had died in her sleep.

The service wrapped up, and Max stayed frozen in place as the mourners quietly departed, until only the immediate family remained. Malee's sister put a hand to her arm and gestured toward him. He watched as her eyes lifted and found him on the slight hill, standing alone in his dark suit, silhouetted against the gray sky.

Malee patted her sister's arm and then stepped past her, walking slowly toward him. He stood stock still, watching her approach, a myriad of emotions warring inside him. She looked lost, out of her depth, and so damn sad. He wanted nothing more than to take her in his arms and hold her. But things had changed between them. A palpable wall had risen, one that held him back. And he hated that. More than anything, he hated the fact that in all this time, she hadn't come to him, not even when this had happened, and she would have needed him most. Was it gone, then? Did she not need him anymore? Was everything they had dead?

When she got to within a few feet, he signed to her, *I'm so sorry about your aunt, Malee. She was a sweet, dear woman.*

"Thank you, and thank you for coming. She liked you, Max."

I liked her, too.

They stared at each other a long moment. A strand of her hair blew across her face, and Max fought the urge to brush it back before she reached up a finger and hooked it, tucking it behind her ear.

Are you okay, Malee?

She gazed off into the distance, and he could see the stress lines on her face. She looked like she hadn't been sleeping, and he wondered if she'd been eating. He worried about her, and more than anything, he wished he could lighten this burden for her.

Finally, she replied, shaking her head. "No, but I will be. I think it will take time, probably a long time. She was very dear to me. She believed in my dreams. She made them possible."

Your shop?

She nodded.

It's doing well?

"It was. I haven't… been there in a while. I can't seem to get in the mood to create anything right now."

Don't give up, Malee. Promise me.

She looked at him, her eyes glazing with tears, and attempted a smile she clearly didn't feel as she nodded. She glanced back toward her family. "I should get going."

He nodded, feeling absolutely bereft at the thought of her walking away.

"It's good to see you, Max."

It's good to see you, too. It wasn't what he wanted to say; it wasn't what he needed to say. But this was hardly the time or place for them to hash out the problems of the past.

She stepped toward him to give him a hug, moving into his arms with a familiarity that almost brought him to his knees. Her head tucked up under his chin, fitting perfectly, just like he remembered. His eyes slid closed, and for the briefest moment it was just the two of them clinging to each other. He held her, breathing in her scent. God, it felt so good to hold her.

It was over all too soon as she stepped back, gave him a shaky smile, and then turned to leave. His hand slid down her sleeve, finally dropping away as she retreated.

Two weeks later —

Max stood at the front window of Brothers Ink, staring across the street at Malee's shop. It had been closed for several weeks now, ever since her aunt had died.

Jameson moved to stand next to him, following his gaze. Max felt his brother's eyes on him, but he didn't turn.

"When are you going to get over her?"

It was a question Max had asked himself a million times. There was no easy answer, so he gave the only one he could. "When I'm sure she's okay."

"Are you waiting for her to move on? To find someone else?"

Max shook his head. "I don't know. I just... want her to be happy again."

"Even if it's without you?"

Finally, he turned to face Jameson, letting all the pain on his face show, revealing how much that tore at him. "Yeah, if that's all that's left. This isn't what I wanted. It wasn't supposed to end like this."

"Then do something about it."

Max let his gaze drift back to the dark store across the street, wondering if asking the woman he loved to choose between him and her family again was even fair anymore.

***

Malee stood at the window in her aunt's now empty apartment and stared down at Brothers Ink. The movers had left with the last of the boxes and the place was eerily silent. In her hand she held two items: her aunt's hand-painted parasol that was so dear to Malee and the thick envelope from the Willis, Wagner & Bailey. She'd just come from their office where one of the attorneys had gone over the portion of Aunt Tan's will that had to do with Malee.

Her dear sweet aunt had left her a quite sizeable amount, along with her parasol and tea set — the box that sat at her feet.

Malee would have the funds to continue her business; her aunt had ensured its future, and with it, Malee's freedom. She would no longer be dependent on her father or any arranged match he might try to force on her. She wouldn't be dependent on any man for her survival. She had the funds to do anything she wanted.

But as she gazed down at Brothers Ink, it all seemed like an empty dream. Without the man she loved, it meant nothing. Her aunt's words whispered in her ear, as if she were standing right next to her, urging her on.

Malee, there is still a chance. But don't wait too long, my child. Go to him. Now. Right now.

CHAPTER THIRTY

Max cooed at the tiny bundle in Ava's arms. Little Lila Rose was six weeks old. Jameson was asleep on the couch, having fallen into an exhausted slumber after working long hours to complete the new house for his budding family.

"She's beautiful, sweetheart."

"Thank you, Max."

His eyes lifted to his sleeping brother. "Daddy passed out before baby."

Ava smiled. "He's been working so hard. I think I'll let him sleep."

A set of headlights flashed across the ceiling.

Ava frowned. "Who could that be?"

Max moved to the window, pulling the curtain back. A compact car rolled slowly up the gravel drive.

Ava peered over his shoulder as the driver climbed out.

"Malee," Max whispered under his breath.

Ava touched his arm. "It takes a lot of guts for a girl to come to a man like this. Don't be too hard on her."

Max let the curtain drop, and he stepped back, his mind whirling through every possible reason she could have for coming here. *Don't get your hopes up, boy,* he told himself. *It may not be what you think.*

There was a soft knock at the door.

Ava stepped over and answered it.

Malee looked surprised for a moment, and then her eyes dropped to the bundle in Ava's arms and lit up, her mouth dropping open as she pointed to the baby.

Ava grinned and nodded, holding Lila Rose up proudly.

Malee tickled the baby's cheek but stilled when her eyes moved past Ava to see Maxwell standing stiffly behind her in the living room, his hands jammed in the hip pockets of his jeans.

"Hello, Max. Can I talk to you?"

"Please, come in," Ava motioned her inside, but Malee shook her head and motioned outside.

"Can we talk out here?"

At last, with a single curt nod, Max yielded. He stepped out onto the porch beside Malee, reluctance written all over him.

Out in the darkness, Max heard the hoot of a faraway owl and his own too rapid, harsh breathing. To the back of the farmhouse, he could see where the land lifted higher, all the way up to the ridge—and the place he still thought of as their spot—now just a black, looming, outline against the shadowy night sky. Finally, he signed to her, *How have you been?*

"Lonely."

What was he supposed to say to that?

"I'm sorry about everything, Max."

I know you are, Malee.

"You're not going to make this easy, are you?"

Easy? None of this has been easy.

"I never meant to hurt you."

He nodded, his throat closing and the muscles in his jaw tightening. *Well, if that's all you came to say…* Maxwell signed impatiently.

When she didn't respond, he leaned against a porch post, his eyes on the horizon, wondering how many more times he was going to have to encounter Malee and pretend he was okay.

"That night I saw you in town… who was that girl you were with?"

Max kept his gaze on the horizon, then finally looked back and signed, *No one.*

He wasn't sure where the sudden anger came from. He knew he wanted to forget the disgust and shock and disapproval that had been written with blinding transparency on her face that night as she'd gaped at him through the passenger window. For one split second, under the intensity of her wide, dark eyes, he'd felt branded with shame, and he'd wanted to hide the mark on his neck and the cuffs on his wrists.

Heat and anger tore through him now, coming to his rescue. *I saw the look on your face that night. You broke up with me, Malee. Not the other way around. We weren't together. But I didn't do anything with her other than a few kisses. There hasn't been anyone since you. And I don't know why I'm even telling you this. You have no right to know anything about what I do anymore. You lost that right.*

She stepped back, and he closed his eyes, already regretting the words he'd spewed at her like that. He ran a hand over his head and then signed slowly, *Why did you come here?*

"I'm sorry, Max."

For what?

"For everything. I was wrong, Max. So wrong."

He stood still as a statue, frozen with fear that this was no more than just words. He refused to let himself hope again, and he fought to keep that extinguished flame of hope from sparking to life again. Finally Max's eyes met hers with a penetrating stare. *I want so bad to trust you… to trust you mean it this time.*

She searched his eyes. "I have a shop now, Max. I should be happy."

He nodded. *Why haven't you opened back up?*

"You noticed."

I noticed. Are you back at the restaurant?

She shook her head. "My aunt left me some money. I don't have to work for my father. I'm not trapped there."

You were never trapped there. He felt the need to remind her of the fact.

She nodded.

So you're free now, like you always wanted.

"I have a business that I love. But do you know what I do? I sit in the back room of the dark, closed shop, trying to create something beautiful, something happy and full of life, but I'm not happy. I'm miserable."

He hung on every word, intently.

"I made a decision. I can sit in that room and make all the beautiful art in the world, but it won't mean a thing if I don't have you. So I'm here, baring my heart for you, hoping you won't throw it back in my face."

She studied his face intently, but he couldn't hold her gaze. He didn't want her to see the hope in his eyes or the fear that he'd be hurt again, so he glanced at the horizon, his jaw tightening. She touched his arm to get his attention, and he had no choice but to look at her.

"If you did, I know I would deserve it, but I'm hoping you won't. I had to come here, Max. Don't you see? Until I have you back, I can't do anything else."

He signed to her, almost resignedly. *Malee, it's not that easy. Your father —*

"I love you. I don't care what my father says, what he thinks."

Yes, you do.

"Okay, I do. But I care more what you think."

You won't be happy. Not if you have to give up your family. You'll come to resent me.

"My aunt gave me some good advice. Do you want to know what it is?"

He shrugged.

"She told me I can't live my life for anyone else; I must live my life for me. She's right. I can't...I won't live my life to please my father. I love my father, but I'm in love you, Max. Please tell me you still love me."

He looked away, and his eyes glazed over.

"Max?"

I still love you. He wasn't happy when he made the motions with his hands to admit it. He turned to face the horizon, one hand on the porch post. He sensed her move behind him, and then her thin arms slipped around his waist and her head pressed against the hollow between his shoulder blades. It was his undoing. He felt all his walls shatter like glass.

Then she was pulling him around. He looked down at her, all the vulnerability plain on his face. She could hurt him again, and he hoped he wasn't a fool for giving her another chance.

She asked, "Will you marry me?"

He searched her eyes and tried one last time to get through to her. His motions were jerky and abrupt when he signed to her. *Look at me, Malee. Really look. My skin is covered in ink. I ride a motorcycle. I work in a tattoo shop. Don't you see? I'm not Thai. I'm an O'Rourke, and this town has always looked down on the O'Rourke brothers. That didn't change until Jameson became famous, and it became profitable for the town to accept us. Are you really seeing me? Do you see what you'd be getting? Because I'm nothing like what your family wants for you. You need to be sure this time.*

She stepped closer to him, right in his face. "I see you. I see all that you are, not just the ink on your skin." She took a breath and signed more slowly. *I see a man that's gentle, with a good heart. A man that took the time to learn sign language for a girl he'd only spent five minutes with. I see a man who looks at me and doesn't see my disability; he sees a woman. I see a man who cares about other's feelings, a man whose heart is full of life and big enough to share his love. I see a man who would never hurt me and who I never want to hurt again. I see a man I am completely in love with. I see a man I want for my husband. I see a man I want for the father of my children.*

He stared at her, his eyes glazing at her words, and then his eyes shifted away. But this time she wasn't having it. She gripped his jaw and turned his head back.

Finally, she asked, "What do you see, Max?"

His jaw muscles worked, and he signed, almost with resignation. *I see a girl who stole my heart the first moment I laid eyes on her. I see a girl I want to live beside me all the days of my life, until we're both in rocking chairs, rocking beside each other, watching our grandchildren run in the yard. So you better be sure, Malee.*

She jumped into his arms, and he buried his face in her neck. When finally, she stopped crying, he pushed her back and signed, *If we're doing this, then we're doing this now, tonight, just the two of us. Will you come with me?*

She nodded, not even knowing where they were going.

No luggage. I'll buy you what you need. Are you game?

"I love you. Yes! Yes! A million times yes! Tonight!

Now! Let's go!"

He took her face in his hands and pulled her up to his lips, kissing her long and slow — a kiss filled with all the heartache of months apart and the sweet taste of reunion.

CHAPTER THIRTY-ONE

Malee and Max stood in front of the hotel room door as he fumbled with the keycard. When the door popped open, he hefted her up into his arms. She squealed, jostling her bouquet in her hand, one arm going around his neck to hold on tight. He grinned down at her, his face tanned by the Maui sun, and carried her across the threshold.

Their suite was lavish with a big bed and a balcony with a gorgeous oceanfront view that right now neither was concerned with.

Instead of tossing her down on the bed like she expected, Max set her on her high-heeled feet. He grinned as he stepped back to the bottle of champagne chilling in a silver bucket. Picking it up, he waggled it at her, and she nodded.

He popped the cork and poured them each a glass while she moved to the balcony and pushed open the sliding door. The diaphanous sheers billowed as the salty ocean breeze blew in. It carried with it the scent of gardenia and plumeria blossoms that bloomed all over the stunning resort property.

Malee breathed in deeply, her eyes on the waves crashing against the shoreline. This was the most beautiful place in the world. She hoped one day Max would bring her back again, perhaps for their tenth anniversary.

Today had been magical.

Max had planned it all out, and it had been perfect.

They'd flown to LA and then to Maui. He'd checked them into this amazing suite. Malee was willing that first night, but they still hadn't had sex. He'd told her they'd waited this long, he could wait a couple more days. The morning after they arrived, they went directly to get their marriage license and then to a jeweler to pick out wedding bands. Because they were at an upscale hotel, the concierge was able to pull together all the other arrangements per Max's requests.

Malee hadn't known any of this.

He'd totally surprised her on the second morning, waking her up when someone knocked on the door of the suite. He'd arranged for a person to come and do her hair and makeup and had even selected a beautiful white flowing dress for her to wear.

When she'd come out of the bathroom, dressed and ready, he'd been standing there looking so handsome in a perfectly fitted suit. The concierge was there with a gorgeous bouquet of white lilies. They rode the elevator down and were escorted to the almost deserted beach.

All this, and it was barely past sunrise.

But the most wonderful surprise of all was who was waiting with the officiant. Malee had broken down into tears when she saw the Buddhist monk standing in his robes, a loving smile on his face, there to bless the couple.

Her wide eyes went to Max, to see him smiling down at her.

He knew this was important to her, and it meant the world to know he'd taken the time and trouble to make this happen.

Although neither of their families were there, it was all the more special sharing it just between the two of them. She knew she would always remember how handsome Max looked and how happy he was as he promised to love, honor, and cherish her for all the days of his life.

He slipped a beautiful wedding band on her finger, and she slipped a matching one on his much larger finger, struggling to get it over the knuckle as they both laughed.

Afterward, the Monk said prayers and blessed the couple with holy water as a single white dove was released into the sky.

Malee couldn't have dreamed of anything more perfect.

They'd had a lovely breakfast under a beautiful pergola with flowing white sheer draping. The table was set with flowers and an abundance of fresh fruits, pastries, crepes, and even a tiny wedding cake. They'd sipped mimosas and watched the sun climb into the sky.

Max tapped her on the shoulder, pulling her from her thoughts. She turned from the glorious view to see him holding out a glass of champagne. He'd removed his tie and suit jacket, and they now lay draped over a chair.

She accepted the flute, and they clinked their glasses together. She took a sip, and then he kissed her. It wasn't long before he was taking the glass out of her hand and pulling her toward the bed.

He sat, tugged her down on his lap, and signed, *My beautiful wife.*

Her face glowed with a radiant smile as his love shown from his face. "My gorgeous husband."

He returned her smile, his white teeth flashing.

She said, "Today was amazing."

You look amazing in this dress. His eyes moved over her. *But now I want to take it off you.* His hands moved to her hips, and he lifted her to stand in front of him, positioning her between his knees. Then he reached around and unzipped the strapless gown. It fell in a flutter, pooling at her feet. She stepped free, and he tossed it aside.

She stood before him in nothing but her silver high heels, a pair of satin panties, and a pale blue garter around her thigh. His hands smoothed up the outside of both thighs, sliding over her satiny skin. He curled one finger under the garter and gave it a snap as he smiled up at her.

She jumped, startled, then grinned back at him.

He drew the satin and lace slowly down while his eyes remained locked with hers.

Malee could feel her heart pounding in her chest and the heat climbing up her neck and face. She'd waited so long for this; they both had. And now, as he drew the moment out, she felt like the most treasured thing in the world.

The garter slipped to her ankle, and she stepped out of it.

She couldn't wait another minute to touch him, and her fingers fumbled with the buttons of his white dress shirt. He reached up to help her, the garter dangling around his wrist. A moment later, she was pushing the shirt off his broad shoulders.

He shrugged out of it and tossed it aside, then slid her garter up over his bicep.

She slipped her finger in it and gave it a snap, like he'd done to her.

He grinned as his hands cupped her ass and pulled her toward him. He held that eye contact as his mouth latched onto one of her nipples to draw and suck deeply.

Her hands slid over his shoulders, and her head dropped back. She was glad his strong arms were wrapped around her, holding her in place, because if they weren't, she was sure she would have melted in a puddle to the floor. The sensation was that good. A sigh escaped her lips as her fingertips dug into his skin.

Oh God, what had they been waiting for? If this was any indication of how good the sex was going to be, she'd just died and gone to heaven. The hot skin of his hard muscled arms burned against her, setting her on fire. She wanted more — more of his firm hands touching, exploring, and more of his hot mouth doing those amazing things to her breasts. His head moved from one to the other, giving it the same attention as the first.

She moaned, the sound rumbling out of her throat.

She felt needy and excited and daring. Her hands smoothed down his broad shoulders and her head dropped forward, her eyes taking in that broad expanse of beautiful masculine perfection. She'd never seen him with his shirt off, and now she took her time, examining the intricate beauty of the tattoos that stretched across his shoulders and back. It was stunning work, and her fingers traced along the lines, skating gently over his skin. She felt a moan rumble up from his chest and felt the vibrations, too, through his mouth wrapped around her nipple.

She couldn't stop one knee from bending, her leg lifting and her inner thigh stroking against his outer ribs as she writhed against him, undulating with a need so strong she couldn't hold back.

A moment later, his arms locked around her, he twisted, and she found herself flat on her back on the soft mattress, the satin coverlet cool against her bare skin. He surged up over her, the look on his face just as needy as hers and fully determined to do something about it.

He dropped to his elbows, his mouth coming down

on hers as his bare torso pressed her to the bed. The weight of him on top of her felt amazing, like this was exactly where he was always meant to be.

His mouth plundered hers as his large strong hands smoothed gently over her skin. She kissed him back with just as much passion, which only flamed the fire and drove him further.

One big palm closed over her bare breast and squeezed. He smothered the moan that emanated from her throat as he continued to tease and torment her, pinching and rolling her nipples between his long fingers. Finally, he tore his mouth from hers to lavish attention on her breasts again. He couldn't get enough of them. He licked, and nipped, and sucked, and squeezed until she was a writhing bag of bones. Her hips lifted instinctively, seeking contact, stroking against his slacks.

That tore his attention from her breasts. He lifted up to stare down at her, almost questioningly, his eyes searching hers. She was breathing heavy, her lips swollen from his kisses, her face flushed.

He moved back off her, and she watched as he stood at the side of the bed long enough to yank the fastenings of the slacks open and shove them and the briefs underneath to the floor.

He was magnificent, his body ripped with muscles, ink running up both sides of his ribs. It was all drool-worthy, but what drew her attention was the proud erection standing tall. Her eyes widened at the sight of it, and fear must have flashed across her face, because a moment later, he was crawling back over her, his hand sliding over her cheek, stroking her reassuringly. He pulled his hand back to sign.

It's all right. We'll go slow. When you're ready. Okay, baby?

She nodded. "Okay."

We've got all the time you need. You know I'd never hurt you, right?

She nodded again, and he dipped his head to kiss her. He pulled back to sign, *Take my hand. Put it where you want it.*

She reached up and took his hand, and their eyes held as she moved it to her breast. He squeezed. Then she slid it down her body over the soft quivering skin of her belly and farther down to her mound. His hand moved in slow tender strokes over her silk panties.

And suddenly she was trembling with need, with desire, and with an eagerness to please him in a way she'd never felt before. She thrust against his hand as they stared into each other's eyes, both of their breathing coming in pants. She could feel his hot erection pressed against her hip, throbbing with need. His hand took hers and brought it to his cock, curling her fingers around the hard length.

She was intrigued to find his skin like satin as he closed his hand around hers and taught her the motion, showing her the firmness of touch he liked. She was a quick learner, and his hand dropped away to plant in the mattress near her head. He kept his eyes on her stroking motions, getting off on watching the way she touched him.

She studied his reaction, the way his jaw clenched, the way his hips rolled in time with her strokes, and the way his nostrils flared as his breathing accelerated. Eventually, he pulled her hand away, pressing her wrist to the coverlet by her head as he sucked in a breath and tried to regain his control.

She lay there motionless, her chest heaving with her breathless anticipation for what was next.

He released her, his hand skating down over her side until he reached the edge of her panties. His fingers curled around the satin, and he gave her a questioning look. She knew what he was asking, and she nodded her consent.

He pulled them slowly down her thighs, his head dipping, and his eyes going to all that was now exposed to him. She saw his chest inflate with his breath and then felt as that breath exhaled slowly out of his lips.

She lifted her knees, and he pulled the panties the rest of the way off, tossing them to the floor. His eyes were still at the apex of her legs as he smoothed his warm palm up the inside of her thigh, applying the smallest bit of pressure to spread her legs. She let him. Then his muscular thigh was moving between her legs, his knee pushing them farther apart.

His hand trailed up the soft skin of her thigh until

his thumb brushed over her most intimate parts now exposed to him. His touch was soft, gentle, tender even.

Her hands reached up to cup his neck, drawing his eyes to hers as she pulled his mouth down to hers. He gave her what she wanted, kissing her deeply, and she was lost in his kiss, so much so that she felt no embarrassment or shyness as his fingers dipped to find her wet.

When he did, he groaned his response into her mouth as his fingers took up a circular motion, coating him with her body's response. Her head fell back, her mouth open, and she arched into his touch. His lips moved over her exposed neck, under her jawline, over to the base of her ear, and down to her collarbone as his fingers kept up their motions, stroking her higher and higher toward release.

His mouth returned to her face, raining soft kisses all over it as she soared closer to her orgasm.

Her hands tightened at the back of his neck, and his name burst from her lips as she finally crested the precipice, hurtling over into ecstasy. Her head tucked into the curve of his throat, and her arms wrapped around him as she floated back down to earth.

When he pulled back and she opened her eyes to look up into his, a small grin pulled at his mouth and then the smile burst wide. She couldn't help smiling back at him, before she hid her head in his neck again.

He brushed the hair back from her forehead and then nudged her back so he could look at her. She read his lips. *I love you, baby.*

"I love you, Max."

Keeping eye contact with her the whole time, he took his erection in his hand and positioned himself at her opening. Then he took both her hands in his, threading their fingers together and pressing them to the mattress as he poised above her. His brows rose, as if he were asking permission.

She bit her bottom lip and nodded.

His knees pressed her wide, as he arched his back, pushing slowly but firmly inside her, his hips sliding into the cradle of her thighs.

It hurt. She knew it would, but she couldn't fight the urge to clamp her thighs together. It did no good. All they did was come up against his solid body.

He felt her reaction, his motions stopping.

But when he began to pull back, she realized that wasn't what she really wanted after all. Her arms clutched at him.

He cupped her face, staring deep into her eyes, their foreheads almost touching. "You okay?"

She nodded. "Don't stop."

He released her with one hand, his palm sliding over her thigh, down to her ankle to wrap her leg around him. He began to ease in and out, watching her face closely for any sign that she wanted him to stop.

It wasn't long before he dipped his head, his eyes going to where they were now joined, as if the pull to watch his erection now covered with her release as it slid in and out of her was just too strong to ignore.

She thought she saw him mouth the words, *fuck*, and, *so beautiful*.

Soon his skin was covered with a sheen of sweat as his muscles worked and he tried to keep most of his weight off of her. His palms planted firmly in the mattress on either side of her, his arms flexing as he began to quicken the pace. The force of his strokes were increasing, too, but she didn't fight it. It felt so good, so right. She didn't think she'd ever want him to stop.

He kept dipping his head to watch, and she did too. It was erotic as hell, and just as beautiful.

Soon, he lifted his head to stare into her eyes. His face was filled with the struggle he was waging to control his release, and she knew he was close. And suddenly she wanted to see the orgasm wash over him, the way he had watched when she'd come moments ago.

She began to rock her hips, meeting him thrust for thrust and deep inside her, she felt herself clenching down on him. That amped his reaction up as he began to pound into her until his body went tense, all his muscles going rock solid as he groaned and came inside her.

She wrapped her arms around him when a few moments later, his body relaxed down on top of her.

His weight felt good, *so* good.

She pressed soft kisses along his salty skin, damp with his sweat, and she felt a tremor in his muscles as he fought to recover from his orgasm. His breath sawed in and out.

Lifting up on his elbows, he stared down at her, brushing the hair back from her damp forehead and smiling down at her. He dipped his head and gave her a barely-there brush of his lips. Somehow it was more touching than the deepest kiss would have been.

He moved his mouth to her ear to nuzzle her there a moment, and then he was lifting his big body off her, falling heavily to his back.

Her damp skin felt cool with the absence of his warm body pressing against it, and she immediately missed his weight.

She rolled to her side, tucking against him, and he lifted his arm, allowing her to burrow under as he wrapped his arm around her, pulling her even closer. His big palm trailed up and down her back, drifting low over the top of her buttocks. Just a teasing touch, but she was finding his touch was magic — at least for her it was.

Her hand moved over his belly and chest as her eyes skated over his gorgeous body. God, would she ever be able to keep her hands off this beautiful man?

His free hand came up to capture her exploring hand and brought her palm to his mouth for a soft kiss. His tongue snaked out to wet the center, and she giggled.

He dropped her hand to sign. *You're happy?*

She nodded. "Very happy."

Good. I didn't hurt you too much?

She shook her head. He hadn't, and if he had, she would never have had the heart to tell him. Not when he looked at her with such concern in his eyes.

She slipped her hand to cup his cheek and stroke his beard, staring up into his warm brown eyes. God, how she loved him.

Then she rose over him to press a soft kiss to his mouth. Of course one wasn't enough, and she knew it never would be with this man. She couldn't imagine her desire for him ever waning, even when she was an old woman.

The thought of being an old woman led her to thoughts of babies and grandbabies.

She lifted up to stare wide-eyed down at him, her mouth a perfect O. "Do you think we made a baby?"

He grinned up at her. *Would you mind it so much if we did?*

Looking at his smiling face, how could she mind? It wouldn't be so bad to have a mini-Max running around. She gave him a shy smile and shook her head.

He grabbed her chin, pulled her down for a peck, and rolled her to her back. His hand came up to sign as he grinned down at her. *We could give it another go, if you want?*

She giggled and pulled his head down for a long kiss.

That was okay with her.

CHAPTER THIRTY-TWO

Max pulled to the curb in front of the Thai Garden restaurant, feeling a weird sense of déjà vu. The last time he'd been here things had gone so badly. He looked over at his wife.

You sure you want to do this alone?

Malee nodded. "I need to do this by myself. There are things I need to say, things he needs to understand. It will be better if you're not there to distract from that."

All right. But just know I'll be right here if you need me.

She leaned over and kissed him. "I love you."

I love you, too, baby girl.

"I may be a while."

I'll wait as long as you need.

She gave him a big smile, then turned and climbed out of his truck.

***

The bell above the door tinkled as she walked in; Malee knew this not because she could hear it, but because her father paused in his sweeping to turn and look over his shoulder.

Scanning the room, Malee found her mother

wiping down a table. She straightened when she saw her daughter. Her face was a mask, showing no emotion as she waited to see what Malee would say.

Malee's eyes darted back to her father. His look wasn't so blank or so hard to read. His chin came up, and his face tightened. He was angry, and probably hurt. She'd left with no explanation and, more importantly, without his approval or permission. She'd informed Lawan in a text of where she'd gone and why, passing the burden of telling her parents to her sister. Something she owed Lawan an apology for. But at the time, Malee knew she couldn't tell her parents. She couldn't risk them getting in her head again. She'd made her decision. If she could have, she wouldn't have informed them of anything about her trip, but she couldn't do that. She would never want them to worry.

Malee walked slowly forward, lifting her chin as she did. She was not about to cower, yield, or defer to her father's idea of how she should behave or live her life. Not anymore. That was over and done.

"Father, Mother, I'd like to speak with you."

Her father set the broom aside. *Did you go through with it? Did you marry that man?*

"That man? He has a name, Father, and you know it."

You dare to speak to me this way.

"His name is Maxwell O'Rourke, Father, and yes, he's my husband now. He loves me just the way I am, disability and all. He makes me very happy. You may not agree with my choices, but I hope you can at least be happy that I am happy."

I was trying to do what was best for you, Malee. Why can't you see that?

"No, Father. It is you who can't see." That had him straightening his back with anger, but she didn't care; he needed to understand. "You were trying to force me into the life you thought I should live, not the life I want to live."

He raised his chin. *And where is this husband of yours?*

"He's waiting for me outside. I wanted to talk to you alone."

Well, Malee, you disobeyed me. I warned you. He will be trouble. You've disrespected me by going against my wishes. You've made your choice. He lifted his chin toward the door. *Go! Go have this life you wanted. I will not be a part of it.*

"Papa—"

She wanted to forgive him. She needed him to ask to be forgiven, or to say he was sorry, or to at least admit he was wrong. But he did none of those things. Instead, he turned away and stalked into the kitchen.

Her mother's eyes followed her husband, but then she turned back to Malee and wagged her hands, entreating her daughter to come to her. When Malee approached, her mother enfolded her in a tight hug. It didn't last long before she was pecking Malee on the cheek and then pulling back to sign, *There is a photograph that your father keeps on our dresser. It's a picture of you up on his shoulders when you were barely three years old. You both were smiling at the camera. It is a good shot, both of you so happy. Every morning he picks up that framed picture, Malee. He rubs his thumb over the glass and stares at it. He does love you.* She patted her cheek. *Remember that.*

Then she turned to follow her husband into the kitchen.

Malee stood a moment, her eyes drifting around the restaurant she'd practically grown up in, taking it all in, not sure if or when she would ever return.

She turned and looked out the window. Max's truck sat idling at the curb, his red taillights glowing through the tinted plate-glass. He was her future, and together they would make a new life. There was sadness in her at the loss of a relationship with her father, but there was happiness inside her, too. And she refused to let the sadness overshadow that. She was in love, and that was a powerful feeling. Pushing the door open, she took a deep breath, letting the negativity roll off of her as she filled her lungs with a breath of fresh air and walked toward her husband and her new life.

CHAPTER THIRTY-THREE

Max moved with increasing rhythm, his thrusts becoming more urgent, more demanding. He held himself up with one hand planted next to Malee's head while he arched back, slipping his hand between their sweat slick bodies to coax his wife to orgasm. It didn't take long; she was already thrashing beneath him when finally she clutched at his shoulders, her head going back and her mouth falling open. Max was right behind her, shooting over the edge into ecstasy as his body locked, and he came inside her. After another slow pump, he settled his weight down on top of her as they both floated back to earth. He pressed a soft kiss to her lips, then slid free and fell to his back next to her. They turned their heads and stared at each other, both breathing hard and smiling.

Malee rolled and threw her leg over her husband, straddling his hips. She sat up, her hands braced on his strong chest, and stared down at him. He grinned up at her. She traced over the lines of his ink, something he was finding she loved to do, and his eyes dropped and followed her delicate finger, the pad trailing along his overheated skin, until he reached up and grabbed her hand, pulling her down for a kiss.

She pushed back up. "This bed is very comfortable; much better than my old one."

He grinned up at her. *Good. It cost enough money.*

"You like it, too. Don't deny it."

Yeah, baby, I love our big new bed. He bounced his hips on the mattress, causing her to bob up and down with the motion, her breasts jiggling, and his eyes falling to them as his big hands locked possessively around her bare waist.

She shrieked and grabbed his arms.

He glanced around the room. They'd moved into the master bedroom at the farmhouse when Jameson, Ava, and the baby moved into the new place they'd built across the property.

They'd painted the room a pretty pale blue color, and Malee had decorated it with framed black and white photos she'd taken of Grand Junction and the valley. She'd also added some framed silks she'd painted. They now felt very much at home here.

Liam and Rory still shared the house, but Rory was on the road with his band and almost never there. Liam was quite easy to live with. He could sign, so that made everything easier; he also wasn't messy, and he was usually in a fairly good mood.

There's something I want to talk to you about, baby. Max gazed up at his beautiful wife as he signed.

"Okay."

I added you to my health insurance the other day.

"You did? Thank you."

There's something I want you to do.

"What's that?"

I want you to go see your audiologist again. See if there's anything they can do for your hearing. You once said there was talk about some implants you could get, but your father didn't approve because of the cost and risk.

She nodded. "I was twelve."

Well, it's been almost ten years. Maybe things have improved since then. Maybe there isn't as much risk anymore. They make advances every day in technology.

She stared down at him, not responding.

Only if you want to, baby. I just want you to know the insurance will pay for it...if it's something you want.

She smiled. "Okay. I'd like that. Will you go with me?"

Of course. You don't ever have to face anything alone. We're in this together.

She bit her lip. "And if I'm not a good candidate for the surgery any longer...will you be upset? Does my disability bother you?"

He frowned. *No, baby doll. No! Not at all. That's not what I meant. I just want you to have every opportunity for the best care available and to make your own decision. Whatever you want, baby. I don't want to push you to do anything. I just want you to know that nothing is keeping you from it, if it's what you want. I'll support whatever decision you make.*

She nodded, her eyes dropping to his chest.

Baby. Please understand, if you have the surgery, you have to do it for you, not because you think I want you to. Okay?

"Okay."

Promise?

"Promise."

He nodded. *I love you. And if you never get to hear my voice say the words to you, I can still sign them to you.*

"I do want to hear your voice, Max. I do. But what if it doesn't work?"

He shrugged. *Then it doesn't work.* When she didn't look like that was the answer she wanted to hear, he tried again. *Baby, only you can know if it's worth it to try. I can't make the decision for you.*

"I love you, Max."

I love you, too, baby.

She grinned and changed the subject with a challenge. "Then prove it."

He gave her a cocky grin, and quick as lightning, he rolled them both until she was pinned under him. He leaned down and kissed her. And then he went about proving it.

CHAPTER THIRTY-FOUR

Malee walked out of the Fourth Street Gym, her hand in Max's. The last of the day's light faded to a purple-blue on the horizon as dusk set in.

Max stopped and turned to look up at the place. Dropping her hand, he signed, *So, what do you think?*

"I like it."

I didn't want to change too much. I like the old school atmosphere the place has always had, but I thought some of the equipment needed an upgrade.

She nodded and stared up at the new sign painted on the brick wall in black and white, illuminated by a new gooseneck lamp mounted above it. "I like what you've done. And I like that you kept the old name."

I'm looking at adding some more classes geared toward adolescents. We've had a great response for the class we have now.

She searched his eyes, smiling up at him. "It's good to see you so excited about this. You have a passion for it."

He grinned. *I guess I do.*

She was so happy for him. Several weeks ago, she'd had her Cochlear Implant surgery and since then had

NICOLE JAMES

gone for her post-op appointments. And finally, next week she would go back to have the initial activation of the device, and she would hear for the first time. Max was making all her dreams come true, and it was so good to see him attain his own dream of purchasing this gym.

"I'm so happy for you, Max." She wrapped an arm around his waist and stared up at the sign again. He pressed a kiss to the top of her head, and they turned toward his big truck. He opened the door for her, and she climbed inside. Her eyes followed him as he moved around the hood and slid behind the wheel.

He backed out of the spot and turned down a street that ran parallel to Main Street. Malee gazed out the window as they rolled through town. Her eyes landed on a green neon frog in the window of a bar, when suddenly Max was slamming on the brakes. She turned to look at him, but he was already shoving the truck into park and climbing out. She frowned as she watched him angrily stalk around the hood to the curb. And that's when she saw him.

A young boy was sitting on the curb, his knees to his chest, like he was waiting for something. Her eyes lifted to the establishment. *Otto's Pub.*

Why on earth was this child—who couldn't be more than seven or eight years old—sitting on the curb in front of a bar as darkness fell?

Malee climbed out of the truck and moved to Max. He was squatted down in front of the boy, talking to

308

him. When his eyes lifted to hers, he gestured toward the bar. *His father is inside the bar.*

She replied in sign, not wanting the boy to understand they were talking about him. *Why is he sitting on the curb?*

He's waiting for his old man.

Max, he's just a child.

I know. Then her husband said something in a quiet reassuring tone to the boy and gestured to Malee. He signed as he spoke. "Malee, this is Ben, the boy I told you about. Ben, this is my wife, Malee. She can't hear. That's why I'm using my hands to communicate with her. It's called sign language."

"She really can't hear?"

"No, son. Can you wait here with her for a few minutes? I'd sure feel better if I knew she wasn't waiting alone."

"I guess so."

"I'm going to go inside for just a minute, okay?"

"Okay."

Then Max stood, his eyes connecting with Malee's. *Stay with him. I'm going to have a few words with his father.*

She nodded, and he strode angrily inside. Malee's gaze followed him then dropped to the child. She smiled, sat beside the boy, and put her arm around him. Glancing over her shoulder, she could see Max through the glass door. He was standing halfway down the bar, yelling at some man.

***

Max stared at the drunk on the stool, Ben's father. By the looks of him, he'd been in here quite a while. Max spoke loudly, wanting everyone in the place to hear what a loser this guy was. "You leave your kid sitting out on the curb while you sit in this bar and get shit-faced drunk! What the hell is wrong with you?"

"Who the fuck are you to tell me anything?" the man growled, his watery eyes focusing in on the big muscular man who leaned toward him. "Wait a minute. I remember you."

"I remember you, too. I know all about your story. I know your wife died, and I know you've spent every night drowning yourself in alcohol ever since. You get social security for the boy, and what do you do with the money? You drink it away in this bar."

"It's none of your fucking business."

"I'm making it my business." Max pointed toward the street. "From this moment on, that boy will never sit on a curb outside a bar again; he'll never wait alone at night for a drunken father to come home; he'll never open the door to an empty refrigerator again. And do you know why? Because he's coming home with me, where he'll be fed and clothed and loved. And you're not going to do a damn thing to stop me. You know why? Because you like to drink, and you like to have that government check to do it on. You push it, I'll make sure he's taken from you legally, and all those checks will stop. So, if I were you, I'd be glad someone was taking care of him; take the checks and leave it be."

"He's my son."

"Not anymore. You want to get help for your alcoholism, I'll be glad to help you. But if you come to my door and try to take Ben, you'll have to go through me. You ain't gettin' that boy back. Over my dead body…or maybe yours."

Then Max slapped a fifty on the bar and growled at the bartender who was looking at Ben's father with distaste. "His drinks are on me. Pour him another."

Ben's father did exactly what Max knew he'd do; he pushed his glass forward for the bartender.

Max stalked toward the door, knowing the man would never give him any trouble that couldn't be bought off with some drinking money. If he were a betting man, he'd bet the guy would drink himself to death before too long.

A man at the end of the bar stood and started clapping as Max walked past, and before he made it to the door, the whole bar was applauding him.

***

Malee stood when Max came back out.

We're taking him home with us, Malee. I can't leave him with that man any longer.

She wasn't sure what had happened in the bar, but if this was the boy he'd told her about so long ago, then she supported his decision, and she was so proud of her husband at that moment.

He knelt and spoke to the boy in low tones. Ben looked back over his shoulder toward the bar for a moment, then nodded and slipped his hand in Max's. Together they walked to the truck.

***

Max pulled down the gravel drive.

He parked and looked over his shoulder at Ben buckled in the backseat. He signed as he spoke. "Ben, when there's a lady in the car, a gentleman goes around and opens the door for her. Do you want to see how it's done?"

Ben nodded, slurping down the last of his milkshake. They'd stopped at a drive-thru and fed him. Meals out were something this child was probably never treated to.

Max winked at Malee, then climbed out of his side. He opened the door for Ben and helped him out, then said, "Okay, buddy. Watch this."

He opened the door for Malee and held his hand out for her. She slipped her hand in his as he helped her down out of the truck, and then Max shut the door.

"Simple, right?"

Ben nodded.

"What other doors do we open for ladies?"

Ben frowned, then pointed at the door to the farmhouse.

"That's right. Would you like to hold the door for her?"

He nodded and ran up the porch steps to hold the screen door open. Once they were in the kitchen, Max squatted down in front of Ben. "Hey, buddy. You're

Dad said he didn't mind if you stayed with us for a while. Would you like that? I'll show you all kinds of cool stuff around the place."

"I guess so."

"You can even stay in my old room. You want to see it?"

Ben nodded excitedly.

Max stood and held his hand out to the boy and took him upstairs.

Max had a big bed covered in a navy blue comforter. There was a dresser with an old football on top and a stack of MMA and tattoo magazines. The room was a basic white that hadn't been painted since the boys were young.

"What do you think, Ben? Would you be okay sleeping in here tonight?"

"I guess so."

"You know, now that I'm married, no one uses this room anymore. How would you like to make it yours?"

"But I have a room at my house."

"I know, son. But this could be your room when you stay with us. You could even put some posters up and maybe we could paint it a different color. Would you like that?"

He shrugged. "I guess."

Max picked up the football and sat on the mattress tossing it in the air. "I talked to your dad, Ben. We just thought maybe you'd like to stay here with us, since your dad is gone a lot of the time. Then you wouldn't have to be alone so much. And I sure could use a helper around the place."

Ben sat on the mattress next to Max and stared at the floor. "What about my dad?"

"Well, I think he'll be spending a lot of time out, trying to find a good job, and if he knew you were safe here and we were taking good care of you, he wouldn't worry about you."

Ben looked up at Max with earnest eyes. "Is my dad worried about me?"

"I'm sure he doesn't like leaving you alone, Ben."

"But I have Mrs. Larsen."

"I know you do, but she doesn't live with you."

"But, who will look after her if I'm gone? I have to go home and check on her. She needs someone. I can't leave her."

"I have her phone number. Would you like to talk to her? Then maybe tomorrow we could go see her. How would that be?"

Ben nodded. "Okay."

Max pulled his phone out. "Give me a minute to talk to her first, okay buddy?"

"Sure."

Max passed him the football. "You want to hold onto this for me?"

Ben grinned and nodded.

Max stood. "If you want to lie on the bed and toss it in the air, that would be okay. But no shoes on the bed, okay?"

Practically before the words were out of Max's mouth, Ben was toeing his sneakers off and scooting back to plop on the big bed. Max grinned and walked downstairs.

Taking a seat at the kitchen table, he called Mrs. Larsen. After he explained the situation to her, he signed to Malee to go upstairs and get Ben.

A couple of minutes later, Ben skipped into the room holding Malee's hand. Max passed him the phone. While they talked, Max pulled Malee aside and signed to her, appreciating the fact that he could talk in front of Ben without him knowing what was said.

He's worried about Mrs. Larsen.

Malee frowned. *Is she the elderly woman who lives next door to him? The one you said looked out for him?*

Yes. He feels like he needs to be there to take care of her.

That's so sweet. She looks out for him, and he thinks it's the other way around.

I told him we could take him to see her tomorrow.

Malee nodded. *I think that's a good idea. What did he say about his father?*

Not much. He was concerned his father might be worried about him. I didn't exactly explain that he was moving in here for good. I don't want to drop that on him all at once. I figured we'd take it day by day and see how he does.

Malee nodded. *He's an adorable boy.*

I'm sorry. I should have discussed all this with you.

It's okay. You did the right thing.

Max looked over at Ben, then back at Malee. *We're*

starting a family, just not the way I'd imagined.

She grinned up at him. *Have I told you lately how much I love you?*

CHAPTER THIRTY-FIVE

Max stood on the porch with Malee and Ben, who proudly held a box of donuts. Max knocked on the wooden door. A moment later, Mrs. Larsen answered. She bent and hugged Ben, who held the box out to her.

"We brought you donuts, Miz Larsen."

"You did? Why thank you! Aren't you sweet? Did you help pick them out?"

He nodded.

She handed him back the box. "Well, go put them on the table, and I'll get us all some plates."

He ran off to do her bidding, yelling, "I'll get them down. I know where they are!"

Max watched as Ben ran through the small house to the kitchen, set the box down on the mint green Formica table, and pulled a chair across the linoleum floor to the cabinet. He climbed up and opened an upper cupboard.

"I'm so glad you're taking care of him," the older woman said, turning back to Max. "Come in, please."

Max and Malee stepped inside. He signed as he said, "Mrs. Larsen, this is my wife, Malee. She's deaf, so I'll have to translate for you, but she can speak."

"How do you do?" Malee said, extending her hand.

"I'm so pleased to meet you," Mrs. Larsen replied. She looked to Max. "I'm glad you told me what happened. And I'm so happy you stepped in. How was Ben last night?"

"He was fine, but he was worried about you."

"That dear boy."

Max put his arm around Malee. "We have something we'd like to talk to you about."

Mrs. Larsen nodded. "Well let's go sit at the table, and I'll make a pot of coffee."

They moved to the kitchen, and Ben served them all donuts like he was a waiter. They laughed as he took such pride in asking them which kind they wanted, and carrying the plates to them.

Mrs. Larsen soon carried mugs of coffee over. "Ben, there's some milk in the refrigerator. Can you pour yourself a glass?"

"Yes."

"Ben, you say, 'yes, ma'am', remember?" Max instructed.

"Yes, ma'am."

Mrs. Larsen beamed. "Why, such manners! I'm so proud of you, Ben."

He opened the refrigerator and got out a half-gallon carton.

"Be careful not to spill," Mrs. Larsen reminded him.

"I will."

When he was seated at the table and they were halfway through their donuts, Max took a sip of coffee and set his mug down. "Mrs. Larsen, Malee and I have a proposition for you."

"A proposition? What kind?"

"Ben is going to be staying with us for a while, and we sure could use some help taking care of him while we are both at work. We were wondering if you'd be interested in the job."

"I don't mind watching little Ben at all. You don't have to pay me."

"You don't understand. We want to offer you room and board. We'd like to move you out to the farmhouse. It's a big house with plenty of space. You'd have your own room. And in exchange, you could help take care of Ben."

"But I already have this place."

Max nodded. "I know. I was thinking maybe you could sell this house or rent it out for an added income."

Mrs. Larsen toyed nervously with the handle of her coffee mug. "Well, I don't know."

"Ben would love for you to come," Max insisted.

"Pleeease!" Ben begged. "I don't want you to be lonely here all by yourself without me."

Mrs. Larsen smiled at the boy and reached over and patted his cheek. "I would miss you, Ben, but I don't know. Moving… that's a big step."

"Would you come out to the farm to at least see the

place?"

Ben sat on his chair, swinging his feet back and forth. "Yeah, you have to come see my new room! Please!"

"Well, I suppose I could do that."

Max reached across the table and covered her frail hand with his. "He needs you, Mrs. Larsen. I'm not sure this will work without you there."

She nodded and looked around her aging, dilapidated home. "I suppose a change would be nice."

Max and Malee both grinned at each other, and Max said, "I think that's a yes, Ben."

Ben put his fists in the air and screamed, "Yay!"

***

As spring rolled into summer, they all settled into a routine. Mrs. Larsen had a room on the first floor that made it easier for her not to have to climb the stairs too often. She took over a majority of the cooking, something she was good at, to the great appreciation of everyone.

She soon had the home running like a well-oiled machine. Ben would come home from school on the bus each afternoon, and they would sit at the kitchen table having milk and cookies. Then Ben would sit and do any homework he had.

Max had found a Grad student from the local university to rent out her home for the summer. That gave them enough time to see if this arrangement was going to work out for all of them.

So far, it was working out great. Ben was happier than Max had ever seen him. Once in a while he'd ask about his father. The man had even come by to the farm one Sunday. Ben had been happy to see him, but also almost leery that he was there to take him away.

They'd invited him to dinner. He'd made the best of it, struggling through the meal and attempting small talk, but by dessert, Max could see he was itching for a drink. In the end, he'd asked Max for money.

Max was leery of setting a precedent of becoming a weekly handout, but he gave him a twenty, and Liam gave him a lift back into town.

Ben seemed a little sad to see him go, and Max felt compelled to offer the weekly standing invitation to Sunday dinner. He'd nodded, saying he'd like that, but had only been back once, on Ben's birthday.

After that, Ben didn't talk about him much. It seemed he'd adjusted well to his new surroundings, thriving even. With the fresh air and regular meals, he'd already grown an inch, and Max and Malee planned to take him shopping for new clothes.

In the evenings, they'd rock on chairs on the front porch or around a bonfire in the backyard. If Rory was around, he'd play his guitar, and they'd all sing and toast marshmallows.

Life was good.

CHAPTER THIRTY-SIX

Max, Malee, her mother, and sister sat in the audiologist's office. Max felt it was important that her family be here for this day — the day Malee's implants would be turned on, and she would be able to hear for the first time.

Although her father had basically disowned her, Malee's mother and sister still kept a relationship with her. Max knew it caused tension at the restaurant, but he was happy they stood up to him in this matter and came. Keit stayed behind to help with the restaurant, but her mother and sister insisted on coming, even if it was going to cause the restaurant to be closed for a day. This was too important of a day.

The audiologist was a sweet young woman named Stacy, who was great with her patients. Malee sat near her, and Max sat in a chair a few feet away. Max's eyes moved over his wife whom he loved so much. She wore a lavender tank that dipped at the neckline to reveal a black tube top underneath, jeans, and flip-flops, her legs crossed at the ankles, one foot bouncing nervously. Her purse sat on the tile floor at her feet. There was a cord attached to her ear from the computer that the audiologist worked at as they mapped out the device.

"Our voices will sound very loud to her, like we're shouting, so talk softly." Stacy signed as she talked so that Malee could understand her until the device started working. She spoke very slowly, one word at a time. "Okay. So, Malee, I'm going to turn the volume up and up until you hear my voice."

She nodded, then jumped and made a face like it was painfully too loud, like a squelch in her ear. "Loud."

"Hang on. Hang on." She made some adjustments. "Can you hear me now?"

"Loud squeaking is all I hear."

"Do you hear me talking?" she said, signing as well.

Malee shook her head, and the audiologist made some adjustments on her computer.

"How about right there?"

"Yeah."

"You can hear me talking?"

Malee nodded, smiling. She pointed at Stacy, an excited look on her face.

"Can you hear my voice?"

She nodded and laughed.

"You can? Okay."

Malee's face scrunched up, and she wiped tears off her cheeks.

The audiologist grabbed a box of tissues off her desk. "Okay. I'm going to pass these around because I think we're all going to need them."

Malee, her mother, and sister all took one.

"Okay, Malee. How about right there?"

"Yeah." Her eyes got big. "I hear myself, too."

"Great! Does my voice sound really squeaky?"

"Yes," she replied, nodding and rubbing her leg nervously.

"Do you hear anything else?"

"A sh-sh-sh." Malee pointed at the ceiling fan and the overhead lighting. "The fan maybe. And the lights make noise. A humming. I didn't know the lights made noise."

"Can you hear out of both sides?"

"Yes."

"How does it sound?"

"It sounds very high."

Stacy smiled. "It will sound high at first. It won't always sound that way. Your brain will start to adjust it for you."

Malee nodded.

"I'm going to say the months of the year. I want you to tell me how the volume is, okay?" Stacy recited all the months and then asked, "Did you understand the words?"

Malee nodded excitedly. "Yes."

"Okay. So what I was telling Max before was that your right ear had no hearing...and your left just a tiny bit."

She nodded.

"Now giving you hearing like this is almost like normal hearing, but you're hearing in an electronic way of hearing."

"That's what it feels like."

"Yeah. So it's kind of like this machine quality to the sound. It takes a little bit for your brain to adjust to the sounds. Once it does adjust, it will not sound like this. But that's why it's going to take some time for your brain to understand what you're hearing. Okay?"

Malee nodded again.

"So…it may sound loud, but by Monday, when I see you again we're going to do that same thing we did before where you hear the beep and you raise your hand."

Malee nodded.

"It'll be different, so not the perfect map yet, but it will get us there, okay?"

Malee nodded.

"So…does it sound too soft?"

"No."

"Does it sound like I'm shouting?"

She nodded vigorously. "Yes."

"Okay…I'm going to have you just listen to me for a few minutes while I talk about this, all right?"

Malee nodded.

"When we finish, you'll be able to control the loudness with your remote control. But I don't want it so soft that you can't hear anything because that defeats the purpose, okay? But I also don't want it so loud that you're uncomfortable."

Malee nodded again, smiling.

Her mother came over, kissed her on the forehead, and said softly, "I've been waiting for this day."

Malee pointed at her mother, looking at Stacy with big eyes.

"Could you hear her?" Stacy asked.

Malee nodded, laughing.

"You said you weren't gonna cry," Lawan told her mother.

"Who's talking?" Malee asked Stacy.

"That's your sister." Stacy then looked over at Lawan. "She heard your voice because she turned her head to look for you."

The audiologist looked at Max. "Do you have pets? Any barking dogs?"

"No we don't."

Malee looked at her husband with big eyes. Then looked back at Stacy, smiling.

"Now Max, you say something. I think she heard you."

"Hi, beautiful. Can you hear me?"

She nodded and started laughing.

He laughed back, his voice a sweet low rumble. "Malee, how does my voice sound?"

"Yours sounds loud."

"Very low and very deep, I'm guessing," the audiologist said. "Does he sound different from mine?"

Malee nodded, grinning. "Different." Then she

laughed.

"What do you think?" he asked.

"It's amazing."

Then it all overwhelmed her, and she put her face in her hands and burst into tears.

The audiologist patted her leg. "Aw, honey. That's okay. It's a big life-changing day today."

Max squatted before her and pulled her hands away. "Hey, baby. Don't cry. I've wanted to say this to you for a very long time. I love you, Malee."

She nodded back, letting him know she heard, then said, "I love you, too."

Tears streamed down her face, and she wrapped her arms around his neck.

CHAPTER THIRTY-SEVEN

Malee stood in front of the mirror at the small church. She was about to renew her vows to Max. They'd decided to do a renewal now that she had her implants and could hear Max recite his vows to her. They'd also wanted to have their families attend.

Malee had gone to her family and asked them to come. Her father had flatly refused to even speak to her, and he'd walked out of the room without a word. She didn't know if any of her family would be able to come, but her mother, sister, and brother were very happy for her and had helped her with throwing together this event.

Lawan fussed with her hair, trying to secure the flower above her ear. Malee smiled at her in the mirror, and Lawan gave her a wink. Then her mother stepped into view, and Malee turned to see there were tears in her eyes.

"Malee, my daughter, you are so beautiful."

"Thank you, Mama."

Her mother pulled her in for a hug. "I wish your Aunt Ratana was here to see this."

Malee pulled back and smiled. "I feel like she is here."

Her mother nodded. "Yes, Malee. I do, too."

"You better go take your seat, Mama. It's almost time."

"I'm so happy for you, baby. Max is a good man. He's not what your father thought at all."

Malee nodded. "I know, Mama. I only wish he could be happy for me."

"I talked to him last night. I thought he was coming around. I had hoped he would show up today."

"Me, too."

"He's a proud man, Malee. It's hard for him to admit when he is wrong."

Lawan pulled her mother's arm. "Don't make her cry. Her makeup is perfect. Let's go take our seats."

"Okay."

Lawan gave her sister a hug. "I love you, baby sister."

"I love you, too."

When they left the room, Malee picked up her small bouquet and looked back in the mirror. She would walk herself down the aisle, and that would be okay, because she would be walking toward Max. She would focus on the smile on his handsome face and nothing else.

She heard the music start up.

The door behind her opened, and she saw in the reflection the man who had walked in.

She turned, stunned to see her father standing in a dark suit.

"Papa. You came."

He nodded once. "I was wrong. It is your life to live as you decide. I want you to be happy, Malee."

"I am happy, Father." Then she laughed. "This is the first time I've heard your voice."

And then he was across the room hugging her. "I love you so much."

"I love you, too, Papa."

He stepped back, holding her at arm's length, and his eyes swept down her. "You look beautiful. I hope I didn't crush your flowers."

She tried to laugh, wiping her happy tears away with the handkerchief she held in one hand. "You didn't."

He extended his elbow. "May I walk you down the aisle?"

"Are you sure?"

He nodded. "I would be honored."

She slipped her hand into the crook of his arm.

"Okay, my baby girl. Let's go."

They stepped into the vestibule, and the attendant pulled the doors back to the chapel. Rory was sitting on a stool to the side of the altar, strumming a quiet melody on an acoustic guitar.

Malee grinned, hearing the musical sound. Her eyes traveled around the small chapel. Max's family was all there. Jameson, Ava, their baby, and Liam were in the front row. Ava's sister and some other friends were behind them, many of them tattooed men. On Malee's side stood her mother, sister, and now, too, her brother, who must have come with her father. And then suddenly it struck her that her father must have shut down the restaurant for this—something he'd never done in his life.

She looked at him and smiled, and they began walking slowly down the aisle.

Her eyes traveled over Mrs. Larsen standing in a pretty dress. Little Ben was there, too, smiling proudly in his new suit as he stood next to Max as his best man.

Her eyes moved to her husband. He looked so handsome, standing there with his hands clasped in front of him, his feet spread. His eyes had widened for a split second at the sight of Malee's father walking her in, but his face broke in a broad smile at the sight of her.

They held eye contact as she walked toward him, and somehow it felt like she was floating down the aisle to him and to a life filled with love and happiness.

EPILOGUE

Maxwell —

I lay on my side on the blanket spread out over the grass. With my head in my hand, I looked down at my sleeping wife and drew a piece of straw grass across her face.

She cracked open an eye and smiled, batting it away with her hand.

I chuckled, then leaned down and kissed her. "You were sleeping."

"I was just resting my eyes."

I twisted my head to look out over the view from our spot. "I'm glad Mrs. Larsen could watch Ben and let us have some time alone today. It's a special day."

She giggled. "Max, are you saying you actually remembered?"

"Of course I remembered." I nodded toward the tree. "One year ago today I brought you up here and told you I loved you."

"And I said it back."

I grinned and dipped my head to brush my lips over hers. "And you said it back."

She tilted her head back to look over at the tree.

"And you carved our initials in a heart."

I grinned. "Hey, I'm a romantic guy."

"Yes, you are." She cupped my bearded face in her hands. "You've done a lot of romantic things for me, all the letters you wrote…" Suddenly she sat up, her mouth falling open.

"Baby, what's wrong?"

Instead of answering, she scrambled to her feet and dashed over to the tree. She dug around, pushing piles of leaves to the side until she came up with a tin box, which she clutched to her chest and carried back over to me.

"What's that?" I asked.

"I'd forgotten about it. I carried it up here the day my aunt died. When my sister texted me, I left it by the tree where I'd set it down."

I frowned. "You were up here that day?"

She nodded.

"Why?"

"I came here to think."

"About what?"

"About you. About how much I loved you. I'd planned to go to you that day and tell you how wrong I was and ask for forgiveness and another chance. But then…"

"You got that text."

She nodded. "Yes. And everything changed."

My eyes fell to the box. "What's in it?"

Malee looked down at it, stroking her hand over it

lovingly. "Your letters."

I grinned. "Really? Let me see."

She sat down next to me and opened the rusted box. "It's been up here so long. But look, they're okay."

I watched her lift the stack and then I held my hand out. "I'll bet there's something you never noticed."

She frowned at me as she passed me the stack. "What?"

I took them and fanned them out across the blanket. "Look at the first letter of each one."

She looked down.

"What does it spell?"

Her eyes moved across them and her mouth dropped open.

"What does it say, Malee?"

In a soft voice she read the words out loud. "Marry me."

"You were it for me. I knew it from the very first note I wrote you."

She looked into my eyes and then lunged across the space dividing us to wrap her arms around my neck and kiss me.

When she pulled back, she looked up at me with sparkling eyes. "I love you, Max."

"I love you, too, babe."

Her eyes moved to the letters scattered on the blanket now. "You're not the only one with a secret."

My brows shot up. "Oh, yeah? You write some cryptic message in your letters, too?"

"Nope. Even better."

"What, baby doll?"

"I'm pregnant."

My smile disappeared, and I stared at her in shock. "Are you serious right now?"

She laughed. "I'm serious."

I threw my head back and shouted to the heavens, "Whoo-hoo!" Then I grabbed her and rolled her to the blanket, crushing all the notes under us. I looked down at her, grinning, and brushed the hair back from her face, searching her eyes. Then my gaze dropped to her stomach, and I smoothed my palm lovingly over her belly.

"I take it you're happy?" she whispered.

"Hell yes, I'm happy. A baby. You're sure?" I grinned down at her as she nodded, then I added, "I ever tell you that twins run in my family?"

Her mouth dropped open, and her eyes got big.

I chuckled. I should tell her I was joking, but the look on her face was priceless. God, how I loved this woman. I dipped my head and kissed her again. I'll tell her tomorrow. Maybe.

THE END

PREVIEW OF LIAM

Brothers Ink

Liam sat at the booth that Brothers Ink had reserved at the tattoo expo in LA. He couldn't take his eyes off the gorgeous tattoo model doing a photo shoot for the crowd. They had her up on a raised dais, reclining on a mock bed with a white fur throw under her. It was the perfect backdrop for the colorful ink that covered her sexy body. As the videographer filmed her, the video was thrown up in a live feed onto a giant screen, like they do behind bands at rock concerts. The entire convention space had a perfect view of her as she rolled around on the fur. And she knew what she was doing, that much was obvious. She had the textbook pinup vibe down pat.

Currently, she was on her back, her bare legs extended in the air and crossed at the ankles, sexy platform shoes with sexier-still thick straps around her ankles. She wore a fifties style two-piece bathing suit, her lips were painted bright red, and her hair was tied up in a fifties style bandana, a la *Rosie the Riveter*.

The cameraman was filming from behind, and she tilted her head back to look at him, her white teeth coming out to nibble at her bottom lip.

Jesus Christ, the woman was sex-on-a-stick. Every man in the place probably had a hard-on for her.

She rolled to her stomach, arching her ass in the air with her arms stretched forward like a cat.

Liam had heard she was selling a pinup calendar at the event, and they were selling out fast, even at thirty bucks a pop. She and the photographer had to be making a mint.

He couldn't tear his eyes from her. What he wouldn't give to run his hands over her skin and trace every tattoo she had with his tongue. Hell, he'd even settle for putting some ink of his own on her gorgeous body.

Twelve hours later…

Velvet stared down at the handsome tattooed man lying among the white hotel sheets. They'd spent an incredible night together. He'd been her secret crush for years, and when the opportunity to spend the night with him presented itself, she'd jumped at the chance.

They'd shared an amazing connection, something she'd never felt before with any other man. And he'd felt it, too. He'd even admitted as much last night.

God, how she longed to lie back down beside him and take him in her arms again. But as her eyes moved lovingly over his muscled, inked body, fear flooded through her. She couldn't risk him ever finding out the truth. Because if he ever found out her secret, he'd look at her with different eyes, and he'd come to hate her, and that she couldn't bear.

So she did the only thing she could. She forced herself to slip out of his hotel room without saying goodbye, without so much as leaving a note.

She knew she was turning her back on what might be the only opportunity she had for any kind of relationship with the one man who had ever made her feel something, and that's what made walking out that door so incredibly hard.

But she knew she had no choice.

The door quietly latched as she slunk out, and the feelings of regret immediately overwhelmed her.

Perhaps he would remember her. After all, she'd heard what men said about her…

Velvet… Nobody forgets Velvet.

If you enjoyed Maxwell, please post a review on Amazon.

Also by Nicole James:

OUTLAW: An Evil Dead MC Story (Book 1)

CRASH: An Evil Dead MC Story (Book 2)

SHADES: An Evil Dead MC Story (Book 3)

WOLF: An Evil Dead MC Story (Book 4)

GHOST: An Evil Dead MC Story (Book 5)

RED DOG: An Evil Dead MC Novella (Book 6)

BLOOD: An Evil Dead MC Story (Book 7)

JAMESON: Brothers Ink Series (Book 1)

RUBY FALLS – Romantic Suspense

Join my newsletter
http://eepurl.com/biN_p5
Connect with me on Facebook
https://www.facebook.com/Nicole-James-533220360061689
Website
www.nicolejames.net

Made in the USA
Columbia, SC
19 February 2019